Ancient Exhumations

+2

Second Edition
Revised and Expanded

by Stanley C. Sargent

Ancient Exhumations

+2

Second Edition
Revised and Expanded

by Stanley C. Sargent

elder signs

press

Ancient Exhumations +2 is published by Elder Signs Press, Inc.
This book is © 2004 Elder Signs Press, Inc.
Preface © 2004 Robert M. Price.
Introduction © 2004 Peter Worthy.
Author's Preface and Acknowledgements, and all stories © 2004, Stanley C. Sargent.

"The Rattle of Her Smile" originally appeared in *Ancient Exhumations* (Mythos Books, November 1999). "Dark Demonize" originally appeared in *Ancient Exhumations* (Mythos Books, November 1999). "The Hoppwood Tenant" originally appeared in *NetherReal* (September 1997) and was reprinted in *Ancient Exhumations* (Mythos Books, November 1999). "The Tale of Toad Loop" originally appeared in *Nightscapes* (January 1998) and has appeared in *Dark Legacy #1* (August 1998), *Ancient Exhumations* (Mythos Books, November 1999), and *Eldritch Blue* (Lindisfarne Press, March 2004). "When the Stars are Ripe" originally appeared in *Nightscapes* (November 1997) and has appeared in *Tales of Lovecraftian Horror* (November 1998), *Al-Azif* (Yhtill Press, 1998) and *Ancient Exhumations* (Mythos Books, November 1999). "The Paladin of Worms" originally appeared in *Ancient Exhumations* (Mythos Books, November 1999). "Self-Correcting Mechanism" originally appeared in *Cosmic Visions* (January 1997) and has appeared in *Ancient Exhumations* (Mythos Books, November 1999). "Famine Wood" originally appeared in *Strange Tales* (March 2004).

Cover art © 2004 by Daniel Alan Ross.
All artwork © 2004 to the artists:
Pages 70, 89, 112, 162, 166, 170, 189: Daniel Alan Ross
Page 34: Daryl Hutchinson
Pages 74, 135: Jeffrey Thomas
Pages 20, 56: Peter Worthy
Page 44, 180: Stanley C. Sargent

SECOND EDITION
10 9 8 7 6 5 4 3 2 1
Published in July 2004.
ISBN: 0-9759229-0-4
Printed in the U.S.A.

Published by Elder Signs Press, Inc.
P.O. Box 389
Lake Orion, MI 48361-0389
www.eldersignspress.com

TABLE OF CONTENTS

Artwork
Cover - Daniel Alan Ross
Illustrations -
Pages 70, 89, 112, 162, 166, 170, 189: Daniel Alan Ross
Page 34: Daryl Hutchinson
Pages 74, 135: Jeffrey Thomas
Pages 20, 56: Peter Worthy
Page 44, 180: Stanley C. Sargent

Dedicated to Robert M. Price, my mentor and great friend

Preface

I like to flatter myself that I "discovered" Stan Sargent as a writer. Sure, that is a lame gesture trying to siphon off glory from the guy who did the real work. But it remains true that Stan had the stereotypical artist's trial of running through several disappointing turn-downs before he got to me. And I had the stereotypical delight of being that editor from whose eyes the scales fell away. In fact they were never there. I liked his work as soon as I saw it. And what's not to like? In my humble opinion, Stan's imagination is every bit as fertile and brilliantly quirky as the young Ramsey Campbell's. Stan's canon of stories thus far have formed a body of coherent tales and mythemes, his own private sub-mythos in the best tradition. In creating these tales, Stan is defying and destroying yet another stereotype, namely that the Lovecraftian Mythos is a preserve for fan hacks. That prejudice, it ought to be obvious, is merely a case of the "anxiety of influence" discussed by Harold Bloom. Lovecraft is the rock from which 20th century horror was hewn. Some, like Stephen King, are big (and secure) enough to admit this. Others (Charles L. Grant, Peter Straub) feel they must dump on HPL and all his works in order to escape from their master's long shadow. Writers like Stan are honest with themselves and their readers: they cut their teeth, as Campbell and Bloch were happy to do, on Lovecraft pastiches. No doubt he will go onto to greener pastures (or is that "more blasted heaths"?), but we will never write off Stan's early tales as mere juvenilia, mere teething rings. They are already winsome, fascinating, and horrific tales in their own right. And they already evidence Stan Sargent's boundless creativity. We don't have to wait for that.

His work, while fitting into a recognizable genre (on purpose!), is already fresh and innovative. And he is a scrupulously careful and indefatigable researcher, again like HPL. His Qom-maq epic, which still leaves me breathless, is a masterpiece of both research and manic imagination. I have enthusiastically published just about every scrap of Stan's work he would let me use. I continue to pursue the same policy.

Robert M. Price
1/99

ix

Author's Preface and Acknowledgements

As far as I'm concerned, the mere fact that this second, expanded (and corrected) edition of my first collection of tales, is being published is amazing. When I first began writing weird fiction, just under a decade ago, I never expected any of my stories would see print. I wrote tales that I, as a reader, would like to read but could rarely find. I had no intention of writing popular fiction honed to fit the taste of the widest possible audience. Writers who do that actually make money and become well-known. Expecting neither of these rewards, I wrote whatever I wanted the way I wanted to write it. It takes a long time to write my stories as they go through several incarnations before I am satisfied, but when they are finally complete, I harbor no doubts that the final product is far better as a result; sometimes the final product bears only a passing resemblance to the original concept and/or plot.

As a result of this nerve wracking, tedious process, I know I write good stories. When I decided to test the waters by sending a few stories to editors, I had confidence in the quality of the stories, but deep down inside I didn't believe anyone else would understand what I was trying to accomplish in my work.

I simultaneously sent my first four tales to two editors. The first to respond didn't hesitate to offer his opinion that my work was "way over the top." He told me frankly that, in his opinion, I was not cut out to be a writer and should stop wasting my time trying to be one. It seemed my doubts that others would understand had been totally confirmed.

A week or so later, I received a response from the other editor. His reaction to the same four stories surprised the hell out of me. He said he loved them all and wanted to print them all, adding that one of the stories, the longest of the four, literally "took my breath away."

That was all I needed; nothing could stop me from writing after hearing that from Robert M. Price, an editor I highly respected. Bob has continued to encourage and publish my work, and I consider him not only my mentor but a wonderful friend. I jokingly promised I would dedicate my first book to him despite the fact that, at the time, I felt sure there was no chance such a book would ever be published. Now that book is being published a second time in a fancier format, with two new stories, and it is still hard for me to believe. I've kept my promise by dedicating both editions of this book to good ol' lifesaver Bob as he certainly deserves that and so much more! Had he not unfailingly encouraged me throughout the years, I would almost certainly have taken the advice of that first editor and thrown in the glove.

The first edition of *Ancient Exhumations* (500 copies) sold out in less than a year after receiving great reviews in "Locus" and "Cemetery Dance" magazines. I was classified as a Lovecraftian Mythos author, which was fine with me at the time, as the work of H.P. Lovecraft had inspired much of my work. Despite the fact that I used several of Lovecraft's characters, alien monsters, and locations in a number of the stories that ended up in *Ancient Exhumations*, none of the tales required the reader be familiar at all with Lovecraft's work; that's the way I wanted it.

Many of my stories did require foreknowledge of Lovecraft's work, however, so I rounded up most of those for inclusion in my second collection, *The Taint of Lovecraft*. My first novella, set in ancient Egypt and heavily researched for historic accuracy, "Nyarlatophis, A Fable of Ancient Egypt," is the longest piece in The Taint of Lovecraft, and I was pretty nervous about how reviewers would respond to it. To my utter delight and relief, Ellen Datlow gave it honorable mention in her annual of the best fantasy and horror of the year. In his review of the book for "Cemetery Dance," Garrett Peck dubbed the novella "astounding" and referred to me as "the most intelligent of the current crop of Mythos-inspired authors, as admirably demonstrated in his first collection, *Ancient Exhumations*." I was elated!

In the preface for *The Taint of Lovecraft*, I announced that, with that volume, I was bidding *adieu* to the Lovecraftian genre. Garrett Peck, Dick Lupoff, Ken Faig, Jr., and others expressed the mixed feelings they harbored about this decision but added that they were curious to see what I would do next.

The two stories (hence the "+ 2" extension of the original title) I have added herein to the original *Ancient Exhumations* line-up represent my "post-Lovecraftian" work. One is set in my fictional Madland County, Ohio, and the other is my tribute to the fantastic writings of Clark Ashton Smith. The latter has not seen print until now, so the jury is still out.

I would like to briefly add a few notes about the tales in this book. Half of them are in Madland County, Ohio at various times within the last 150 years or so. Madland County is a fictional place, although the Mad River, after which it is named, does run through the part of southwestern Ohio in which I spent my first eighteen years. The landscape and descriptions of farmhouses, barns, etc. in these tales all derive from my memories of my maternal grandparents' 120 acre (originally 200, but they sold it off it chunks over the years) property, their rambling old farmhouse (now a state historical site as is the log cabin built by my forebears in the early 1800s), their barn, etc. I'll provide a couple examples.

The burrow in the bank of the creek that used to scare the hell out of me ended up in "The Paladin of Worms," as did the farmhouse, both interior and exterior, as well as the century-old tree that stood just beyond the large porch that fronted the house. Another example is the eerily sallow wooded area around which "Famine Wood" revolves. My grandfather and father forced me to go hunting with them (only once!), and these are memories of the place they took me as seen through the eyes of a twelve-year-old who did not want to be there. That remote section of my grandparents' land totally creeped me out. Luckily we returned home with nothing but a big bag of wild mushrooms my grandfather had miraculously spotted growing beneath the at times knee-deep groundcover of dead autumn leaves. The description in the story of a fallen tree and what lay beneath its bark derives from my actual experience that day as well.

"Self-Correcting Mechanism" reflects the pessimistic, to say the least, attitude I often harbor when I consider mankind's progress. The planet in the tale is named in honor of my wonderful friend from 5th grade on, Cathy Denny. She always wanted to be a writer but became a very popular and award-winning college-level teacher and just never found the time to really do much writing. I am so glad she got to see her name in a preview copy of *Ancient Exhumations* just a few days before she died of cancer. The story, for what it is worth, stands as my tribute to Cathy, the woman my mother always insisted I should have married, something Cathy and I chuckled about on many occasions (yes, she knew I am gay).

My fascination with the cultures and religions of ancient Mexico and Central America led to the writing of "Rattle of Her Smile." All of the mythological information cited in the story is historically accurate with the exception of my interpretation of the broken image between the statue's feet. I someday plan to stand face-to-face with the statue described in this tale if I ever get to the anthropological museum in Mexico City. The exterior of the tomb-den in which

Coatlicue lurks is based upon a mausoleum built into the side of a grassy mound that caught my attention when I went to visit Lovecraft's grave in Providence, Rhode Island.

"When the Stars Are Ripe" is my attempt to compress into a single, comprehensible creature the several differing descriptions Lovecraft provided for his Shub-Niggurath entity. I proceeded to transform Lovecraft's beastie into a species rather than a single entity, and I am quite pleased with the nasty explanation I created for their existence.

My day-long visits (I had to go back a second time before leaving the country) to the fabulous ruins of mighty Persepolis in 1979 led me to study more of the history of the Persian Empire and inspired some of the scenes and creatures of "Dark Demonize." The griffin demon's name is a play on the name of and a loving salute to my beloved friend Sheila Achs.

As mentioned above, the landscape and barn described in "The Tale of Toad Loop" directly reflects the landscape of my grandparents' land and the barn in which I so often played.

After originally writing "The Hoppwood Tenant," I shipped it off for Bob Price's appraisal. He didn't like the ending, and after re-reading it, I didn't either. I returned to the middle of the story and tried again. When I realized the plot was becoming that of a typical monster tale in which someone stumbles upon a giant alien which kills them before moving on to terrorize the countryside, I stopped and tried to devise the most unexpected turn of events I could imagine. The result is what you will find herein. Some readers find it silly, while others have taken the time to appreciate the not-so-subtle social comment I tossed in at the very end for good measure.

I managed to type about six single-spaced pages of "The Black Massif" before realizing the story required further fermenting in my mind before I could continue as the plot I had in mind was not a worthy tribute to the great Clark Ashton Smith. Moving on to another project, I expected to return to this tale in a few weeks. It wasn't until five full years later that the bulk of the storyline came to me. Like I said, I'm slow but sure, and I feel the final narrative was worth the wait.

Peter Worthy originally came up with the idea for *Ancient Exhumations* as a collection and inspired me to pursue the idea. Thanks to Peter and David Wynn of Mythos Books, the book was published and another followed.

I owe much to the several artists who have added so much to both editions of this book. Most of the interior artwork that appeared in the first edition is reprised in this second edition; only two small, insignificant pieces of my own didn't make this edition. As we wanted a glossy color cover for this edition, Daryl Hutchinson's original and extremely fine black-and-white cover drawing could not be carried over to this newer edition. My dear friend (and a real trooper!) Dan Ross came to the rescue by not only agreeing to create a fabulous, all-new color cover for this edition but additional interior illustrations for the two extra stories. I consider all of the artists who contributed to this book very good friends who have once again proven they are ready and willing to chip in and help whenever called upon. Thanks, guys!

In closing, I wish to acknowledge the great debt I owe to all the wonderful people who have unwaveringly encouraged, supported and believed in both me and my work. Were it not for them, I wouldn't be writing and you wouldn't be reading this or any other book by me.

I offer my very special thanks to, among others, Sheila Achs, Lucas "Rocco" Alexander who is married to the greatest singer in the world, warm-hearted master and kind friend Hugh B. Cave, my buddy James Chambers, sweet Maggie Cooper, buddy Ken Faig, Jr., unpredictable Rick Faust, poet-musician James Gruetzmacher, the ever-elusive Greg Kroll, my delightful friends Dick and Pat Lupoff, super couple Ray and Wendy Meluch, my mentor extraordinaire Bob Price, great friend and author Joe Pulver, my fairy-godmother Wilum Pugmire, the poetic Ann K. ('Ankh') Schwader, Helen Simone and Tinkerbell, the ever-generous and giving Barbara and Jeff Stevens, my brother buddies Jeffrey and Scott Thomas, the threesome of John Wise, Danni and John Smith, my talented and wonderful friend Peter Worthy and his fantastic wife Jan, and last but never least my dear Hans-Krishna von Hagen and our pal Ralph. You folks kept me going on those numerous occasions when I doubted myself and when my world fell apart, and I lovingly thank you all!

In addition, I wish to thank David Conyers for his generosity, his help, and especially for introducing me to William and Deborah Jones. As they say on TV, "The following is brought to you by ...", in this case, William and Deborah! It is great to work with such cooperative, knowledgeable, and friendly people! Thanks for everything!

Stanley C. Sargent
San Francisco 6/23/04

Introduction

I know I can say without fear of contradiction that Stanley C. Sargent as an author and an artist is one of the few class acts to emerge from the amateur press in recent years. This is no easy task. I've been involved with the small press in most of its incarnations since late 1996/early 1997 whether it is traditional print or the evolving e-press, and I've 'paid my dues' as well as taken some hard knocks too. What I mean to say is that I have learned what it takes to make it in the business of writing, editing, and illustrating, and it is by no means as easy as some people think. Those who deserve the plaudits don't always get where they ought to be. Don't take that as an expression of discontent or disrespect for the amateur vein; I wholeheartedly believe it is the sole garden, if you will, that welcomes and propagates new talent and original ideas as well as departure from the mainstream of professional print. I just meant to say that it is no kinder a business than any other, but sometimes there rises a voice so unique that you cannot help but listen to the song it sings.

The title of this collection brilliantly sums up the elements of the stories herein. Attention to history and his love of it all come through in all of Stan's work, imbuing tales such as "The Paladin of Worms" with a life all their own. Each piece is full of atmosphere, rich in details and meticulous in construction, an enchantment he works extremely hard to bring forth. He is a writer from the 'pen to paper, ass to chair' school; there is no effort too small, no amount of research too much for him. You'll be hard put to find any historical inaccuracy in the backdrops of the tales set in the past as he is an indefatigable researcher and it certainly shows. It is this attention to the small background elements that makes Stan's work such a pleasure to read.

His monsters are rarely ghosts – they erupt into this world disturbed by the intrusions of scholars, artists or sometimes merely by people being, well, people.

Almost ten years on, I can still remember that first batch of stories he sent to me. The first made me laugh out loud and the second caught the dreamer in me. I was hooked from that moment on. Read these pieces and see if you can blame me. The quality and imagination in them are addictive, and there is always a professionalism about his work that many modern 'pros' seem to lack in their hurry to tell their tales and smear the reader with gore.

Every story grows in stature and scope as he develops the plot, his terrors gaining a great and physical detail with each word. Read "The Rattle of Her Smile" to see exactly what I mean. All the tales in this book are woven with elegance, showing us how even in these modern times we can be haunted by the past. Indeed, that there are things the ancient world can still teach us.

I did not 'discover' this talented literary voice, that honor remains Bob Price's alone, but I readily recognized the pursuit of excellence and was determined to see his efforts reach a wider audience. I hope in some small way that I succeeded. He deserves it so much. For putting me in touch with Stan in the first place I have to thank my friend, correspondent and fellow collector *Mythosian*, James Ambuehl.

In closing, if I were to be asked to give a single sentence on the output of Stanley C. Sargent, it would be this — he writes tales to aspire to.

Peter Worthy
June 19, 2004
Scotland

The Rattle of Her Smile

". . . the unintelligible is necessarily hideous."
— Maurice Levy: *Lovecraft: A Study in the Fantastic*

Two years ago, I began gathering information for the biography I planned to write, based on the life of Ashley Farland. I wanted my first book to be a bestseller, and Farland seemed the perfect subject — an internationally acclaimed artist whose bizarrely evil sculptures were rumored to be inspired by the supernatural. My fifteen years as a journalist had given me the ability to write well, my subject was a celebrity, and as a bonus, he had vanished mysteriously a few months before I contracted for the book. I assured my editor I could discover Farland's whereabouts, whether he had vanished from his ancestral home in Aylesbury, Massachusetts to continue his work sequestered from all outside intrusion, or had met with foul play. In keeping that promise, I exchanged my assumption that the world is a safe and familiar place for the sure knowledge that it can be, at times, a nightmarish realm of unsuspected horror.

The public is most familiar with Farland's work through the popular coffee table collection of photographs published over five years ago. That volume purports to represent the best of Farland's often horrific efforts, yet many of his best pieces were deliberately deleted from that book as being "too repulsive and shocking" for widespread appeal. Aside from those censored sculptures (Copulating Demons, Soul Less Torment, The Ecstasy of Agony, etc.), which currently reside in various private collections, every gallery and museum of import, both here and abroad, boasts at least one Farland among its acquisitions.

I easily accumulated a tremendous amount of material concerning Farland's family and career, yet I had not discovered the slightest clue as to what had become of him, information absolutely vital for my book's success. I finally received a break in late May, when a letter arrived from the only man with whom Farland had maintained any regular contact during those final months. The letter was an invitation to meet with Dr. Jeffrey Markson, an expert on Pre-Columbian art whom Farland had befriended some eighteen months before his curious evanescence. All of my previous attempts to contact Dr. Markson had met with failure, so it was with great excitement that I accepted this opportunity for the potentially important interview. I could not help feeling puzzled at this unexpected invitation to meet with Markson at his home in Middleboro, Massachusetts, for although he had shied away from contact with the press throughout his entire career, he had obstinately refused to discuss Farland in any way even when the authorities officially declared the sculptor "missing." I wasted little time in responding to the offer, fearing Markson might change his mind; I caught the first available flight to Providence via Boston's Logan Airport. Once in Providence, I rented a car and immediately drove to Markson's address in the tiny town of Middleboro.

I had come across photos of Markson in the course of my research, but I was still surprised at the haggard appearance of the man who greeted me at the door. I knew Markson to be only fifty, yet he looked much older. Although he was obviously uncomfortable over the coming discussion, he nonetheless did his utmost to act the gracious host, introducing me not only to his charming wife, Barbara, but also their quietly observant teenage son, Tyler.

After an exchange of pleasantries, Mrs. Markson offered to bring tea to the two of us in the library, to which we then adjourned, accompanied by "Jenkin," the professor's ubiquitous German shepherd. I immediately accepted a seat in a comfortable chair near the warmth of a low fire, but the nervous Markson preferred to remain standing.

"As I am sure you are aware, Mr. Hathorne," he began, "I have avoided any mention of Ashley Farland for some time." After a moment's pause, he added, "I am willing to breach this subject only now that my health is failing. According to my doctor, my life expectancy is limited to under a year. I have therefore decided, contrary to my wife's advisement, that it would be wrong for me to pass on without first communicating any information I possess concerning Ashley and my interaction with him."

I offered my regrets over his failing health then, noting his reluctance to say anything further on the subject, I waited in silence for him to proceed.

"It is essential for you to understand that not only was Farland one of the most brilliant artists mankind has ever produced, but also a man haunted by that same talent. It tormented him to such a degree that he often reminded me of the demently driven surgeon of Mary Shelley's acclaimed novel. Over time, he grew increasingly dissatisfied with everything he produced, fanatically propelled by an urgency to surpass all of his previous accomplishments. He felt compelled to expand the boundaries of art so that his sculptures might approach and even achieve, as he called it, an 'intrinsic essence' of their own, independent of the consideration or even existence of any outside agency.

"He first wrote to me shortly after he became fascinated with Amerind art. We had met briefly while attending a series of lectures at Boston University, at which time I had expressed my admiration for his work, so he later felt free to seek my aid in attaining a deeper understanding of the antique styles of the Maya, Olmec, and Aztec cultures. I was quite flattered by the attention of such a well-known artist, realizing only later the true extent of his fanaticism.

"For several months I provided him with the information he requested, most of it fairly general in nature, but in those final months, he demanded research of a more specialized nature.

"He came upon a peculiar statue of an ancient Aztec goddess in a museum in Mexico City and, from that time on, its visage haunted his every waking thought. You may have seen photographs of the gruesome thing, eight feet tall and universally considered the most abhorrent piece of carving ever created by man. Yet it was more than just the piece's defiance of every tradition and definition of art that appealed to Farland's psyche; the abomination has a vile and evil presence about it. When he later found mention of a similar statue in a copy of the fabled *Necronomicon*, he believed he'd stumbled upon some ancient secret. I now regret helping him gain access to that and other equally damnable books, as they most certainly contributed to his psychological deterioration."

I was surprised at the direction Markson's tale had taken, having expected to hear more of a man obsessed, not possessed.

"He insisted on discovering everything about the goddess depicted in the monument, even going so far as to familiarize himself with the bizarre theories proffered by such pseudo-scientists as that Von Daniken fellow. Luckily, he quickly recognized such trash for what it is — a mishmash of conjecture, fantasy, ignorant misinterpretation, and quackery. By that time, I'd become rather irritated at his excessive demands upon my time, so it was with a certain relief that I informed him of the dearth of legitimate information pertaining to that particular subject."

Markson hesitated, once again lost in thought. He absentmindedly began to seat himself opposite me, then thinking better of it, he continued his pacing back and forth. After the passage of several minutes, I felt it prudent to disrupt his reverie.

THE RATTLE OF HER SMILE

"If you don't mind, Dr. Markson, I am not at all familiar with the statue to which you are referring. Would you mind providing me with a few details concerning its history?"

He started as if he had forgotten my presence. "Pardon me, Mr. Hathorne, it's just that for some time I have made great effort to forget any and everything connected with Farland, such that I now find it rather disturbing to recall it all.

"All that aside, however, you have asked about Coatlicue. She must actually be seen in all her heinous distortion to be appreciated." He turned and strode over to a bookshelf to remove a small volume, which he opened to a marked page before handing it to me.

"I describe the statue as if it were an atrocity, but you must decide for yourself whether or not I exaggerate."

At that moment, I glanced down at the revolting form which leered menacingly up at me from the page before voicing my agreement with Markson's assessment of the thing. I continued to stare at the photo even after he had resumed speaking, overcome with a vivid presentiment of timeless evil.

"For her history we must turn to the Post-Classic legendry of the Aztec as documented by the Spanish and augmented by contemporary folklore. Certainly this insidious creature had been highly revered by the Aztec, who recognized her as a great Earth Mother.

"According to legend, her original consort was another creation god, Yigcoatl, known to the Plains Indians of the Southwestern United States simply as 'Yig.' He proved too passive for the blood thirsty Coatlicue who, despite her gravid state, immigrated to the desert of Mexico where she gave birth to four hundred male offspring of a divinity less than her own. These sons are simply described as 'diamonds,' representing stars of the southern night sky. The goddess had previously conceived a daughter, Coyolxauhqui, whose paternal origin remains obscure. Her appearance differed from that of her brothers to the extent that her symbol was the lunar disk.

The story goes on to state that Coatlicue established residence in the heights of Coatepec, the 'Serpent Mountain,' where she came across a curious ball of feathers. She tucked the ball in her bosom for later examination, but when she subsequently sought to retrieve the thing, it had slipped down and impregnated her. Upon hearing such a bizarre explanation for the pregnancy, Coatlicue's four hundred offspring, at the behest of their sister Coyolxauhqui, beheaded their mother."

I found myself growing strangely uncomfortable as the story progressed, never dreaming that the rest would prove even worse.

"The headless Coatlicue was immortal, so she gave birth on the spot to a male child who sprang forth from her womb, dressed in full armor and ready for revenge. That male was Huitzilopochtli, the great god of war and incarnation of the Sun, who thereafter defeated his matricidal siblings. The Aztecs believed each dawn marked the supernal reenactment of Huitzilopochtli, as the Sun, driving away and defeating the stars and the Moon. I needn't add that Farland was intrigued by every aspect of this odd mythological vignette."

He paused to finally seat himself in an overstuffed chair opposite me. "And what became of Coatlicue after all of this?" I asked.

"She, as I stated, couldn't die. The two great gouts of blood that gushed from the terrible neck wound congealed into two giant rattlesnakes whose heads created a new face, or rather faces, for the goddess, when joined nose-to-nose. As you can see in the photo before you, the statue depicts her with her new head, bearing a face in both front and rear. Her hands were also severed, the blood from each wrist condensing into a single reptilian head.

"Legend claims the goddess' statue came to life during blood sacrifices to her, but due to her strong aversion to light, the statue had to be kept within the heavily curtained interior of "The Black House," the temple dedicated to her in Tenochtitlan, the Aztec capital city. In 1519, the Conquistadors witnessed ritual sacrifices to Coatlicue that so sickened and enraged them that, to the horror of the worshippers, the idol was cast roughly down the temple's steps and buried on the spot. The fractured likeness of Coatlicue was only rediscovered in 1824, buried beneath Mexico City's Cathedral Square. She was reassembled as you see her here," he said, indicating the photo in my lap.

Markson remained in his seat, but leaned forward to wearily cover his face with his hands. A moment later he gazed intensely into my eyes, adding in a whisper of growing intensity, "It was with this she-fiend of hell that Ashley became obsessed, almost enamored; his ultimate goal being to sculpt a likeness of Coatlicue so perfect that, with the aid of incantations from the *Necronomicon* and other profane incunabula, it could actually be animated and imbued with life!"

Shocked at this last statement, I asked, "Are you telling me that Farland was mad? Certainly no sane person could entertain such a concept! You are describing nothing less than a megalomaniac, possibly even a dangerous one."

Enigmatically he replied, "I have never contended that Farland was mad, and I would not do so now."

"But ..." I began, only to be silenced by Markson's upraised hand. He lifted a large bundle of papers from an adjacent desktop and extended it toward me.

"It is all here, recorded in his letters to me. I feel it would be more profitable for you to read them for yourself rather than hear an encapsulation of their contents from me. I want you to take them with you; I have no further use of them."

Overwhelmed by his stern but generous offer, I objected, insisting I could just as easily study and return the documents after making copies of any I deemed necessary for quotes in my text.

He became agitated suddenly and pressed the letters upon me. "Please understand, Mr. Hathorne, as I will soon be beyond any concern for such things, Barbara has pleaded with me to dispose of these letters so she will not be left with them."

"But they could easily become very valuable in the near future," I told him. "You must consider your son's future if nothing else."

Markson, unmoved by my argument, stated he hoped his son never found opportunity to read the letters — they were mine. As I relieved him of the bundle, the professor rose to mark the conclusion of the interview, though I felt the need to query him on one final point.

"Sir, in your opinion, just what has become of Ashley Farland?"

Markson carefully weighed his words before responding ominously. "I fear I cannot answer that question. I know he had completed his sculpture of Coatlicue; in his last letter, he asked if I would attend its 'christening.' The appointed date, however, fell during the final week of the exams preceding summer break, so I wrote him not to expect me.

"I tried unsuccessfully to contact him by phone several times before the scheduled date, finally contacting the sheriff of Aylesbury. It was from him that I learned Farland had not been seen for nearly a week, having failed to collect supplies he had ordered from the town grocer, although he had insisted they arrive well before the date on which he planned to unveil his creation. I haven't the slightest doubt that his experiment backfired in some way or other; I only pray that death was the worst that overtook him." As he continued, there seemed to be a hint of nervousness in his voice.

"You must read these letters with an open mind. If I've learned anything in my life, it's that a rigid mind is a most terrible weakness. Farland accepted much we normally consider preposterous, but his real error lay in his certainty that such things could be controlled and manipulated. I admit to the acceptance of certain aspects of the supranormal, yet I failed in turn to convince Farland of the peril he courted."

Noting my shocked expression, he gave further challenge.

"Before you decide I too am unbalanced, I suggest you take the opportunity to look into the recent case of three staff members at the university who entered an ancient Cretan tomb despite similar warnings; they too have vanished without a trace.

"I advise you to abandon your search. Ashley Farland was intent on delving into areas better left alone and unknown, and now you must ask yourself if this book is worth the risk of your sanity ... or your life."

I sat for a moment, unsure if I had been threatened, then Markson turned and walked toward the doorway to the hall. I followed, taking the letters with me. I hoped Mrs. Markson would arrive with the promised tea that I might have more time to question the academian further, but I was disappointed.

"I will say no more on the subject, Mr. Hathorne. You may consider this interview at an end."

Allowing me no opportunity for response, my host escorted me to the door and bid me good night. I left feeling sure that whatever disease had ravaged his body had also affected his mind. I felt so sure of this that I felt no need to investigate the other cases of disappearance to which Markson had directed me.

Markson's unexpected gift occupied all of my attention in the weeks that followed. To my delight, he had amassed Farland's letters in precise chronological order, methodically binding them in notebooks. The initial page of each letter was carefully dated in an altogether different hand, apparently Markson's, the oldest being dated nearly two years before Farland's disappearance.

The earliest letters reflected Farland's fascination with Amerind art, just as Markson had stated, the sculptor's inquiries being interspersed with his lengthy dissertations detailing his search for some means to elevate the "intrinsic essence" of his artistic endeavors. Much of this latter text struck me as being the result of his dissatisfaction not only with his work but also with the critical acclaim he had achieved. He repeatedly bemoaned the waste of his talent and effort in creating "relics" which, after momentarily exciting a few critics and gallery owners, ended up being little more than dust gatherers in some collection.

At the same time, he kept Markson quite busy researching various aspects of Amerind history and art, the topics ranging from the several schools of Mayan painting and sculpture, to the sand paintings of the tribes in the Southwestern United States. It must have been quite taxing for Markson to attend to his schedule of classes while still finding time to write an endless number of responses to Farland's requests for more and more information.

Nothing that Farland had written seemed all that exceptional until a tour of Mexico City's Anthropological Museum brought him face to face with the eight-foot likeness of Coatlicue. It was carved "in the round" and represented the only image of the goddess known to have survived. Her name, I discovered, translates as "She of the Serpent Skirt," a reference to the raiment apparent in the museum guidebook photo. Farland had been so overwhelmed by the eidolon that he began to write Markson daily, urgently pleading with the scholar for more information about it. Markson seems to have done his utmost to comply with these requests, but in the meantime, Farland instigated his own brand of study, involving theories and speculations he considered too "outré" for the conservative professor.

I still felt repulsed by the same effigy that had made such an impression on Farland, finding it impossible to imagine anyone worshipping such a monstrosity. Just what was it that had so intrigued Farland that he would abandon all other pursuits? The answer had to lie somewhere within his final correspondence with Markson.

Farland had explored several "forbidden" texts located in private collections both here and abroad, his reputation and association with Markson providing *carte blanche* access wherever he went. He seems to have felt no obligation to share the results of this private researches with Markson, simply integrating it all into a set of interlocking revelations he believed would provide him the means to instill life in his sculpture.

The letters became almost a chronicle of intensifying dementia. Markson seems to have made periodic attempts to point out the irrationality of his friend's delusions, but to little effect. In several letters, Farland even scoffed at the scholar's warnings, inferring the professor predicted certain disaster should he persist in his sorcerous efforts. Farland planned to model his carving after Coatlicue in the steadfast belief that the original's geometric contours themselves contained an inherent power. He claimed the discrete non-Euclidean geometry of the statue could create an elision in the space-time continuum, a minor gateway through which an adept could entice interdimensionally peculiar life forms. He stressed, for Markson's benefit, that he could control any life forms he might so entice and protect himself should his sculpture awaken with the appetites of its predecessor. Unfortunately, he neglected to elaborate on those methods. Still, I could not comprehend these two intelligent men taking this nonsense seriously. Farland had made little attempt to convert Markson, merely pointing out documented instances of bi-cephalic serpents, a mutation real enough though exclusive to rattlers; he neglected, however, to mention that such freaks of nature never reach maturity despite both heads being quite functional. I had to assume, therefore, that something else, something he was unwilling to discuss with me, had convinced Markson to accept the reality of the supernatural.

It occurred to me that Farland might have experimented with the same hallucinogenic drugs taken by the Aztec priests for their ceremonies. Under such influence, the terrible stone entity might appear to achieve at least an immanent mobility; yet nothing in the letters directly indicated drug use of any sort, and it seemed unlikely that Farland would have settled for peyote, knowing the Aztec priests had greatly preferred bufotenine. Bufotenine is produced only by a rare and poisonous giant marine toad (*bufo marinus*), which would have proven extremely difficult for Farland to obtain. If he had indeed experimented with drugs, I believe his conversion to supernatural beliefs would have been an overnight process rather than the gradual evolution expressed in his writings. The only other alternative I could see was that something he learned while exploring forbidden lore had affected him deeply enough to have altered his entire mindset.

An important adjunct to the letters was my own study of the Aztec, beginning with Prescott's familiar *The Conquest of Mexico*. But to get beyond the general, I was compelled to reference more than one treatise written by the friars of the post-conquest period. Many of these, unfortunately, had never been translated from the original sixteenth-century Spanish, but I managed to struggle through, armed with my knowledge of contemporary Spanish and a dictionary pertaining to the linguistic quirks of the period. What I read therein put me off my appetite.

Coatlicue, I found, was more than a creation goddess; she was the embodiment of Mother Earth to the Aztecs. As she, along with the other important deities, bestowed favor upon those who fed them, thousands of people were butchered annually in bloody sacrifice intended to quell the appetites of the divinities. For offerings to Coatlicue, the victims' still-beating hearts were cut out and burned with copal incense in braziers before her idol — the very idol now residing in the museum in Mexico City. The victims' mutilated bodies were tossed down from the pyramidal heights to be fought over by the mob waiting below. Whoever gained possession of the corpse would flay it and display the skin publicly; the dermally-stripped torso and limbs were used to flavor a ceremonial soup that was consumed by all in imitation of Coatlicue, who it was believed also feasted upon dead bodies. Her ghoulish propensity is reflected by the severed human hands and hearts strung on her necklace, along with the pendant human skull that dangles between her flaccid breasts. Although this cannibalistic penchant of the goddess was literally interpreted by Farland, many scholars believed the Aztecs were simply employing a metaphor to explain earth's reclamation of organic matter; dead bodies decomposed in earth, thereby replenishing the fertility of the soil. This symbolic interpretation explains the references in Aztec prayers to "She who receives the bodies of the dead, who devours the flesh of the skeletons." Farland, however, rejected this theory, preferring a living abomination over a mere analogy.

And it was upon a new version of this fiendish aberration that Farland dreamed of bestowing life as his ultimate masterpiece. "What," the artist had asked in a letter, "if the Mona Lisa had been provided with the resources to explain her enigmatic smile?"

"What," I had to ask myself, "if Picasso's abstracted mutations had come to life?" Even that would be preferable to Farland's Aztec monstrosity!

I no longer harbored any doubts about the state of Farland's sanity; I concluded he had become quite certifiable. I remained puzzled, however, by Markson's part in all this. How was it the professor was so sure Farland was dead, and what was the meaning of the implied threat in his parting words to me?

After a second read through Farland's correspondence, I felt I had reached an impasse — I still had no idea what had become of him. From clues spread widely throughout the letters, I gathered he had set up some sort of studio, appropriately in his family's subterranean burial vault, in early April. The letters mentioned that the entrance lay secreted behind a trio of dogwood trees, in a wooded area not far from the house. I saw no other option than to visit the property myself, gambling that I might still contrive some conclusion for my book. Should Aylesbury prove another dead end, I would stop by Markson's home in nearby Middleboro for a second, more impromptu visit.

A week later, I was back in summer-heated Providence, where I rented an air conditioned car before heading for Aylesbury. After a nearly two-hour drive, I found it necessary to seek directions to the Farland property, but the local townsfolk proved uncooperative, some even turning their backs upon my inquiries. The town's metropolitan area consisted of only four blocks of tiny business and office buildings, in the midst of which I spotted the sheriff's office. As part of my initial research into Farland's disappearance, I had spoken to Sheriff Waterman of Aylesbury, who had been decent enough on the phone. I parked my car outside his office, hoping Waterman would be available and willing to provide me with directions.

Sheriff Waterman, a short slovenly man, squirmed uncomfortably behind his desk as I introduced myself, then explained my predicament. I eventually managed to extract sufficient directions despite the slurring of his speech due to the wad of tobacco he was chewing. I then asked him if there had been any progress in the search for Farland.

"Progress?" he drawled. "I know he's more gone now than he was when you called me from Californier, but that's 'bout all."

He spit, missing the spittoon, then wiped his chin. "Listen, mister, you go sniffin' 'round out there and chances are I'll be a lookin' for you next, an' I don't relish the nuisance. There ain't nothin' out there worth writin' 'bout; Farland's gone and, well, he ain't exactly been missed 'round here. Take my advice — go home, write yourself a dirty novel, and forget all 'bout this one."

I did not take the sheriff's advice, but I had wanted to ask just what Farland had done to make himself such a pariah. The artist had generally been described elsewhere as affable, though self-involved and moody at times. I felt sure the local disdain for Farland had curtailed the sheriff's efforts to locate the man, thereby increasing the odds of my uncovering some further evidence. If I could solve the mystery or, even better, find the artist himself, the success of my book would be guaranteed, along with my own celebrity.

Following the directions I had been given, I stayed on the post road until I spotted a private, unpaved drive off to the left, about three miles out of town. A few minutes later I parked my car before the dilapidated Farland house, a stark Georgian structure with upper stories nearly obscured by an overgrowth of ancient oaks. Finding the front door unlocked, I entered, leaving it wide open behind me to allow more light into the shadowy interior. A quick perusal of the ground floor revealed that at least three of the first-floor rooms had been occupied, possibly as recently as the previous year — just about the time Farland vanished. The thick dust and heavy fall of cobwebs over the stairs indicated the upper stories had not been used for several years.

In a sunnier room in the back, there was a bed which I assumed had been Farland's. In that same room, I found a small collection of books and handwritten notes scattered across the top of an old fashioned desk. Among the confusion I also noticed a daily calendar which noted the date as June 21, the Summer Solstice; "Markson at 11" had been scribbled across that same page. I recalled that Farland had last been seen on June 10, although he was not pronounced officially missing until June 22.

The notes were in total disorder and contained passages in several oddly unfamiliar languages along with numerous signs and symbols I assumed were magical emblems. Among the books Farland had collected for reference was *Pallida Mors*, a vampiric bible with a sanguine history, along with other, equally intriguing banned titles such as *Unaussprechlichen Kulten*, *Cultes des Ghoules*, the *Popul Vuh*, and the *Biblia Sinistre*. Although not an antiquarian, I recognized the great value of some of those rare tomes, at least one of which was bound in skin, probably human. Tucked among the pages of the *Popul Vuh*, I found what I assumed was Farland's attempt to decipher a series of Mixtec pictographs from *The Borgia Codex* in relation to certain passages from von Junzt's demonic text.

Thinking I would have ample time later to study the paperwork with more care, I returned to my rented car in search of a light. The glove compartment yielded a working flashlight, so I set out for the wooded area behind the house, determined to locate the crypt's hidden entrance before dark. According to Markson, Farland worked on his sculpture of Coatlicue in the makeshift studio he had built within the crypt. Considering the artist's obsession with that particular sculpture, its presence or absence should determine whether Farland was still somewhere in the area.

I searched for nearly an hour before finding the trio of dogwood trees Farland had mentioned in one of his letters. I was tired, drenched in sweat, and covered with tiny cuts from thrashing through bramble bushes and shrubs by the time I finally came upon the trees that marked the entrance to the family sepulcher. Unable to find a path through or around the trees, I forced my way between the rough, twisted trunks of two of them, my skin and clothing already miserably torn. Finally, I found myself facing the rusting metal bars which served as gate to the Farland family crypt.

The inner structure lay deep underground, but the entry shaft had been carved directly into the rocky earth of a mound that served to camouflage its presence. Farland had chosen to work in the isolation of a 300-year-old corpse lair, he claimed, for the eerie ambiance of the place.

I made short work of the lock and chain that bound the heavy bars of the outer gate to an earth-imbedded framework, and prepared to enter the dark tunnel.

Suddenly I felt overcome by a claustrophobic anxiety that I had not experienced since childhood. I shone my light into the dank shaft to reveal rough-hewn walls siding a dirt floor that extended some ten or more feet before abruptly ending at a massive door engraved with the family name. I timorously entered and approached the inner door, praying it would be locked. The latch handle turned easily, but I had to apply my full bodyweight in order to shove the heavy barrier of the door inward, whereupon there was revealed a pitch-dark expanse that reminded me of nothing more than a black abyss of

Hell. A gut-wrenching odor, far worse than any normal fumes I would have expected even in a sealed tomb, assaulted me immediately as I stepped inside, forcing me to lean momentarily against the moist wall before continuing.

Whatever form Farland's experiment had taken, I could see instantly that it had gone very wrong, for the inner crypt was a total shambles. Areas of the ancient walls and ceiling had recently caved-in, leaving piles of stone and masonry heaped and strewn across the floor. Only a few support columns remained in place to prevent the earth-burdened roof above from crashing down and filling in the large room. As I maneuvered through the rubble, avoiding unstable structural supports, the beam of my flashlight defined only the slimmest shaft of light through the aggregated shadows.

As my eyes adjusted to the darkness around me, I slowly began to spot a few half-buried sculptor's tools among the debris; I was definitely standing in Farland's studio, or what remained of it. I discovered crude torches protruding from the farthest wall, by which I managed to illuminate the place somewhat. Thank God I had thought to bring matches with me. How the man could possibly accomplish such intricate carving by the feeble light of torches was beyond me, but Farland had somehow managed it marvelously, for within a spacious recess cut from the raw stone of the room's circumference, I beheld his awesome work standing apparently undamaged in the midst of the dust-covered wreckage.

I pushed aside endless curtains of diaphanous cobwebs, often stumbling over loose stones that lay hidden beneath at least six months' accumulation of grime blanketing the limestone floor. A fallen plinth blocked my near approach to the statue, but even when viewed from a distance I was impressed by the unbelievably detailed features of the figure and the awesome skill of its creator. Only the pale translucence and immobility of the eight-foot idol tainted the illusion of true vitality, and I wondered at the nature of the material from which it had been carved. Even the gentle transparency of alabaster could not approach the inherent luminescence of its substance.

What amazed me most, however, was the great beauty Farland had culled from such a hideously deformed figure. I found it unexpectedly fascinating rather than frightening, feeling at ease in its presence even in such dank and eerie surroundings. It frustrated me that I could not descry an unobstructed pathway to it through the rubble, as I felt an urge to run my hands along its delicate squamate contours. I wondered what effect this new Coatlicue would have upon the viewer when seen up close under proper gallery lighting, for in its own bizarre way, it was breathtakingly beautiful. I sensed no innate evil in

Farland's depiction of the distorted creature, unlike the foul revulsion elicited by the original even in photographs.

I must have stood entranced before the enlivened sculpture for some time, far removed from thoughts of aught else. Then, while attempting to lean closer that I might better observe certain aspects of it, my foot slipped on a small rounded pebble and I fell roughly forward across a pile of broken masonry. As the dust cleared, I tried to right myself in order to stand up, but I slipped in the course of my efforts, such that my groping palm came to rest upon an oddly shaped object in the dirt. Carefully lifting my hand, I turned my light that I might illuminate whatever it was I had found, recognizing immediately a spinal column with the shoulder blades and one arm still attached — human bones. Caught totally off guard, I screamed and grappled my way awkwardly to my feet.

The light revealed the nearly complete skeleton of a man lying at the base of Coatlicue's statue; the head and hands were missing altogether, and I swung the light over the entire area in an almost desperate attempt to catch sight of them. Frantically driving out memories of what the original goddess had strung upon her necklace, I concluded that Farland had been caught in a cave-in and died, his skull and carpal bones subsequently being displaced in the collapsing of the walls and ceiling or carried off by some vermin. Certainly some type of scavenger had to be responsible for the fleshlessness of the bones, I told myself. Then I grew nauseated envisioning the latter possibility but knew it was preferable to further suggestions which, although becoming more horrifyingly believable each moment, I dared not allow myself to consider. A glance at the statue itself, half in anticipation of seeing Farland's severed head and hands displayed there, helped calm my fears; Farland had not allowed the goddess neck adornment of any kind, let alone the gruesome kind I had half expected to see ensconced upon her breast.

Further exploration of the tomb only added to my growing fear and trepidation. In several corridors branching from the main room, I encountered numerous drawers in which individual members of the Farland family had been entombed since the 1600s. The marble seal had been smashed in every instance, the pall disinterred, and the body savagely torn from the coffin and disseminated haphazardly about the area. It was with relief that I noted the presence of skulls and hands among the skeletons so rendered asunder. Yet many of the bones displayed wedge-shaped lacerations for which I could not account. It was clear that the mayhem of my surroundings could not be attributed to the simple crumbling of the interior structure over time; the destruction was the result of some terrible paroxysm of unrelenting rage — but by whom or what, and to what end? Could the damage derive from an attempt to obliterate any sign of violence? Had Farland been murdered?

I had all but concluded that the wisest thing for me to do would be to report my discoveries to Sheriff Waterman, when I banged my shin upon a stone and blurted out an expletive that echoed the length of the chamber in which I stood. From the far extreme of a dark corridor I had not yet explored came the sound of labored breathing in response, accompanied by an auditory shuffling and scraping. The sounds became amplified in a cadence of heavy shambling that made me realize someone or something's attention had been attracted by the sound of my voice.

I could only inhale in short gasps as I stood frozen to the spot, no longer capable of denying the icy fear that slowly crept over me, gripping both my mind and body in a vice of terror. I suddenly found myself willing to admit belief in anything if only the thing approaching me would just go away.

The flashlight had been wrenched from my grip as I fell, landing a few feet away, its beam pointing directly at the source of my terror. I could have easily reached out and grasped the light had I not been immobilized with absolute terror.

The thing came closer, until its lumbering mass was partially silhouetted at the edge of luminescence provided by the torches in the main room behind me. Before the thing's outline broke over the top of the flashlight beam, I managed a faltering retreat, back into the main room, snatching the flashlight from the floor as I ran. Once there, a mad curiosity kept me from backing further toward the exit, for I could not leave without knowing beyond doubt the nature of the thing that had emerged from charnel darkness.

I prayed the slime-drenched thing I had seen emerging from the blackness had been distorted by my imagination but as it neared, its form clarified, additionally lit by a phosphorescence like that emitted by decaying organic matter. When I beheld the full detail of the thing in the glare of my flashlight, an insane shrieking simultaneously assaulted my ears. The screaming was deafening and went on and on until, finally, I realized it was coming from my own throat. This realization made me laugh — hysterically, uncontrollably, psychotically. It struck me as ironic that I should be raving so uncontrollably when confronted by a totally voiceless presence in a silent tomb.

I looked up and beheld Farland's living, breathing masterpiece. Her necklace initially caught my eye. It was strung with a pair of mummied hands and a rotting, maggot-infested heart. At her waist depended the long-sought-after object of my search, or part of it, for I could not mistake the head of Ashley Farland, despite the overall gray-green cast of the skin and the bits of putrid flesh peeling away from the underpinning bone.

In all honesty, I cannot say how long I remained in a half-mad state, my mind pummeled by the nauseous "uncleanliness" standing before me. I found myself studying Coatlicue while each of the two mammoth rattlesnakes of her head studied me; I wondered whether the front pair of eyes served as vehicle for intelligence or, indeed, if the abomination had a need for brains at all. Her movement and function might be directed by nothing more than ravenous lustful hunger.

I can only describe the reptilian bitch as a gigantic caricature of the human form and an insult to nature itself. The structure of her wide, distorted head incorporated the features of two gargantuan rattler heads rampantly joined at their snouts to form a face of living blood. The lipless orifice created by the merging of the mouths penetrated the width of the poll to provide for a face in front as well as its duplicate in the rear. Large fangs depended from the jaws of the two-faced monster, curving outwardly, away from the center of each of the idol's malefic 'smiles.' Horny ridges above the jaws acted as cheek bones, and below the protective dual ridge of the brow nestled lidless, unblinking nyctalopitc eyes inlaid with vertical pupillary slits.

Great pendulous breasts lay like deflated bags upon her chest above a row of innumerable swaying rattlers that formed a clicking fringe belting her bloated waist. Her thick arms terminated in open-mawed reptilian heads resembling vicious handpuppets with unnaturally large fangs. These were only surpassed by the discolored claws extending from the toes of her swollen feet.

Aside from the nauseating necklace, her only raiment was a convoluted mass of writhing snakes of normal size, their vaguely triangular heads bobbing and weaving threateningly as they slowly dove in and out of the Gordian weave the Aztecs had dubbed her "skirt." The sibilant hissing of their extraordinary numbers blended into a resonance reminiscent of the rustling of dry, brittle leaves as their ugly heads swayed calculatingly, keeping to a measured beat only they could hear.

Seeing this total abnormality heft its bloated bulk toward me caused some function of my brain to lapse, rendering me incapable of movement. I stood there, agape, unable to defend myself or run away, like the fabled rabbit trapped in the hypnotic glare of a viper. Its breath reeked of fetid meat and worms, and I grew dizzy, helpless before the approach of conglomerate lunacy. It was all so unreal and impossible, that I doubted the reality of the experience. I seemed to view the scene from afar as the accursed beast grappled for me with its grotesquely mutated limbs.

Suddenly another sound intruded upon the sibilant silence, and I turned

to determine its source. From behind me came a flash of gray and brown with teeth barred in a deadly snarl. The dog hurled its body into the air, landing on Coatlicue's mottled chest, where the animal began to rend and tear the scales from the underlying vulnerable flesh. The hound seemed familiar until finally, to my amazement, I recognized it as Markson's German shepherd, Jenkin.

The brave beast did not have the slightest chance against a creature of such overwhelming proportions, and I listened as Jenkin cried out again and again at the painfully venomous bites inflicted upon him by the viperous denizens of the monster's skirt. Only moments later, he emitted a final agonized yelp before falling, lifeless to the floor. Coatlicue was obviously agitated, but I detected no sign that she had been seriously harmed.

I knew my chance to escape had come, so I began inching myself away, moving slowly toward the door to the entry shaft. Coatlicue bent down awkwardly to rip into the canine carcass, her attention distracted momentarily away from me. Walking backwards, however slowly, proved impossible without stumbling in the half light, for when only ten feet from the outer door, I tripped and fell headlong into a pile of rubble.

At the noise, Coatlicue snapped to attention, abandoning her nauseating feast in an effort to catch me. I had underestimated her intelligence for she immediately maneuvered herself around to bar my way to the exit. I stumbled again in my haste to move further away from her, and my groping arm tore one of the burning torches out from its cresset, knocking it to the ground at the foot of the statue off to my right. The instant the flame touched what I had thought was a sculpture, its true nature became all too clear. No wonder I had not been able to guess its composition — it was not stone at all! The thing I had seen and found so beautiful was nothing more than the slough the monster Coatlicue had shed immediately after her rebirth! The dry discarded skin burst into flames of such intensity that even the real Coatlicue was driven back and away from the exit. The light, combined with the heat of the fire caused her to twist and convulse such that countless adders were flung from her skirt by centrifugal force. Each landed with a slapping sound upon the floor around her before quickly slithering off to the shelter of the room's darker recesses.

The blaze terrified Coatlicue. She seemed to totally lose control of her body. Her head suddenly rose up in fury. The composite rattler heads that comprised her head wrenched and ripped apart. Each of the bleeding heads flailed wildly back and forth, the forked tongues snatching tastes of smoke-filled air. Taking advantage of the monster's disorientation as she lumbered in ever-widening circles, I dashed for the exposed portal to freedom. I had nearly made it through the door before being viciously struck again and again from every direction by the poisonous fangs of the cowardly refugees of Coatlicue's skirt. I managed to drag myself through the second doorway before passing out, so desperate to reach that cool night air that I did not even bother to fling the hateful scaled biters from my flesh. Once outside, I threw myself through the trees and headlong into the weeds.

I awoke with a start on the following afternoon, only to find myself laid out upon Farland's makeshift bed in the main house amidst the lingering reek of Coatlicue's pervasive stench. I tossed back the blanket that covered me and prepared to stand, only then realizing both my legs were heavily bandaged. Before I could even formulate the several questions this situation brought to mind, Markson entered the room and welcomed me "back from the dead."

"You? You saved me?" I blurted out. "But you wanted me to find that, that thing — you set me up to walk right into a death trap!"

Markson pulled a chair next to the bed where I rested. "Now whatever brought you to that conclusion?" he asked defensively.

"Well, for one thing, your name and time of arrival was written on Farland's calendar, yet you told me you had declined the invitation before making any plans with him." The pieces of the puzzle began to fall together as my head cleared.

"You lied to me — not only were you expected, but you were also present at the revival ceremony," I blurted out in accusation. "You were there, and when you saw that horror actually come to life, you ran, leaving Farland, your friend, at its mercy! You left him there to die in order to save yourself!"

Markson sighed, then looked directly, openly at me.

"Half of your accusation is true; a part of me did hope you would disappear, but my conscience wouldn't allow it. When Sheriff Waterman phoned to inform me he'd provided you with directions to this place, I realized I could not be a party to murder, not even indirectly. I simply couldn't bear the thought of meeting my maker with your blood on my hands."

"What about Farland's blood? Where was your precious conscience when you abandoned him to his terrible fate?" He may have saved my life, but I felt hatred for him, as I would for any coward who could forsake another in such a manner.

"You judge me too harshly, Mr. Hathorne. I am no hero, but I am not a coward either.

"I admit I attended Farland's little ceremony as you call it, but I came here hoping to convince him that the risk was too great. Given the opportunity in person, I felt sure I could persuade him of the danger involved with his plan, but he insisted the invocation must commence exactly at noon on the Solstice. At that particular moment each year, the sun and Earth are at their closest proximity, and Farland was sure the solar influence was intricately linked with Coatlicue as she was the mother of Huitzilopochtli, who represented the sun.

"There's no need to describe the conjuration in detail, and I would never dare cite the unspeakable forces he called upon for aid. Suffice it to say, the statue was somehow invested with the reptilian goddess's pestilential essence. You've seen her, so you know."

I tried to interrupt, growing impatient with his explanation, but he would not allow it.

"Please allow me to finish," he sternly silenced me. "You have accused me of murder, man! You owe me at least an opportunity to defend myself!"

I nodded my assent though I still doubted the veracity of his words.

"You will recall that Farland stated in a letter to me that he was prepared for the worst should the revived goddess retain her lust for bloody sacrifice. You may also recall that he failed to explain the means by which he planned to protect himself, should it become necessary. That is because he intended all along to offer me up as a sacrificial victim to assuage her monstrous appetite."

I drew back from him in disbelief. I could not imagine anyone, even Farland in his madness, capable of formulating such unimaginable treachery.

"You are shocked, as well you should be, but that is the shameful truth. I stood in disbelief as Farland bound the flailing spirit within the confines of the eidolon, totally unmindful of my precarious position between the two. Once he was convinced the demon was fully congealed within the sculpture, he threw himself upon me from behind, hurling me directly into the path of the ravenous creature. I heard him call out to the goddess, begging her to accept me as his blood offering.

"Somehow, I regained my balance and managed to right myself enough to stagger away from the oncoming horror, still unable to believe Farland's betrayal. He brandished a blade with which he then attacked me, fully intent on depriving me of my heart."

I became fully engrossed as he revealed the circumstances of the struggle, slowly but surely realizing he was telling the truth.

"Luckily, Farland had underestimated the strength adrenaline bestows upon those who are desperately afraid. He came at me, we struggled, and he stumbled, falling back into the arms of his own fatal creation."

The ailing professor stopped briefly, overcome by the bitter memory. I averted my gaze as tears streamed down his cheeks and began to reassess my earlier evaluation of the man. The cold unfeeling man I had originally interviewed was now gone, replaced by a warmer, more vulnerable human being who had faced an impossible dilemma from which he could never recover.

"There was no way to save him. I would have, even then, if there'd been any way possible at all, but once she'd enveloped him in her terrible embrace, there was nothing I could do. I turned and fled, stricken with madness and horror."

"I contrived to eliminate all trace of my presence here that day, obviously without realizing Farland had made note of my expected arrival time on his calendar. Knowing she was unable to tolerate the light, I returned before sundown and locked her in the tomb, accomplishing the deed with a thick chain and strong padlock on the outermost gate. No one remembered the crypt was there, so there was little chance of her inadvertent release. I knew her anatomy would deprive her of the dexterity necessary to tamper with the lock. I then tried in vain to put the entire nightmare series of events behind me."

Amazed at the naiveté of Markson's plan, I objected. "Didn't it occur to you that such a famous person would not just be forgotten? That some type of investigation would certainly follow?"

"I knew any outside investigation would be sidetracked by Sheriff Waterman. You see, I went to him that day, immediately after fleeing the crypt; I told him everything, though I doubt he believed it all. He actually helped me place the lock and has kept my secret since that day. You have no idea just how terrified the good citizens of Aylesbury were of Farland. They considered him some sort of devil incarnate, so they were glad to be rid of him regardless of the means."

"It was only later, when I learned of your determined quest to discover Farland's whereabouts, that I panicked. I knew I didn't have long to live and I could not allow my family to become involved in a scandal. Who would have believed a tale such as mine without unleashing the Coatlicue from her prison? Still, I could not bear the thought of leaving Barbara and Tyler the terrible legacy of a suspected murderer."

He looked up at me with a shamed expression on his face. "I felt obliged to tantalize you with the letters and other small clues, so you would follow the trail to the demon's lair wherein you would disappear, just as Farland had done. But as you see, I couldn't follow through.

"As to your rescue, I happen to be one of those persons who is always prepared, which means I brought a healthy dose of anti-venom and a hypodermic along with me. Just in case.

"Diamondbacks are not native to this area, you know," he continued. "Have you put that clue in perspective yet? No? Well then, do you recall how the Aztecs described Coatlicue's four hundred sons?"

I thought a moment, then recalled a passage from Coe's *Mexico* on the subject.

"She gave birth to four hundred male offspring, described simply as 'diamonds' — my God! I see it now! I'd taken it for granted that "diamonds" was just a euphemism for stars. Incredibly, the bitch was giving birth right before my eyes!"

Markson smiled, relaxing a bit. "The term 'skirt' seems to demonstrate the black humor of the Aztec priests, doesn't it? In truth, Coatlicue had already birthed the four hundred progeny of her new incarnation before you arrived, yet they still clung to their mother as a source of nourishment — creating the semblance of a skirt. They were unwilling to be weaned, however, until your little fire posed a threat to their safety." He chuckled slightly to himself. "I'll wager she was more than happy be rid of her malevolent brood."

His face clouded over slowly before he added, "I also brought Jenkin with me when I came here today."

I told him of Jenkin's daring charge at the beast and how he'd miraculously provided me an opportunity to escape. I offered my condolences at his loss of such a loyal companion. He had assumed Coatlicue had killed the dog, but he did not seem surprised it had sacrificed itself on my behalf.

"A brave dog and loyal friend, old Jenkin. I'll miss him in the time I have left."

He paused to gain his composure. Before he could continue, I placed a reassuring hand upon his shoulder. I felt only sympathy and understanding for him at that point.

My next question was an obvious one: "What do we do now?" The subject change helped revive my new found friend's spirits.

"Well, you needn't be concerned about a few diamondbacks being loose in the neighborhood. I am sure Sheriff Waterman will be happy to arrange a snake hunt. It will not only be good fun for the townsfolk, but they will jump at the chance to rid the area of any creation of Farland's, I'm sure.

"As for the our lady of the crypt, that shouldn't be too difficult either. The good sheriff and I originally discussed sealing up the crypt forever with concrete, a plan I think we shall now instigate." He turned and gave me a reassuring look. "Don't worry, I've locked her in again for now. I told you I came prepared!

"She nearly brought her house down upon herself when she was locked in the first time, what with all the banging on the walls and rampaging through the vaults in her fury! So I doubt she'll try that again for fear of collapsing the roof on herself. Poor thing," he joked, "those catacombs are over three hundred years old, you know, and not so strong anymore. Her essence may be immortal, but the Conquistadors buried her for centuries and so shall we. There's not much else we can do without knowing just what manner of entity she really is, and I see no safe way to find that out. Farland hoped to bring his statue to life, but in reality, he, like the Aztecs before him, merely provided a vessel for that alien abomination to inhabit."

I finally asked him about the change that had come over Farland. What did he think could have happened to him?

"It seems he forgot the most important thing — that an artist's finest creation is himself. Maybe he never understood that art's true value lies in its ability to remind its admirers of the sublime heights man is capable of reaching. Art need be no more than proof that man's perception, insight, and sensibility — his soul — can reach an incredible degree of transcendence. The greatness of every civilization throughout history is measured by its artistic accomplishments. Empires fall, and their advancements and learning often fall to the wayside, forever lost in time, but somehow the remnants of their art survives, a silent testament to the genius of that particular people. Farland couldn't see that; he thought the art itself was more than the mind and soul that created it, and thus he was willing to sacrifice his values, morals, and goals to achieve that art."

I must now agree with Markson's assessment of Farland, although it took a long time for me to fathom it all.

Markson proved as good as his word, supervising the concrete pouring himself, just a few days later. Sheriff Waterman and his deputies volunteered to do the work early one morning, guaranteeing the job could be completed long before dark. Waterman told me later that Markson had etched a five-pointed symbol into the still-wet concrete at the last moment as an added precaution, although he did not know the significance of it. I regret not taking the time to ask Markson the meaning of that symbol before he passed away just one month later.

Waterman added that I should have joined him and the others for what they called their "Diamondback Jubilee." The hunt was so popular that several of the local men set out every day for a week. Waterman finally declared an end when he realized over four hundred rattlers had been killed.

Markson never asked how my book would end. Actually, that was something I could not decide myself, so I finally gave it up altogether; instead, I took the advice of another friend, I wrote a dirty novel — I sent him a signed copy in thanks for the suggestion. He called just last week to say he had enjoyed the book and, since it's selling well, everything seems to have worked out for the best.

Yet at times my experience in the crypt comes back to me in nightmares during which I relive the entire episode. It all happens in slow motion, so I see each detail clearly. One image haunts me such that I felt compelled to return to my study of Aztec mythology. The original statue depicts a nearly obliterated form descending from beneath the skirttail of the goddess, and it is a clearer vision of that same form that I see in my dreams. It appears to me as a palely glowing, blue-white human face with serpentine features; its lineaments are those of a woman. I wish Markson were here to tell me what it means, as I fear it is the face of Coyolxauhqui, the jackal-minded daughter of Coatlicue. Had she too been reborn and did she escape the tomb along with her brothers before the crypt was plugged with cement? All I know is that after one of these dreams, I dare not venture sleep again until early morning, long after the moon, Coyolxauhqui's symbol, has set. Until then, I sit by the window, staring out at the night sky, wondering — *how long has the moon had a tail?* ✦

Dark Demonize

"Look at the images of those holding up my throne and you will understand ..."
— Inscription from the tomb of Darius I at Naqsh-i-Rustam

By two a.m., Martin was so exhausted that he began reading some of the weirder passages aloud as he translated the ancient manuscript:

> *To call forth the Efreet Fahramoosh, the Mage must clutch the Eyes of a Corpse while reciting the Doehl Chant, that through the thus-enlivened Orbs, he may gaze upon his Enemies from afar. By then crushing the cadaverous Organs of sight while performing the Banishing Ritual of Windy Vaju, the Efreet is dismissed.*
>
> *The Daemon Badmazeh can be cajoled to rejuvenate useless or severed Limbs if summoned by a Mage who consumes the still-animate Tail of a Lizard as he incants the Ritual of Renewal. The Daemon is banished by the Banishing Ritual of Mah.*

He had finally reached the last page of the chapter concerning the calling up of imps, demons, and djinn. With an end in sight, Martin found the strength to continue:

> *By imbibing a Token of Blood, then uttering 'Aiyedeuh' but once, the Daemon Brachamashoot is raised as an intangible Manifestation from the Depths of the Black Abyss that he may grant two Boons. The Daemon may then be discharged in part by speaking the Word of Summoning once more. The Word must not be intoned thereafter for one full Cycle of Mah, lest the One closest to the Mage be afflicted with malefic Possession; if the Word is not spoken again during that Period of Time, the Mage is forever freed of the Daemon.*

"Yeah, right," Martin chuckled to himself, "and praise be to Ahuramazda!" He yawned as he closed the centuried treatise. In his opinion, the text was nothing more than a collection of old wives' tales and occult gibberish, an opinion certainly not shared by his boss, Professor Waltham.

Professor Alfred Waltham claimed he had purchased the two-volume grimoire for the price of twelve goats from an elderly bedouin he had come across somewhere on the desert plain of Marv-i-Dasht, near the ancient ruins of Parsa in central Iran. Two years of drought had left the nomadic herdsman desperate for any means to provide for his starving family; no circumstances less dire, Waltham had assured Martin, could have persuaded the man to part with such venerable writings.

Although neither he nor the bedouin could read the weathered incunabula, Waltham was so convinced of their value that he abruptly terminated his study of the nomadic tribes to return to Miskatonic University in May, 1933, three months earlier than planned. He subsequently hired Martin Dodd, a graduate specialist in pre-Islamic Middle Eastern languages, to undertake the translations that Waltham felt certain would ensure great academic fame for the both of them. It struck Martin that the old scholar craved the recognition of his peers a bit too obsessively.

The bedouin had insisted the manuscripts were all that remained of the *Kurush Nameh* or *Book of Cyrus*, a legendary collection of occult secrets reportedly compiled by the Magi, the powerful priest magicians of the Achaemenid Shahs, at the behest of Cyrus the Great ("Kurush" in the Persian language of Farsi). The majority of modern scholars dismissed the *Kurush Nameh* as pure fable, the same scholars who had for so long denied the very existence of the *Necronomicon* of the mad Arab.

Martin knew the Indo-European Achaemenid kings had shattered the powers of Babylon, Egypt, Greece, India, and Arabia, finally bringing some twenty-three nations under the rule of the world's first real empire.

Kurush founded the Persian Empire in 520 b.c. Among his more notable successors were Darayavaush (Darius the Great) and Khschearscha (Xerxes the Great). Each king had enhanced the notorious fortress capital at Parsa, which Kurush had carved out of a mountainside, erecting sculptured palaces of an ever grander scale in hope of outdoing his predecessors. Hundreds of gigantic friezes and sculptures depicting mythological beasts adorned the sprawling metropolis at its height. Giant two-headed griffins, bulls and lions locked in deadly combat, sphinxes, and other composite zoomorphic sentinels of stone decorated the temples and palaces, stone reminders of the might of Persia's kings. Most impressive of all, however, were four colossi that guarded the cyclopean Gateway to All Lands at the city's entrance. These gigantic winged bulls towered twenty-two feet above their pedestals and mimicked the likeness of King Xerxes himself with their braided beards and cylindrical, fretted tiara crowns. The Greeks had so despised the sprawling metropolis that they dubbed it Persepolis, the "Eater of Cities."

One of the more fanciful embellishments to the Kurush legend asserted that the king had ordered the foremost sorcerers and magicians of subjugated kingdoms brought before him, beginning with the necromantic high priests of the Babylonian deity Marduk. Through torturous means, he is said to have extracted secrets that would provide his armies with unparalleled military prowess. The secrets were recorded by the Magi within the pages of the *Kurush Nameh* and entrusted to the fearsome adepts of Atar, god of fire.

Persia's seemingly endless victories, attributed to the powers of the Magi, continued well into the fourth century b.c., at which time the Magi withheld their knowledge from Darius III, a leader deemed by them to be weak and ineffectual.

When Alexander the Great besieged the Persian Empire in 320 b.c. and slew Darius III, the Macedonian conqueror became so entranced by Persepolis that he chose it as the capital of his empire as well. Yet in the midst of a subsequent celebration feast, Alexander had inexplicably ordered the site burned to the ground, an action that still puzzles scholars today. Legend has it that the

fearless conqueror was so repulsed by horrific secrets offered to him by the Magi that he ordered the city be put to the torch that very night; the god of fire himself would provide the means to obliterate such unnatural horrors for all time.

Bedouin tradition claimed the Magi of Atar split the *Kurush Nameh* into two halves and assigned each half to a trusted member of their number. These guardians were immured within a secret hypogeum located beneath the holy of holies. When the burning temple collapsed, the guardians were baked alive by the hellish heat from the inferno above, and the *Kurush Nameh* was thereby lost to mankind, seemingly forever.

However, in 1931 a team of European scholars began disinterring Persepolis from the layers of ash and rubble that had covered it for centuries. Waltham purchased the manuscripts from the bedouin four years later, after touring the partially resurrected ruins.

The bedouin claimed to have discovered the texts in 1931 during a looting expedition to the site. While digging for buried artifacts, he stumbled upon the entrance to a subterranean chamber near the stairway of the Tripylon. The ancient flooring had collapsed under his weight, and he had landed between the charred remains of two human skeletons, each of which had an iron box clutched tightly to its long-dead bosom. Believing the boxes contained gold or jewels, the thief snatched them from their bony cradles, climbed to the surface, and escaped with his discovery. Thereafter, he swore the ground shook furiously as he fled the ruins, frightening the superstitious fool half out of his mind. The following day he learned from the excavators that a minor earth tremor had caused a cave-in during the night, a cave-in which obliterated all signs of the looted chamber.

Skeptical of this story, Martin had pointed out that although the lavishly inscribed texts praised "Mighty Kurush, Shah of Shahs" and an encoding device dating from the Achaemenid period had been used to write the text, these factors alone were not sufficient proof of the texts' age or authenticity.

After straining over the faded, flaking, hand-lettered leaves, often for twelve hours each day, Martin had grown accustomed to headaches and chronically blurred vision. Still, it bothered him to realize that, despite his own Herculean efforts, Waltham would undoubtedly take all the credit for any noteworthy discoveries in the translation.

The bulk of the first volume yielded a veritable encyclopedia of folk medicine, providing hundreds of herbal remedies for various diseases. The final chapter, however, concerned only divination and the raising of imps, djinn, demons, and an unclean spirit Martin equated to the "peri" of Persian folklore, a term not in common usage until the 1770s. He had as yet only scanned the contents of the second volume, but it appeared to deal with religious doctrine and practices concerning a hierachy of cosmic entities who once held domain over primordial Earth. One section warned that these alien entities would "resurrect themselves," during the time of specific astrologic convergences, to extinguish mankind and reestablish their own planetary dominion. Martin suspected the esoteric material of such sections would eventually require anagogical interpretation in order to reveal some encrypted message intended only for the initiates of the innermost mysteries. The medicinal information might prove valuable, but the rest he deemed worthless religious mumbo jumbo.

As he began to pack up for the night, he slipped the translated pages into an envelope. Although Waltham would be ecstatic over his progress, Martin wondered what the old coot would think of the more preposterous sections. He envisioned the professor requisitioning cadavers' eyes and lizards from the university Board to prove the accuracy of the incantations.

While closing the envelope's clasp, Martin accidentally sliced his index finger with the edge of the flap. He dropped the offending item and jammed the bleeding finger into his mouth. As he chided himself for his carelessness, an odd thought occurred to him: he was literally "imbibing" his own blood! That in itself fulfilled half the requirements to summon one of the demons!

He reopened the envelope and spilled the contents out onto the desk. With the bleeding finger still jammed in his mouth, he located the appropriate passage. As a lark, he recited the entire formula aloud, sounding out the unfamiliar summoning word phonetically as 'eye-dee-yoowh':

> By imbibing a Token of Blood, then uttering 'Aiyedeuh' aloud but
> once, the Daemon Brachamashoot is raised as an intangible Manifes-
> tation from the Depths of the Black Abyss that he may grant two
> Boons.

A nauseating stench seemed to seep into the room. As Martin glanced around, trying to determine the source of the sudden odor, he sensed he was no longer alone.

Near the middle of the room, approximately seven feet above the carpeted floor, an ashen puff of smoke appeared. As Martin watched, the smoke darkened and expanded, like ink disbursing in oil, until an insubstantial globe was roughly defined. The globe lopsidedly increased its size, stabilizing only after it achieved a diameter of more than two feet. Within its hazy parameters, an agglomerate of vividly swirling colors, some outside the familiar spectrum, blended and whirled in a convoluted dance.

Martin leaned cautiously toward the thing. Within its swirling mass, he detected two tiny violet points of light glowing brightly. The points solidified into a pair of seemingly tangible orbs, eyes! Martin realized he was gazing into a pair of darkly brilliant demon eyes! Intimidated, he drew back and blurted out, "What in the hell ...?"

Before he had even finished his exclamation, something slammed against his head with the force of a hammer's blow. The impact knocked him back, hurling him from his seat and onto the floor. He stared dazedly at the phantasm as he regained his seat.

Some remote area of his brain recognized the blow as a vehicle of communication, an uncouth means of relaying information. A response to his unfinished question, in the form of visual, auditory, and olfactory impressions, had been crudely and painfully propelled across the room and imprinted upon his mind. If this was the only way the two thousand year old demon could "speak," Martin considered, then it might be prudent for him to limit the number of questions he directed at the damned thing.

Martin recalled reading earlier in the ancient text that demons were distinguished as either benevolent "eudaemons" or malevolent "cacodaemons." He suspected he was dealing with the latter in this case. Yet he wondered if a being incapable of a true physical manifestation could pose a real threat to him, aside from giving him a splitting headache, that is. At the same time, he was shocked to find himself considering the possibility that he was in the presence of an actual demon rather than experiencing some sort of waking hallucination induced by extreme exhaustion. Excitement and curiosity had plainly overcome his instinctive incredulity.

With less force than previously, Brachamashoot introduced himself and complimented Martin on his insight. It assured Martin that it meant him no harm, reminding him that the summoner was the master of the summoned, not *vice versa*. Brachamashoot apologized for the excessive force of its initial communication, an error it would not repeat. If Martin would simply state both of his wishes aloud, the demon assured him, they would gladly be granted.

Faced with such important decisions in the midst of such an unexpected and unimaginable situation, Martin hesitated, recalling stories he had heard and read as a child about unscrupulous geniis. Yet, despite his uncertainty, he was sorely tempted to test the abilities of the demon.

In less than a month, Martin planned to improve his social standing through marriage, so he dared not wish for anything that would endanger that situation. His wishes must be carefully defined, not vaguely or hastily stated, just in case he was not dreaming after all.

With forced resolve, Martin put aside his doubts; he knew what he wanted most, and he asked for it. "I want to be financially comfortable and secure for the rest of my life. Not excessively rich, as I'd hate to explain the source of the money to the I.R.S., just quite well off. The money must all be legally obtained, tax free, and mine exclusively to use as I wish." He ended with a broad, self-assured smile, convinced the addition of the final specifications was a stroke of genius.

The confident wisher stared patiently at the demon, now a boiling ball of color suspended in the air just a few feet from his desk. The colors deepened, then intensified, expanding without warning into a tidal wave of brilliantly tinted flame. The room was suddenly flooded with a blinding spectral inundation, at the very center of which, floated Brachamashoot's disembodied eyes.

Martin automatically raised his arms to protect his face from the multihued mass that engulfed him. Moments later, he lowered them cautiously as his surroundings returned to normal. The demon withdrew, receding until its previous, more acceptable proportions were resumed.

Reacting to a sudden discomfort, Martin reached down and plucked his wallet from his back pocket. He opened it timidly, hardly daring to speculate on the uncharacteristic bulkiness of the thing. To his surprise and wonder, the wallet was jammed full of hundred dollar bills.

He stared blankly at the cash, unsettled by the unwarranted concern for wealth that he sensed in himself. Money had never been a problem for him at all. His investments always did well, and he would soon be entitled to the whole of the sizable trust his Aunt ... — how could he forget her name? — had established exclusively for his benefit decades ago.

Then it struck him. Why, he had no aunts and beyond that, he had never had enough money to make an investment! Confused, he tried to sort through his memories for the truth until it dawned on him that this was the demon's doing. It had manipulated reality itself, altering both the past and the present as a means of fulfilling the wish! How wonderful!

Calming, Martin reminded himself that a second "boon" still awaited formulation. His second, and last, wish should involve Ellen, his bride to be. Even with money of his own, he still needed her. Sweet Ellen, she would be more of an acquisition than a mate; her real desirability lay in her ability to usher him into the upper echelons of society that had previously been quite inaccessible to him, a poverty-stricken nobody with a graduate degree in an impractical branch of linguistics.

It was vital that he tie Ellen to him permanently, so that she could not abandon him even if she should come to realize he was only using her. He grappled with his thoughts, trying to state his intentions appropriately.

"My second wish is that after Ellen and I are married — and we absolutely must be married — we will never be apart for long. If she should ever try to leave me for any reason whatsoever, I will go to her and she will take me back." Although the wish had been stated hastily, he felt fairly confident about its wording. As long as he could feel sure Ellen would never abandon him, then everything would work out just fine.

Martin prepared himself for a second deluge of brilliant color, only to be disappointed. After a moment, he decided that directing the future was easier, not to mention less dramatic, for the demon than restructuring the past. Having fared so well, Martin decided he had better quit while he was still ahead. He boldly announced, "I assume both my boons have been granted," then, as a precaution, he added, "Respond ONLY if I am mistaken." Nothing slammed even lightly into his head. Considering their interaction concluded, he rose from his seat, faced the insubstantial cloud before him, and said, "Okay, then we're finished. You may go now."

The roiling sphere remained completely unchanged as it continued to hover silently in the air.

"Oh, I forgot!" Martin blurted out. Glancing down at the translated text on the desk, he recited the summoning word a second time in order to dismiss the now-superfluous demon. As the tone of the final syllable dissolved into the air, the demonic manifestation followed suit, the eerie set of eyes lingering only a few seconds longer than the rest.

Pleased with himself, though still not one-hundred percent convinced he was not dreaming, the exhausted linguist packed up his documents and left the office. On his way out, he stopped by Waltham's office briefly to leave the professor a copy of the day's translations.

*   *   *

In the days that followed, the money rolled in and no one else seemed to notice the past had been tampered with in any way, all of which made it easier for Martin to accept the reality of his bizarre experience. The very next day, while visiting his parents, he had decided to test Brachamashoot's reliability by making a casual reference to his aunt, whose name turned out to be Alice. His parents had not only been familiar with this recently-created woman, but his father had actually demonstrated a certain amount of resentment toward Martin as the sole beneficiary of his sister Alice's trust fund. It was incredible, illogical, and maddening at times, but he loved it. He relished knowing something no one else would ever know, something important; it gave him a growing sense of power. Sure, the demon was the one with the power, at least technically speaking, but it was Martin who had called the little devil out of a two thousand year limbo and given it instructions! Without Martin, the demon was a real nothing and nobody!

It was Ellen who was most affected by the change in Martin's personality. The reserved, easy-going man she had come to love transformed in a very short time into an overbearing, boorish extrovert. He dismissed her attempts to discover the reason for his sudden transformation, and persistence only elicited his anger. She finally convinced herself that the pressure of the upcoming marriage was the source of his problem; Martin would surely return to normal once they settled down together in his lovely home.

Professor Waltham found Martin's prideful new persona quite insufferable. He decided the indispensable young man had been working too hard, so as a wedding present, he allowed Martin a week off with half-pay for his honeymoon. Surely the young linguist would feel more like his old self after a few days' rest; in the meantime, Waltham would simply avoid any unnecessary contact with him.

The wedding took place just three weeks after Martin's encounter with the demon. By that time, most of his friends felt disinclined to attend the festivities, and some actually refused the invitation. Luckily, enough family members and friends of the bride were in attendance to prevent the church from appearing too empty.

Despite the misgivings of some guests, it was generally agreed that the wedding went well. Still, a few guests seated near the front of the church later claimed the groom had emitted an inappropriate gasp as he raised the bridal veil, although they admitted he might simply have been overcome by the beauty of his lovely new bride.

Martin kept his fearful suspicions to himself throughout the balance of the wedding. He could not completely rid himself of the notion that he had seen the fleeting image of a dark cloud in Ellen's eyes just as he lifted her veil. It could only be imagination, he scolded himself, a result of nuptial day tension. It was not until later, when he and Ellen were alone, that his worst fears were confirmed.

* * *

After the wedding, the newlyweds stopped off at Martin's home to change and collect their luggage on the way to the airport. Once there, however, the plans for a honeymoon trip to Niagara Falls were ignored. Although Martin had been Ellen's lover for some time, both were suddenly overcome by a relentless desire to consummate the marriage. Before they knew it, they were locked in passionate embrace.

Martin was shocked to find that Ellen, usually a boorishly unexceptional lover, had suddenly become an exciting wildwoman. With Ellen in control, their lovemaking entered the realm of crazed sex. She taunted and teased him with the savagery of a she-beast, accepting nothing less than total satisfaction. Their ecstatic, obsessive grappling completely overrode the intuitive alarm that tried to warn Martin that something was wrong.

Ellen launched into an incredible stream of orgasms, boosting Martin's already inflated ego with lavish praises of his sexual prowess. He found it strangely exciting to taste the sweat — his own — that trickled down his upturned face and into his mouth. When it dawned on him that they were actually participating in nothing more companioned masturbation, he looked to his new bride, curious to see if she shared his revelation; her eyes remained closed, clenched in ecstasy. Irresistibly drawn to her once more, he dismissed such thoughts as he bent to kiss her.

An instant later, he began screaming and whimpering like a terrified child as he wrenched his body away from Ellen's. He tumbled from the bed to the floor, afraid to take his eyes off the source of his horror and disgust. He clumsily propelled himself further away, stopping only when his naked back slammed abruptly against the far wall.

He watched his bride rise up leisurely from the bed, smiling in amusement at the antics of her distraught lover; she beckoned enticingly for him to return to her. Martin might have given in, might have decided he had been fooled by some trick of the dim shadowy light, had not two small serpents still remained entwined about her mouth, reveling in the moisture that they found there.

Martin closed his eyes in revulsion, clenching them tightly as he crawled blindly toward the hall on quivering hands and knees. He banged into the door, maneuvered around it, and flung himself out into the hallway, slamming the bedroom door behind him and bracing it with both feet. Ellen called sweetly to him from the other side of the door, a siren doing her best to lure her confused Ulysses back into her inhuman clutches. Martin eventually nodded off after barricading himself against the door with as much of his body weight as possible.

At dawn he awoke, dressed himself hastily in dirty clothes he fished from the hamper, then fled the house. Martin no longer wondered if he was dreaming; he prayed he would wake up.

*   *   *

Martin had no idea where he should go, but he knew his body craved sleep, the ultimate escape. Once he had put several miles between him and the thing in his bed, Martin felt secure enough to rent a room at a cheap, anonymous roadside motel.

Once alone in the room, he threw his weary body upon the unfamiliar bed, which greeted him with a refreshingly cool sterility. The tension and fear drained slowly from every part of him, but his mind resisted his unwillingness to think about what he had so recently seen and done. He had never thought of himself as the heroic type, but the cowardice he had shown in running away struck him as shameful. Sleep came only after he convinced himself that he had not just run away in fear, leaving his helpless wife to fend for herself; he left because he had needed time to think, to understand the situation before making any rash decisions. He would go back and do whatever was necessary, but first he needed to rest and piece it all together.

Yet in sleep he found no rest. His mind kept working on the problem, continuously replaying the events of the previous day and night. He relived his memories of the wedding, this time easily recognizing the dark eyes of Brachamashoot superimposed over Ellen's when he lifted the veil, and later in bed. But how could it be? He had dismissed the demon long before, and it could not come back ... unless ... He considered the timing of events; the wedding had taken place twenty, no, twenty-seven days after his experience with the demon. The book had clearly warned the reader not to repeat the summoning word before twenty-eight days, one full cycle of the moon goddess Mah, had elapsed.

He had not said it again. He had taken great care to avoid even thinking it!

The wedding, the answer had to be there. He tried to recall every detail, searching for something he had overlooked. As he recreated the actual ceremony, it suddenly came to him. It was so obvious that he could barely believe it. Of course, he had not said the summoning word itself, but he had said words that sounded so very similar that he might as well have said the real thing. He said "I do," which, when spoken quickly, sounds exactly like "Aiyedeuh." Everything was fine until he said those two words, the two little words that they say all men fear. If they only knew! He had needed no demon to trick him; he was quite capable of tricking himself!

The rest of the warning came back to him as he jumped out of bed, fully awake: "The Word must not be intoned thereafter for a full Cycle of Mah lest the Person nearest to the Magus be afflicted with malefic Possession; ..." After lying dormant for countless centuries, the demon must have jumped at the opportunity to take possession of dear, unsuspecting little Ellen.

Martin berated himself for his own naivety, his overblown self-confidence. How could he be so stupid as to think he could match wits with a disembodied evil spirit that was thousands of years old? He did not feel optimistic about his chances of outmaneuvering the damned thing now, but it was either that or resign himself to a literally hellish future.

Less than two hours later, Ellen knocked at the door of his motel room.

She had dismissed her cab and headed directly to his room, not bothering to inquire as to its whereabouts at the office. She reminded Martin of a dog following a scent. There was really very little he could do but return to the house with her.

Once in the car, the thing nestled deeply behind Ellen's eyes announced its presence, utilizing Ellen's mental faculties to speak to him in perfect English. As Martin had suspected, Brachamashoot had taken possession of the new bride and had every intention of retaining that hold permanently.

Repressing his fear for the time being, Martin asked Brachamashoot how he had located him so easily, only to have the demon remind him of his second wish that he and Ellen could never be separated for long.

The anxious groom, only mildly concerned about Ellen's welfare, demanded to know the purpose behind the possession.

Brachamashoot smiled pleasantly through Ellen's features. "If I am to experience physical pleasures," he began, "I require a physical body."

Martin tried to interject, but Brachamashoot interrupted him. "Although you don't seem very concerned about your lovely bride, I feel obligated to tell you she is totally oblivious to my presence and will be permitted to return from time to time when needed." He paused. "Oh, don't frown so. It isn't as if you truly cared for her — or anyone other than yourself for that matter."

When Martin gave no reply, the demon impersonated Ellen's coquettish manner as he whispered, "You will find my presence less repugnant when you realize I can make it possible for you to realize many of your fondest dreams."

* * *

Upon their return, Brachamashoot outlined his plans for the "three" of them. Although he controlled Ellen's body, the demon was quite aware that he would not be able to imitate her personality convincingly enough to fool those who knew her well. Whenever such situations arose, he would simply allow Ellen to emerge. Brachamashoot assured Martin that she would remain totally unaware of the demonic cohabitation, although she would experience regular lapses of memory.

When Martin expressed concern that Ellen might seek professional help to regain her memory, Brachamashoot assured him Ellen would never willingly seek professional help. While browsing among some of the more repressed areas of Ellen's mind, Brachamashoot had discovered Ellen's most secret shame; her mother was not dead, as everyone outside the immediate family had been led to believe — in truth, she was alive but not really well in a very private mental institution on the continent. Ellen's worst fear was that she had inherited similar neurotic tendencies, Brachamashoot confided to Martin, so she would never seek any type of therapy that might confirm her suspicions.

In the meantime, Brachamashoot would use his special abilities to his and Martin's mutual benefit. They would both have everything they wanted.

While the demon rambled on, Martin considered the various advantages that such a situation might provide. Having always been attracted to more hedonistic lifestyles, he found this opportunity to live out his fantasies rather enticing. Together, he and this kindred spirit could explore the worlds of drugs and alcohol, debauchery, and every sort of depravity and perversion! Best of all, with Brachamashoot's incredible powers, he would never suffer any unhappy consequences as a result of even the most abominably sinful behavior!

Excited anticipation slowly replaced the fear and loathing Martin had initially felt towards the demon. He recognized that he and Brachamashoot were alike in some ways, and Brachamashoot provided him immunity no matter what he may do. While Martin had always been afraid to explore alone and unprotected, now he could do anything he pleased and still retain his wealth and status in the community. With Ellen under control, the outside world would see him as the perfect husband in a fairytale marriage. It was just too perfect, he thought as he returned the demon's facetious grin.

Martin distrusted Brachamashoot instinctively, although he appreciated the demon's unquenchable appetite for pleasure. Together they launched upon a series of picaresque adventures, wallowing in the unfettered exploration of deeds both ignoble and despicable. They experimented with every intoxicating substance their money could buy, quickly progressing from alcohol to absinthe to morphine and deadly night shade. They worked their way up from common whoring to vandalism, robbery, and arson, culminating in a scenario that included torture and murder. Their anonymous sexual exploits involved not only prostitutes but willing and unwilling members of both sexes, and eventually even animals and reptiles.

Brachamashoot's powers over the minds of others never ceased to amaze his human companion and, as promised, they remained totally immune from any and all unpleasant repercussions arising from their actions. Eventually, however, Martin began to feel the unreality of their existence, and, although he fought against it, he eventually had to acknowledge his increasing dissatisfaction, alienation, and even loneliness.

Poor, pathetic little Ellen, as gullible and trusting as ever, was allowed to emerge only occasionally in order to accompany Martin to social functions and public appearances, at which times Martin made sure she always put on a good show. She would always be disoriented and confused due to the overwhelming gaps in her recollection, but everyone could see how dependent upon her attentive husband she had become. When alone with Martin, she sometimes expressed the fear that she was losing her mind, but he always managed to assure her that she just needed rest and that everything was fine. It was not long before he began to dread the infrequent moments he was obligated to spend in her zombie-like company. She had always been too clingingly dependent, and now he loathed her and her perpetually adoring attitude.

Eventually, Martin even grew dissatisfied with his revels with Brachamashoot. He did his best to hide his disillusionment from the demon, his lack of independence transforming first into resentment, then into intense hatred.

Brachamashoot sometimes treated him as an inferior and constantly joked about the feeblemindedness of humans. Slowly but surely, Martin realized that, much like Ellen, he had fallen under the overriding control of the demon.

Martin returned to his translation work with an entirely new goal in mind. He was determined to find a key somewhere within the manuscripts that would provide him with the means to rid himself of Brachamashoot once and for all.

It was in the second of the thaumaturgic manuscripts that he learned of the Chimaera, a brand of "archdaemon" tremendously more powerful than lesser demons like Brachamashoot. He decided he should summon the most powerful Chimaera of all, the one referred to as the "steward of Nyarlathotep,

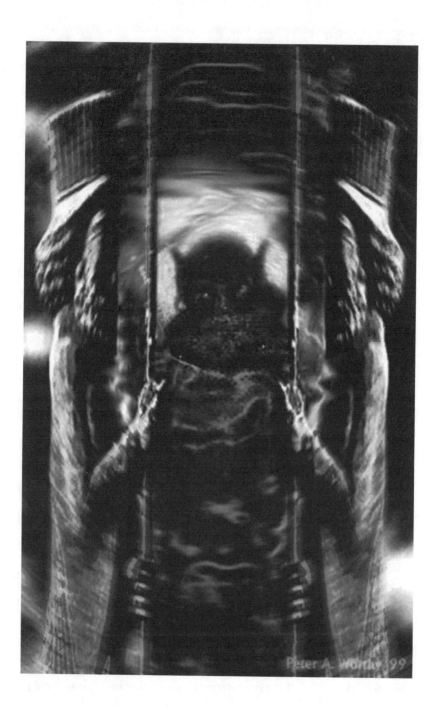

Peter A. Worlar 99

the Black Faceless One, the Avatar of Chaos." This particular archdemon, called Achsheilah, should easily be able to dispose with Brachamashoot's parasitic presence. The book warned that Chimaeras were extremely dangerous to all but the most experienced Archimagus, but a desperate man is rarely a cautious man, so Martin jotted the pertinent passages down for himself before turning the day's translations over to Waltham.

Martin immediately began to gather the candles, chalk, dagger, and live doves required for his second sorceric adventure. A full ceremony was required this time, which he planned to perform in the privacy of the large basement area under his house. Little sound would escape its thick cement walls and flooring, lessening the likelihood that the neighbors would hear should Brachamashoot become unruly.

When all was in readiness, Martin tiptoed upstairs to check on Brachamashoot as a final precaution. With a chill, he noted two undulating ridges rising and falling under the sheet that covered the sleeper. Brachamashoot did not require sleep, but the body did, so the demon was free to occupy himself elsewhere while Ellen slept. Her body was guarded at such times by the two tiny snakes Martin had spotted the night of the honeymoon. The reptilian watchmen emerged each night from Ellen's possessed mouth, slithered protectively up and down the sleeping form, then returned to the oral cavern when the body was rested or when danger threatened their unconscious, and thereby vulnerable, charge. Once inside, the snakes signaled Brachamashoot, whose return was imminent.

As Martin observed the gentle movements beneath the covers, he experienced an odd mixture of revulsion and arousal as he considered the sensual implications of such clammy vermin freely exploring the intimate mounds and valleys of Ellen's supine torso. He quickly drove the latter fancies from his mind and gingerly retraced his steps. Confident now that Brachamashoot did not suspect his intended treachery, Martin closed the bedroom door and hurriedly returned to the basement.

Once there, he drew two large concentric circles on the exposed concrete of the cellar floor with chalk, according to the book's instruction. The larger circle, just over eight feet in diameter, was sketched to encompass a smaller circle, nearly seven feet in diameter. Within the inner figure, he sketched an equilateral triangle with points touching but not intersecting its encircling boundary. Even if Martin's visitor from beyond proved dangerous, it would be safely contained by and within the circumference of the outer circle. Finally, he switched off the light.

The ritual reminded Martin of something out of a Dennis Wheatley novel, but recent occurrences had made him a desperate believer. It had taken a lot to bring him to this — standing in a dark basement alone, draped in a black hooded robe, lighting candles and tracing protective symbols in the air with his hands. Each movement and intonation was carefully executed, as Martin no longer underestimated the chicanery of the book's foul spawn.

Next, he slit the throats of three doves and spilled their blood precisely in the space between the two inscribed circles. This would invite the immaterial archdemon to construct a temporary physical vehicle for itself out of the blood and thereby allow it to communicate in a manner comprehensible to a human.

As Martin chanted the archdemon's name, the area within the triangle began to glow, heated by some unseen force. The doves' blood slowly began to creep in streaming rivulets across the floor to meet in the exact center of the geometric figure. Once there, it coagulated and boiled into a steaming glob. Abruptly, three streams of the sanguine matter shot out to envelope the feet, eyes, and beaks of the three carcasses. These were ripped from the mutilated bodies of the fowl as the streams retracted, then absorbed into the bloody mass.

Martin watched in sickened amazement as the apparition fashioned a body for itself from the oozing glob. A swollen conglomerate slowly rose up, balanced precariously on three spindly, mismatched legs, the remaining legs dangling uselessly from the malformed midsection. A half-dozen dove eyes jammed together near the top of the blob, facing Martin, all six of their pupils moving in unison. A few inches lower down on the crimson mass, the gaping beaks settled together in a grisly horizontal formation.

For a few moments, the gawking mockery of a head bobbed uncontrolled in the air, then all three beaks opened simultaneously, intoning in screechy-toned chorus, "Who dares summon me?" The demand was made in an archaic Persian dialect that had been obsolete since the reign of Xerxes.

The book admonished the conjurer to show no fear in the presence of the otherworldly, lest the spirit gain the upper hand. It had also described Achsheilah as possessing a form that inspired "wonder and great respect," which this image certainly did not. Revolted rather than inspired, Martin felt sure something was wrong. He forsook English momentarily to deliver a bluff to the aviary caricature.

"Begone, you coprolitic lackey! You insult the mighty Achsheilah by this impersonation!" he shouted.

DARK DEMONIZE

A sudden intensification of heat caused the flooring beneath the disgusting creature to glow white hot. The hideous little monstrosity quivered and shook with such ferocity that its borrowed limbs, beaks, and eyes were dislodged and fell to the floor. The torso disintegrated, transforming into a deliquescent puddle of black viscous blood. The puddle emitted suffocating fumes that seared the onlooker's lungs and exposed skin with an ammonia-like burning.

Martin stood firm despite the pain in his lungs and watched the fumes twist and swirl as they condensed, forming the outline of a huge beast situated within the inner circle. The ammonia-like odor quickly dissipated, replaced momentarily by a crisp atmospheric sterility not unlike that produced by the presence of ozone, and as the last wisps fell into place, the final touches were added to the menacing manifestation of a surreal but living creature.

The shock of recognition caused Martin to step back in amazement. He had expected such a highly ranked demon to bear an impressive cast, but how could he have ever guessed? Before him stood the very symbol of ancient Persian cruelty, dignity, and power — the fabled griffin! The haughty amalgam turned its truncated head solemnly to the side, its gaze directed beyond its savage beak, boring directly into Martin's soul. Its blunt eagle head, feather-maned and lion-eared, blended gracefully into the fullness of the neck and torso of a lion. There were other aviary features in the form of a pair of gigantic wings that rose and fell in time with the thing's breath, and deadly talons that extruded from its paws. The dim candlelight defined a beautiful, majestic creature, Martin realized, one infinitely more worthy of his attention than Brachamashoot.

The demon griffin loomed larger than an elephant, its wings cramped by the basement ceiling, allowing it little room to maneuver within the circle. Yet the teratological giant was not awkward or ungainly; rather, it seemed as if time passed at a subtly slower rate for the beast, lending an almost elegant grace to its every move.

Despite its fabulous appearance, however, the beast was quite familiar to Martin, who had seen it again and again among the monuments of Persepolis, monuments (it was now obvious) patterned after living models. Martin realized the source of the fabled might of Persia — by enlisting the aid of invulnerable mutant beasts such as this, the Persian monarchs had conquered the world!

As Martin stared intently into the creature's eyes, a series of vivid images were conveyed to him telepathically — the savage destruction of the Greek Acropolis in 480 b.c. The darkness around him dissipated, supplanted by the unsettling vision of giant mutant bulls, four-winged djinn, bloodthirsty flying griffins, and even an enormous phoenix swooping down to descend upon the helpless citadel like a whirlwind of devils. Believing themselves abandoned by the gods, the terrified Athenians had fled the deadly onslaught of Hades' spawn, but at the direction of their Persian masters, the terrifying monstrosities massacred them to a man. Then, their fury unabated, the horde eagerly demolished the very epitome of Athenian art and architecture, quickly reducing the marvelous temples and sculptures to hopeless ruin.

Even when viewing the scene over two thousand years after its occurrence, Martin was sickened by his vision of the slaughter. Although he had been aware of an immense but indistinct black shadow looming approvingly over the scene from the very start, only now did he recognize it as the shade of Nyarlathotep, the Faceless Avatar of Chaos, delighting in the carnage created by his multifarious hell herd.

Achsheilah, who had patiently observed the awestruck human, suddenly stirred. "*Khayli khoob,*" it uttered in deep, mellifluous, yet obviously feminine tones.

As if released from a trance, Martin peered suspiciously at the demon. Unless his ears deceived him, the griffin had clearly and concisely said "very good." Martin hesitantly responded by greeting the griffin in English.

Achsheilah stared at him with evident irritation until Martin realized his rude mistake; an answer should always be given in same language as the question. He switched to the creature's native tongue, Farsi, blurting out the traditional introductory "*Salaam,*" hesitantly appending the respectful word for addressing a female.

Instantly Achsheilah responded with the proper response of "*Salaam a laykum,*" then formally inquired as to Martin's wellbeing.

Martin stumblingly inquired if the griffin spoke English. Although somewhat perturbed at Martin's curtailment of the greeting ritual, Achsheilah acquiesced by declaring in perfect English, "After almost twenty-three centuries, I despaired of ever returning to this world again. Your needs must be grievous indeed."

Martin compounded his rudeness by ignoring the griffin's remark, asking instead, "Are there more like you or are you one of a kind?"

"There are many thousands of Chimaeras," she said condescendingly, "although we bear various forms. Collectively we are known as the Annihilating Swarm of the Lord Nyarlathotep."

Martin was taken aback. He had come across forbidding mentions of both Nyarlathotep and his Annihilating Swarm while translating the second volume of the *Kurush Nameh*. Nyarlathotep, an intrinsically evil pseudodeity, was intriguingly referred to therein as "the black faceless messenger" and "the crawling chaos." His Swarm had been described as "a legion of invincible hell-beasts" garnered from a profane, poisonous world said to have once existed near the constellation of Orion. They served as his henchmen, capable of utterly exterminating whole worlds on command. In all of history, only the insidious Persian priests had ever dared harness the monstrous herd for their own ends. Martin began to comprehend the staggering potential of the secret he had stumbled upon; nothing on earth could stand in his way with these titans at his command! But for the moment, he reminded himself, he had a more immediate use for the archdemon.

He carefully described his predicament to the solemn Chimaera, who listened patiently to the lengthy tale without comment. Finally, Martin concluded, "As you can see, I have summoned you to provide me with a means to rid himself of this parasite."

The griffin lowered her head as if considering the situation, then unfurled her gigantic wings as if about to take flight, the feathery tips again scraping the ceiling. "This Brachamashoot is not unknown to me. He is weak, yet once in possession of a living host, he cannot be exorcised. Only the death of the host can separate them. Your wife must die; there is no other way."

The finality of the statement left Martin dumbstruck. Was he actually desperate enough to kill Ellen? Could he stoop so low? Sure, he had his own money now and social standing, but she had done nothing to deserve such treatment. On the other hand, he rationalized, Ellen was not even a whole person anymore, just Brachamashoot's intermittent puppet. She had been fading away for some time now, and it might be more merciful to put an end to her plight. But Brachamashoot would never allow it!

As Martin struggled over the proposition, he found himself receiving precise instructions for overcoming the demon sleeping in the room above. If he crept up on the still-sleeping Ellen, he could use masking tape to cover her mouth. The snakes would not be able to alert Brachamashoot of the danger, and in their confused state, it would be easy to snip off their heads with a large pair of pinking shears.

Without further hesitation, the determined scholar turned to the workbench behind him, collected tape and shears, then marched up the stairs. He returned minutes later, bearing an immobile Ellen in his arms, her lips still sealed with tape.

Still following Achsheilah's telepathic instruction, Martin approached the outer circle and, after closing his eyes, heaved his burden into the inner circle.

Using her paws, the griffin guided the insensible form within the confines of the triangular inscription chalked upon the floor, holding the prone body in place with a single taloned paw.

When the adhesive strip fell from Ellen's mouth, Martin sensed Brachamashoot had returned, probably summoned by Achsheilah. The surprised demon awoke with a start and assessed Martin's betrayal as the floor beneath his body began heating up, just as it had earlier, quickly progressing from a scorching red to a white hot intensity. A volley of curses and screams poured from the demon's emancipated lips while Achsheilah, unaffected by the searing heat, calmly scrutinized Martin's reaction to the scene.

Stationed safely outside the magic sigil, and away from the furnace-like heat of its interior, Martin turned and retched, overcome by the stench of burning flesh. Wiping his mouth, he peered through the wavering heat at the incendiary horror his wife had become, aware now that the tortured screams he heard were no longer the demon's but hers. He stood riveted to the hideous sight, watching Ellen's pale soft form shrivel and blacken, then melt into a gelatinous pool of steaming gore, her disintegrating eyes fixed all the while upon her betrayer. Hours later, or so it seemed to Martin, the last traces of the incinerated victim finally evaporated in a puff of blackened smoke.

"Wha ... what about her soul?" Martin stammered hoarsely, barely able to speak.

Disinterestedly, Achsheilah replied, "Her essence, or soul as you call it, has been cast into the Black Abyss where it will remain forever."

Martin felt a wave of guilt but shook it off immediately. What was done was done.

"So it worked?" he tendered. "I am finally really free of Brachamashoot?"

The griffin yawned an enormous yawn before responding. "He has been separated from the Ellen essence and has fled to another part of the same abyss. He cannot return unbidden."

Relieved, Martin smiled at the towering anomaly before him, subtle thoughts of power already reinfesting his brain. These thoughts were interrupted, however, when he suddenly became aware that money, paper money of varying denominations, had begun raining down upon him out of nowhere.

"Achsheilah!" he cried, "what's going on? What does this mean?"

The griffin sighed, obviously quite bored, before explaining that Brachamashoot's banishment did not preclude the fulfillment of Martin's wishes. Although bested, the demon was acknowledging his continued obligation.

Relieved, Martin laughed a little too loudly, then began gathering up the loose bills and gleefully stuffing them into his pockets. Yet a moment later, a troubled expression furrowed his brow and he stopped. Something, some unseen force, was tugging and pulling at him, dragging him inch by inch toward the perimeter of the magic circle.

"Achsheilah!" he called out nervously, "stop pulling me toward you! What sort of foul trick is this?" he demanded angrily.

With feline indifference, the griffin coolly replied, "I do nothing to you, human. Your second wish stipulated you should never be long separated from your Ellen. Brachamashoot is reaffirming that wish as well, so your essence is compelled to join Ellen in the Black Abyss."

Panic struck Martin as he clung desperately to one of the metal support poles upholding the structure of the house above. The force being exerted upon him increased, and he knew he would not be able to resist its draw much longer. He pleaded with the demonic griffin to help him, swearing he would do anything if only she would save him.

Achsheilah seemed irritated by Martin's slobbering display of weakness and fear. "None may interfere with the obligations of another demon," she stated. "It is the law."

Martin's hysterical begging continued as his grip upon the pole gave way to the irresistible emanation pulling him to the circle. Torn from the brace, he teetered at the brink of the chalky curves, as if poised before the entrance to Hell.

The she-griffin eyed the whimpering human with total disdain. "I will admit that, despite your disgraceful demeanor, you have unknowingly provided me a great opportunity. You have foolishly opened an ancient portal through which my herd can return to tread upon your world once again. I will show my appreciation by granting you a merciful death; you will not burn as you caused your spouse to do. I swear your death will be a swift one."

Instantly, Martin's body hurtled through the air and into the circle. Achsheilah casually reared up on her hind legs and snatched him from the air with her front paws. Keeping her promise, she swiftly silenced his howling with a single forward thrust of her lethal beak, neatly severing Martin's head from his body. She flung the twitching torso away, beyond the outer reach of the circle.

Returning to all-fours, she gripped Martin's head gingerly in one paw and began to push it back and forth across the floor, using the bleeding stump to reconfigure details of the sigils drawn upon the floor beneath her feet. In just a few moments, she altered the symbols to create a dimensional port through which she and her unnatural ranks could gain access to Martin's world at any time in the future.

Having completed her artwork, Achsheilah lifted the bloody head up once more and addressed the late scholar. "My word I have kept, but your head I will not, for it bears a less than regal quality." With that, she dropped the mutilated head to the floor and disdainfully trod upon it.

Martin Dodd's decapitated corpse was discovered three days later. Ellen Dodd's whereabouts were never established. The police theorized that the crime had been committed by some unidentified Satanic cult intent on human sacrifice, but the murder or murders were never solved.

The mutilated remains of Professor Richard Waltham and two of his undergraduate assistants were discovered exactly one month later, victims of an apparently related crime. Yet the police have never explained how the trio died of drowning, locked inside Waltham's library, where no amount of water was present. The most bizarre aspect of the case, however, that the victims' heads were found attached to the wrong torsos without any indication of surgery having been performed, was never divulged to the public.

Waltham's original manuscripts, along with Dodd's translations, became a permanent part of the rare book section of the Miskatonic University Library in 1936. Copies of Dodd's translations have since been available to the public for the price of postage and copying costs. The lengthy list of individuals who have requested copies over the years includes such notables as R. Hess, R. Speck, C. Manson, M. Pahlavi, E. Amin, J. Jones, M. Qaddafi, and S. Hussein, to name but a few. The librarian in charge of the manuscripts, a giddy individual, frequently mentions the "top secret" copy ordered by J. Edgar Hoover, pointing out that Hoover's body had to be buried in a lead-lined coffin for reasons never adequately explained.

Nothing has as yet emerged from the portal that Martin Dodd initially opened, although it remains open to this day. The Annihilating Swarm undoubtedly still prowls the threshold, patiently awaiting the day when it will pour through the gate, plunging our world into a final, tragic apocalypse that will cleanse all organic life from the face of the Earth. The Faceless One will surely be pleased.

The Hoppwood Tenant

"**W**hat the hell kind of critter makes a hole like that? This damn thing goes way back into the hill. The mouth alone is big enough for a man to squeeze through, 'though I'll be damned if I'd be one to try!" exclaimed Delbert.

His younger friend, Pete, stared into the fissure that retreated into the dark interior of the mounded hillock. The pair had discovered the tunnel by accident as they tore through a fall of dead brush in search of game.

"I doubt you'd likely fit what with all them extra pounds you've put on since you was married," Pete joked. As he cleared more shrubbery from the narrow entrance, he noted that the top of the slit-like opening rose more than five feet above the ground.

"Don't know who or what made this," Delbert offered, "but it goes right through rock that's weathered smooth, so it's been here for some time; I'd hazard it dates way back to when the redskins lived here. We all know the Hoppwoods never 'llowed no huntin' in these woods for better'n three generations. Maybe that critter ol' Miss Hoppwood was always rantin' about lives right in this here hole."

Pete ignored Delbert's last remark.

"There used to be bears around here, they say. Maybe it's nothin' more than an ol' bear's den — or maybe Big Foot lives here!" Delbert suggested.

"Bears don't *dig* caves, Del," Pete observed, "they only squat in ones they find, natural ones. This one ain't natural, though, 'cos the entrance is lined with rough cut stones. Must o' been Indians that made it 'cos the Hoppwoods just let all this grow wild — wouldn't even hunt 'round here themselves!"

The pair had been trespassing since dawn. The owner of the land, Miss Hoppwood, had passed away two days earlier, and the men simply could restrain themselves no longer; they had to be the first to hunt the virgin wood.

ANCIENT EXHUMATIONS +2

Their fantasies, involving hordes of pheasant, rabbit, 'possum, and quail, had proven altogether unrealistic, however; as they had failed to sight any game at all, despite traipsing through miles of tangled undergrowth and waist-high brambles. As dusk approached, only their fascination with the curious tunnel kept them from realizing their exhaustion.

"I *bet* this is where Miss Hoppwood meant her tenant lived," Delbert insisted.

His friend's gullibility struck Pete as absurd. "Don't hand me that! Ever'body knows the Hoppwoods was all nuttier than a squirrel's lunch and just made up all that stuff about a monster living here to scare off trespassers."

"Well, we're trespassin' right now," Delbert snickered. "But they couldn't o' made it all up 'cos the Indians declared this land off limits long before any settlers got here. My grandpa said it musta taken something pretty awful to drive the redskins out. He swore even the most fearless braves'd rather o' been skinned alive than set foot in these woods."

"And you believed him?" scoffed Pete.

"Well," Delbert responded, "what with you delivering Miss Hoppwood's supplies for so long, you musta heard more of her tales than anybody else. What did the old witch have to say about her 'tenant'?"

Pete suddenly struck a fighting stance. "Don't be callin' Miss Hoppwood a witch! I mean it." He gritted his teeth as he attempted to calm his sudden fury. "She may have been an old woman who never got married, but that don't make her no witch!"

Delbert, realizing he had gone too far, apologized, but felt obliged to add that it wasn't natural for any woman to remain a virgin all her life. He believed such things led to off-color gossip.

The apology seemed to satisfy Pete, who spoke of the deceased beldame with a certain reverence in his voice. "She weren't no witch; she was a real nice old gal once you got to know her. Truth is, I felt sorry for her, living alone out here for all these years. She was awful lonely; that's the only reason why I listened to her wild tales. It was her grandfather who told her all she knew about the Indians and their dealing with the monster, and she believed ever' last word of it."

"Okay, so what'd she say?" Delbert queried impatiently.

Pete tested a sapling birch to see if it would support his weight before he chanced to lean against it. "Her gramps was real friendly with a big shot Hopewell called a 'shaman.' Grandpa Hoppwood wanted to settle on this land somethin' fierce, but this shaman claimed the place was bad medicine. He said some kind of monster had dug itself into the tribe's biggest burial mound and wouldn't leave. When the tribe's best warriors tried to drive it out, they was wiped out to the last man quick as a flick. So this shaman feller, he got himself all doped on magic weed, figuring he'd fix things up 'tween the monster and his people. He took on the form of his animal soul, whatever that is, and dropped right in on that there monster for a visit.

"The critter put pictures and noise in the shaman's head to show him its home on a dark world located way the hell out from the sun where it was colder'n a witch's tit. It called the place 'Hugot,' 'Hugoth,' or something like that. Its kind lived there underground 'til some things that was part insect and part crab came from another star and dug him up. The insect-crab things were small but powerful strong and mean. They slapped great big wings or sails on the monster's back and rode him clear through space 'til they got to Earth, using what the shaman called 'winds of the sun.' They landed right here in these very woods. The passengers were lookin' for some metal they was fixin' to mine, and when they didn't find it here, they up and tore the wing-sails off the monster and just left it here to fend for itself while they went on up North. Since it couldn't bear the light, the monster climbed in the nearest shelter, which turned out to be a hollow burial mound, and made itself right t' home."

Delbert, who didn't believe a word of what he was hearing, felt compelled to scoff at such silly superstition. He ventured, "And it's been holed up here ever since, right? Well, what's the damned thing supposed to look like anyway?"

"Accordin' to the shaman feller, it was big as hell with slimy black, rubbery skin. But mostly, he said it stood on four great big leg posts and 'minded him of an elephant that'd been squashed flat; it didn't have no eyes nor face; it depended on its sense of smell and on hearing vibrations through the ground. And seein' as how it was so rubbery, it could squeeze through small places or stretch out like an umbrella when it was of a mind ta."

Pete paused as if he had completed the story, but Delbert wanted more. "Go on," he called, "tell me how the Hoppwoods ended up with the land. Did they kill off the shaman guy and just steal it, or what?"

"They didn't kill nobody, you jackass. The monster'd been driv' out of one home, though, and wasn't about to 'llow that again. The shaman made a deal with it, so's it promised not to kill no more as long as it was left in peace right where it was. Old Man Hoppwood had to swear an oath never to allow nob'dy to bother it, otherwise the Indians wouldn't o' sold him the land, which they 'ventually did. To seal the deal, the shaman gave Grandpa Hoppwood a vision of the monster just ta put the fear o' God in him so's he'd keep his oath. Must o' been *some* vision, 'cos the Hoppwoods all made it their sacred duty to keep ever'body out of these woods. Wonst her parents died, Miss Hoppwood was a-feared to marry lest her husband dishonor the oath. She made it her mission to ensure her tenant wasn't never bothered."

Delbert gave Pete a skeptical look. "So what do you think?"

Pete paused again before replying, "Well, mostly I just tried to be polite and listenin', actin' like I believed all she was sayin'. She was a sweet ol' gal, a little off maybe, like the rest of her family, but that didn't make 'em bad people. That's why I get a fire in my gut ever' time you call her a witch."

A full minute passed before Delbert deigned to ask, "What with Miss Hoppwood gone, I guess that makes you the expert on her tenant. So tell me, how much of her story do you believe now that we've found ourselves a mound right here where she said it was, probably a burial mound too? Do you s'pose there's a big rubber alien in there waiting to gobble us up for botherin' it?"

Pete contemplated the possibility for a moment before answering. "I sorta doubt it, but if you're right and this is a burial mound, we might find ourselves some treasure in there You hear tell of the gold folks say the Indians fished off the bed of the Mad River?"

That prospect had not occurred to Delbert. He suddenly had visions of making a fortune selling Indian gold. Only Pete's next declaration disturbed his reverie.

"I'm going in there and take a look-see," Pete said. He leaned to one side, allowing his backpack to slip over his shoulder and to the ground. Next, he squatted down and searched through the pack until he located a traffic flare and a box of kitchen matches. Smiling as he rose, Pete asked his friend if he would like to accompany him, knowing full well the chubby Delbert could not possibly squeeze through the slight opening. He was also aware that Delbert was the type to let others do all the work for him.

"Well, I sure as hell ain't stickin' my head in no hole so's I can 'howdy-do' a damn bear or Lord knows what else. You're the brave one, so go on. I'll stay right where I'm at, thank you very much." It suddenly occurred to him that Pete might become lost or injured inside the tunnel, in which case it would be up to Delbert to rescue him; the thought made him uneasy.

"Hold on a tick," Delbert insisted. "Seein' as how you'd get lost in an out-house, I've got an idea." He leaned his shotgun against a nearby rock and re-moved his backpack. After rummaging around inside, he removed a length of sturdy rope. Offering one end to Pete, he tied the other end securely about his own waist.

"Wrap that tight 'round you and make a good knot 'fore you take another step," Delbert directed his companion. With a joking smile, he added, "That way, if you get into mischief in there, I can pull your skinny ass out and be a hero without even gettin' my hands dirty!"

Pete laughed and shook his head. Realizing the sense of the plan, however, he applied the rope as instructed. He then turned to Delbert with a feigned look of sadness on his face and teased, "You'd miss me more'n you can say, wouldn't you, Del Honey?"

He jumped back to avoid the fist that came flying in his direction. Both men laughed uproariously. Delbert began to make a deprecatory remark in response to Pete's joking flirt but found he was laughing too hard to get it out. Calming a bit, he said, "Now cut the sweet talk and get your fanny in that hole if you're a-going — *Honey.*"

Pete chuckled as he approached the cave's entrance, lit the flare with a match, ducked his head low, and thrust one foot into the crumbling portal.

From behind, Delbert called out in all seriousness, "Watch yourself in there, now!"

Pete smiled and replied, "Will do, ol' buddy."

As Delbert watched his friend disappear into the darkness, he wondered if greed had overridden his better judgment. Pete was his best friend, after all, and he certainly did not want to lose him or see him hurt. He decided he was worrying too much, so he abandoned himself to imagining the fortune in gold that would soon be theirs. Standing on his toes and weaving from side to side, he managed to follow the faint glow of Pete's flare as it traveled inward, then disappeared.

"Do you see anything yet?" Delbert shouted impatiently. A muffled, unintelligible response drifted back to him. "I can't understand what you're sayin'!" he responded. "Speak up, damn it!" He held his breath, realizing the slightest sound would drown out Pete's answer. Reluctantly positioning himself closer to the opening, he yelled, "What?" into the darkness of the hole.

"I said the tunnel opens up real big —this whole damn hill's hollow!" Pete shouted. "There must be at least half an acre of open space in here, and it's all one big room. I can't determine how far up it goes 'cos the light from this flare's too weak to cut through the pitch dark. There's four great big, slimy, black columns holdin' something up, but I can't define just what." A choking cough followed. "The smell in here's 'nough to gag a maggot!"

Delbert anxiously pushed for further details.

"It's full of graves too, Indian graves like we thought. Looks like they just dug shallow circles down about a foot and a half into the ground and threw the bodies in. None of 'em's covered over or nothin'. Sure wish I had a better light." His voice sounded much farther away now. "There's things in some of the

Daniel Alan Ross '99

graves that sparkles ever' time the light passes over, but ... hold on!"

Delbert held his breath, excitement coursing through every inch of his body. Surely the sparkles meant some of the graves contained gold, although mica would sparkle as well. He, or rather they, were going to be rich! Unable to bear the suspense any longer, he cried out, "Hey there, Pete! Whatcha doin' now? Do ya see any fer-sure gold anywhere?"

"There must be a hundred or more skel'tons laid out in here," came the faint answer, "most of 'em just thrown in ever' which ways in the graves. Something 'bout 'em don't look right though, not right at all."

"Whatcha mean?" Delbert called back.

"The bones, 'specially these here skulls, is all mashed, like they been run over by a steamroller." There was a pause. "I don't mind tellin' ya, this place is beginnin' to make me feel a mite skiddish. I'm startin' to think I best get outta here!"

"Don't leave! Not just yet," Delbert called out impatiently. "You've gone this far, you might as well get something for your trouble. Take yourself a minute more and see if you can find some gold gewgaws before you trot your prissy ass back out here." When no response was forthcoming, he called out worriedly, "Pete? Hey, Pete! Tell Del what's goin' on!" Before he could help himself, he added, "Did you find any gold yet? Dammit, Pete, answer me!"

"I hear ya!" echoed back to him. "Yeah, some of these bones is wearin' trinkets that are prob'ly gold. But it don't exactly put me none at ease that they's all squashed, same as the bones.

"All the while I'm tryin' to look around, I'm feelin' more and more nervous 'bout what's above my head. I built myself a little fire over at the foot of one of them big round columns I told you 'bout; there's a lot of loose brush that's built up over the years in here, so I figured I'd use some of it to help see better. Soon as the blaze gets big enough to light things up a bit, I'll feel a whole lot better. That damn coal black ceiling gives me the shivers and quakes.

"You know, if I didn't know better, I say it looks like ... huh? What the hell! Columns can't move! Oh, Jesus God Almighty Christ! No! No!"

Delbert turned white, his ears assaulted by a hail of throat-wrenching screams abruptly cut off yet still echoing through the mound's interior. He knew this was no prank, as only unimaginable agony could cause such shrieks. He tried to call out to his friend, but he could not get the sound beyond the thick lump of terror that now lodged in his throat.

"Pete?" he finally managed to whisper; his second attempt was somewhat louder. A sudden jolt of adrenaline made him cry out Pete's name over and over hysterically. It occurred to him that he should go in there after Pete, but his body refused to obey that command; his overloaded brain had simply shut down.

The next moment, Delbert heard something emanating from deep within the mound, a sniffing or gurgling sound — he could not be sure. Whatever it was, it ripped the last remnants of hope from his heart, leaving him short of breath and in a panic. He had no idea that a stream of urine was running down his leg.

"Pete," he called again. "What's wrong? Are you all right, Pete? Somethin' in there with ya, ain't it? Come on, answer me, Pete!" He was sure he now heard an additional sound from within the mound, a lapping noise like a cat makes as it eats. On top of that, he was sure he heard breathing, *really big* breathing.

Recalling the rope tightly wound around his waist, Delbert began to pull its length toward him, reluctantly at first, then more quickly. He soon gathered more than enough rope to account for the distance Pete had traveled, credible proof that Pete was no longer on the other end. He dropped the rope as if it were red hot.

He felt his body growing cold, icy cold all over. Involuntary whimpers began issuing from his throat. "Petey boy," he mumbled. "Somethin's got my Petey boy and I gotta help him." He repeated those same words over and over until they rose to a screeching crescendo.

The rope suddenly rose up from the ground and stretched itself taut. Before thought could spring into Delbert's confused mind, his body lurched forward several feet, slamming into the narrow entrance of the cave.

He struggled, frantically fumbling to untie the rope before it cut his wedged body in half. He had no doubt that whatever held the other end of the rope was not human.

A second mighty draw on the line somehow managed to pull Delbert's entire body through the tiny entrance into darkness. He twisted wildly in an effort to gain solid purchase, but his torn and bleeding form flipped mercilessly against the dirt floor and jagged walls. For one instant, he seemed suspended above an empty, lightless abyss, but shooting pain returned him to the reality of the moment as his head, arms and shoulders struck unseen obstacles again and again.

An eternity later, he came to an abrupt halt. Broken and bleeding, he lay face down on the cold, damp ground, savoring even its rough unevenness. A few feet away, he recognized the stub of Pete's still burning flare; reaching out despite his agony, he pulled it to him. The comfort he received at having light instantly faded when, after forcing himself to rise, he recognized the source of the unevenness beneath him — he had been lying on the bloody, horribly shattered bones of a human being. Amongst the bones of a crushed hand, he recognized the friendship ring he had given Pete several years before.

He screamed and jumped to his feet, mindless of the protests from his damaged limbs. Trembling, he raised the burning flare upward in an attempt to illuminate the darkness above his head, the likely source of whatever had murdered his friend. As he squinted into the shadows, his body began to convulse as he stared fixedly into the incredible mass of teeth set firmly in the face of the huge round piledriver that was furiously descending upon him from above.

In the Fall of 1920, a peculiar pilgrimage took place in Hoppwood County shortly after Lyla Hoppwood passed away.

Nate MacGregor, whose pasture directly sided the Hoppwood property, telephoned Sheriff Boyle to report that a "foldin' cardtable, black and 'bout forty foot tall" was crossing his land at a slow lumbering gait, heading due north. His fields, he claimed, were littered with tons of boulders, sod and uprooted Sycamore trees that had fallen from the earthen mound set atop the headless, faceless intruder.

Sheriff Boyle knew the only Sycamores in the area were on the Hoppwood property. He had also received notice that same day that two young local men, now missing for two days, had been last seen walking in the direction of that same property. Putting two and two together was not hard, especially after the Sheriff discovered a huge patch of newly uprooted earth in the woods near the Hoppwood mansion. It looked as though someone had used a cookie cutter to impress six-foot circles into the ground, circles containing the mutilated skeletons of apparently hundreds of long-dead Indians, plus two very fresh corpses. The Sheriff could not help but recall the queer tales Miss Hoppwood, her daddy and his daddy before him had told concerning their unique "tenant."

As word of the exotic traveler spread, people turned out in droves, hoping for a glimpse of the outlandish spectacle that had the whole town talking. All had heard, although few had truly believed, the stories the Hoppwood family had told for generations. In light of this new evidence, however, skepticism quickly waned. Initial reactions to the strange loping oddity were a mix of fear and amazement, but once folks recognized the bizarre creature as a long term resident and one of their own, a degree of sympathy for it began to develop; after all, it had lived in their midst for decades without bothering a soul until a

couple of shiftless poachers had invaded its lair. Surely they had deserved whatever fate they had received. The poor creature was obviously only tramping across the land now in search of privacy and a more secure shelter.

Spectators traveled from farm to farm just to catch a glimpse of the wonder, their awed whispers becoming cheers of encouragement as the bizarre being paraded before them. Although its newfound fans were convinced Miss Hoppwood's displaced tenant meant no harm to anyone, one unfortunate incident did occur. A young couple, outsiders without local connections, were instantly crushed flat by a previously unseen appendage that telescoped down from the creature's torso. They were strangers to the community and had foolishly ventured too near the mammoth, column-like legs, so they only had themselves to blame for their deaths.

Despite a seeming lack of eyes or ears, the unearthly pilgrim marched on, mile after mile, unerringly headed toward the only suitable refuge in the area, the unexplored subterranean caverns on Nub Jenkins' farm.

By the time the spectacular creature arrived and eased itself into what was believed to be the largest the of Jenkins' caverns, it had been unanimously accepted into the hearts of the citizens of Madden County. The cavern was voted an historic landmark the next day, and the beast itself pronounced an endangered species to be kept secret and protected at all cost. Nub and a handful of volunteers encircled the cavern area with barbed-wire fence, dotting its length with signs that alternately declared, "No Trespassing" and "Do Not Disturb Tenant."

As Nub put it, "Mind ya, the critter may look like some black titan's unmade bed, but that ain't no call for actin' prejudice to'rd it!"◆

The Black Massif

In a matter of just a few years, the brilliance of the Sun noticeably diminished in contrast to the simultaneous slow but constant increase in the heat with which it bombarded the satellite worlds imprisoned by its gravitational hold. The subsequent diminishing of the polar ice caused the boiling seas and oceans to gradually swallow more and more dry land around the globe until finally nothing remained above-water but the fragmented continent of Zothique and a few remote and uninhabitable peaks representing the remnants of the highest mountain ranges.

Those possessing prescient abilities — sorcerers, wizards and necromancers of various corners of the world — foresaw disaster and escaped the impending flood by fleeing to the sanctuaries of the small towns, isolated villages, and ruins of formerly great metropolises that, like the scars of wounds as yet unhealed, dotted the landmass of Zothique. Once there, those powerful magi recognized the precarious nature of their situation to the extent that they joined forces to project an invisible protective shell around the whole of the continent. By controlling the temperature and the weather within this safeguarding enclosure, they maintained a tolerable, self-contained environment for themselves and the unsuspecting citizenry of Zothique; the rest of humanity was abandoned, condemned to cruel demise in the searing blast of ever-increasing, scorching heat. As the temperature outside the sheltering carapace rose to lethal levels, the oceans receded until they eventually evaporated entirely. Within a matter of a few years, the once-lush surface of Earth was reduced to a vast and lifeless desert but for the oasis of Zothique.

Having avoided the immediate emergency, the newly-migrated wizards proceeded to distance themselves from one another, fragmenting the land into feudal estates that they might resume the age-old struggle to wrest as much land and property from each other as possible without regard for the cost. These new masters boldly commandeered the defenseless natives of Zothique, using them as chattel for a seemingly endless stream of campaigns for dominion orchestrated by and for the benefit of the rulers alone. Confusion overwhelmed a land that had long ago lost the secrets of technology and, as a result, civilization quickly reverted to the equivalent of the Dark Ages of a previous millennium.

THE BLACK MASSIF

Fortunately, not all of the power-endowed sorcerers who sought refuge in Zothique were concerned with petty conquests. Among those who survived the rising tide and ensuing heat were those known as the Six, a half-dozen of the greatest living thaumaturgic luminaries, both male and female. The Six were unfailingly dedicated to the preservation and ennoblement of mankind. This optimistic congress of Six believed humanity, despite its long and disparate record, possessed the potential to evolve into a wise and benevolent race, should it be allotted sufficient time. With the intent of encouraging this transformation, the Six had copied and conveyed the bulk of the decimated world's greatest occult libraries and scientific archives to their new stronghold.

Realizing the vast potential the combination of their forces presented, the Six bonded that they might utilize their collective power to utmost effect. By combining the retrieved knowledge of occult studies and ancient scientific information, they made an unparalleled discovery — a means of manipulating the time-space continuum that allowed them to travel through the temporal abyss to any time and location on Earth. They therefore set out to comprehensively search the technological records of their predecessors in hope of finding a solution to the dilemma facing the vestiges of mankind. Such visits were, of necessity, of short duration, as the Six were wise enough to use extreme discretion when venturing into the past. They focused their excursions upon the essential exploration of the most scientifically enlightened eras, particularly the centuries immediately preceding the Great Fall, the holocaust that had set mankind's progress back innumerable centuries. It was imperative they consult the ancient records of empirical science without altering or disturbing the past in even the slightest detail, least they catastrophically disrupt the hypersensitive flow of time.

As they unobtrusively studied the information gleaned from the ancient scientific records, the Six began to appreciate the dire ramifications of the solar engine's extreme acceleration. The Sun, they began to realize, was racing at an unimaginable pace toward its own demise. At the current rate, the nuclear fusion of the core would soon cease due to exhaustion of the hydrogen that fueled that process. Yet the most learned minds of past millennia had determined, based upon centuries of astronomical observations, that the Sun contained sufficient hydrogen to maintain its normal state for another four or five billion years. Something had gone very wrong with the temporal scenario, and the Six were determined to unravel the mystery that they might avert the end of the world.

The tremendous increase in the degree of unbearable heat radiating from the fiery disc clearly foreshadowed the onset of premature stellar disaster. Without fuel, the collapse of the stellar core would relinquish its gravitational grip upon the gaseous outer shell known as the corona. The unrestrained corona, being the hottest part of the Sun, would explode as a nova that would incinerate the entire solar system in a fiery holocaust. The remaining debris would contract as it cooled, eventually condensing into a dark cloud of cold nuclear waste material devoid of all life. According to revised calculations, this terminal conflagration would occur in a mere twenty years' time.

Undaunted, the Six immediately launched further frantic quests into the past in hope of discovering some means by which to avert the impending disaster. After a seemingly endless stream of further temporal explorations, a plausible solution finally presented itself — if an extraordinary quantity of hydrogen could be extracted from Earth's atmosphere and chilled to an extreme, the resultant liquid hydrogen could then be held in stasis through the application of a blend of magical and scientific techniques long enough for its volume be enhanced exponentially. Were the resultant mass then plunged directly into the heart of the Sun, it just might rekindle that star's diminishing process of internal fusion.

All agreed the plan was a monumental gamble as the Sun might very well explode the instant the unnatural injection of hydrogen pierced its outer core, but they also agreed that this was the only feasible option and thus presented a risk worth taking. It was not long however, before they realized two major hurdles still jeopardized any chance that their plan might actually succeed.

First, all of their efforts would have to be in place and ready within fifteen years' time if they were to have even the remotest chance of accomplishing their goal. Yet even this stringent schedule paled in significance once the Six realized that even the cumulative impact of their combined strength would not be sufficient to execute their plan; a seventh member possessing equal power was required to accomplish so much so quickly.

Without further delay, half of the Six undertook assignments to the past that they might discover the mysterious cause of the Sun's premature aging. The other three assumed the task of seeking possible candidates for the vital seventh member of their consortium. This continent-wide search began with a series of telepathic broadcasts intended to specifically tune into minds possessing a particularly stringent set of intellectual requirements along with an inborn penchant for manipulating the inestimable powers vital for the prevention of Armageddon.

The quest for someone possessing the proper qualifications indicated that only three potential candidates existed among the whole of Zothique's population of several hundred thousand. The three magi assigned to the task of ferreting out the candidates included Magla, Rymol and the great Anama, the most powerful and eldest of the Six. Riding upon *zoothllamas*, a fast and reliable hybrid camelid, they immediately set out to locate and assess the three prospective members.

Rymol, the first to locate his target, met with disappointment. The candidate he found was a bed-ridden elderly woman far too fragile and weak for consideration. Sadly, Magla's efforts met with failure as well, for she was drawn to a man who had lost both arms in a futile slaughter meant to expand the miniscule holdings of a necromantic despot. All hope became focused upon Anama's endeavors.

The mental trail lured Anama to Quilac, a collapsed wreck of a city near the southernmost tip of the continent, a city that just a century before had been a thriving metropolis of nearly a million citizens. The old sorcerer, accustomed to the calm beauty of a suburban countryside, was shocked and sickened by the misery, poverty and suffering he encountered everywhere in the dark, debris-littered streets of Quilac. Determined, he unwaveringly dove into the muddled mass that represented the degraded vestige of a once proud populace. Although filled with a mixture of pity and revulsion, he continued his search, praying that he would locate the last hope of humanity somewhere within the pest-ridden ruins.

Having traversed the greater part of the city, Anama found himself in a lawless area that had once comprised the very heart of the city's financial district. In the toppled remnants of once-towering skyscrapers, it seemed those he encountered were naught but muggers, derelicts, prostitutes and muttering madmen. Dirt-encrusted raving maniacs staggered through the streets by day, clinging to life despite the miserable condition of their existence. As the light of day waned, more degraded and misbegotten souls slowly emerged from the shadow-haunted tumult of crumbling office buildings and shops, forced from their hiding places by the threat of starvation. The unbearable hunger he saw in their eyes told him they would eventually set upon one another with cannibalistic passion.

He battled an innate desire to flee the disturbing squalor of the sprawling madhouse. Could, he wondered, even a mind like that which he so desperately sought long resist being absorbed into the ranks of such human garbage?

By carefully exploring the thought-patterns of each subhuman creature he encountered, Anama soon learned the population served as little more than a reserve from which its cruel ruler filled the ranks of his ever-dwindling, ramshackle army. Those forces, devoid of all discipline and training, were then decimated in one horrific battle after another, leaving only the old, the severely disabled and the very young to root out a feeble existence in the twisted ruins. Still, Anama pressed on. Intuition told him he was close to achieving his goal in the surprising form of a teenage boy.

The object of his quest materialized the following morning when, while passing a particularly gloomy and trash-cluttered side street, Anama spied a seated, upright figure half-buried in a pile of reeking garbage. It occurred to him that the filth-encrusted creature somehow anticipated his arrival.

The cautious wizard moved to confront the grime-covered sleeper, then bent down to seat himself upon a square of broken concrete directly facing the dozing figure. Closing his eyes as well, Anama carefully extended his consciousness to penetrate the dark figure's mind.

In respectful deference to the other man, Anama assured the drowsy mind that, despite this intrusion, no harm was intended. In turn and as a further token of good will, the trespasser permitted his host limited access to the wellspring of his own thoughts. Anama instantly recognized the unique and amazing potential of the young man. Without doubt, he had found the one he sought. The elderly mage commenced a review of his companion's life that he might gain further insight into the man's mentality.

His given name, Anama learned, was Shafar. The offspring of a middle-aged prostitute and one of her many faceless clients, Shafar had been in another urban pesthole to the North and raised by a brood of cold and jaded whores, that his mother might continue her profession without the hindrance of a child for which to provide care. The scope of his childhood memories understandably proved vague and incomplete for, at the tender age of five, Shafar was sold to an antiques merchant from Quilac, a nearby city in a lesser state of deterioration. This self-proclaimed dealer, known as Druda, was in fact little more than a common junkman.

Within a short time, Shafar's duties became clearly defined; he was to clean, restore and salvage as much of the discarded remnants, i.e., junk, that Druda acquired and shipped from the remote corners of the world to a dreary, windowless warehouse in Quilac that was destined to be young Shafar's home for nine years.

Under Druda's tutelage, the boy became proficient at reconstituting for resale not only thousands of odds and ends but also the rare treasures he occasionally extracted from what appeared to be nothing more than great heaps of garbage. The concept of beauty, once incomprehensible to a youth familiar with only the disparate wreckage of two deteriorating metropoli, came to Shafar like an epiphany. The artistic masterpieces he all but magically withdrew from the masses of rubbish Druda collected instilled an obsessive appreciation for artistic excellence deep within the impressionable boy's soul.

Shafar felt puzzled and saddened to realize there was no one with which he could share his miraculous revelation. He vowed to devote his life to the preservation of all that was beautiful in the world.

Although unaware of the cause of his servant's transformation, Druda began to look upon the youth with burgeoning admiration, noting his uncanny ability to pluck items of value from what appeared to be little more than mounds of worthless debris. The boy appeared to relish the great efforts required for him to restore and renew the shattered and broken relics of bygone ages, but not as much as Druda relished the revenue he received from the sales of those same items. Using his wits, the heavyset, aging dealer began purchasing the estates of private art collectors. He also sought to acquire the booty looted from the wreckage of art and historical museums buried beneath the rubble of the world's demolished cities. He showed his appreciation by allowing Shafar to keep a few of the small baubles he gleaned from piles of refuse.

During the following nine years, the unlikely pair developed a relationship akin to friendship, culminating in Druda's promise to make Shafar his heir. Yet, as fate would have it, Druda collapsed while away on a buying trip in a distant land and died a few days thereafter and thus died before officially making good his promise. Druda's greedy relatives immediately claimed all of the dead man's possessions and sold them along with the warehouse before tossing Druda's penniless teenage servant into the street.

Before being turned out, however, Shafar concealed within his clothing all that he could of the most valuable pieces of silver and gold jewelry Druda had given him. By selling these items bit by bit, the lad was able to feed himself. For the following two years, the self-reliant youth had survived by using his wits. Donning miserable rags and retreating to the most obscure hiding places in the shunned emptiness of precariously fragmented skyscrapers, he pretended to be a madman on those rare occasions when necessity forced him into contact with others. By such means, he successfully avoided mandatory recruitment into the ruler's military force. His spirit was driven by the certainty that destiny would eventually provide the means for him to keep the world's most precious treasures out of harm's way.

Anama gasped; every aspect of the filth-ridden boy's mentality either met or surpassed the strict qualifications required to become the seventh member of his wizardly group. He was literally a fifteen-year-old magical prodigy, just the miracle for which he had prayed. The boy's obsessive dedication to salvaging the classic art of the past struck the old wizard as an unexpected but admirable and harmless additional quality.

The visitor slowly opened his eyes, only to find his gaze caught in the wake of his companion's now-open, fathomless eyes.

Shafar smiled softly, the red of his smiling lips barely visible beneath the dark shadow that obscured the greater portion of his face. In salutation, he solemnly uttered, "I recognize and welcome you, honored master. You have traveled far and now that you have trod the pathways of my mind, I pray you will accept me as your humble student. I am as eager to learn as you are to teach."

The ancient mage, pleased by Shafar's greeting, responded with, "You will surely be enchanted by the green hills of our destination, though the land itself be far more extensive than even a lover of beauty such as yourself could ever hope to add to his collection. With your help, however, we may preserve that beauty for future generations."

Anama and his newfound apprentice wasted little time in removing themselves from the corrupt degradation of Quilac; that very hour they began the long journey to the retreat of the Six.

Having first beheld the filth-ridden, malodorous waif who accompanied Anama upon his return, all were astonished to find that, once he had been scrubbed and provided decent clothing, Shafar was actually an incredibly handsome young man.

One by one, the Six gently, and as unobtrusively as possible, probed the prospective member's mind. They unanimously agreed with Anama's initial assessment of the boy; he was as bright and benevolent as he was beautiful.

As a prelude to what would prove an entire decade of arduous training, Shafar took part in an elaborate ceremony symbolizing his rebirth as a novice sorcerer. When instructed to choose a new name, an evocative name, Shafar renounced his former identity in favor of Evoquitus, a nominative he considered a clever takeoff on the instruction he had been given.

Although each member of the Six would eventually instruct Evoquitus in various magical and technical methodologies, the greater part of his education was administered by Anama himself. Before all else, however, the young student was required to learn to read and write in a number of languages lost for eons, including the classic tongues such as Arabic, Latin, English and Greek, that he might study the lore of ages past in its original form. In addition to becoming adept in the most obscure and cryptic magical manipulations, Evoquitus eventually became well versed in higher mathematics, geology, astronomy, cosmology, advanced physics and more. His favorite pastime, however, was the study of ancient history and the elaborate art of long forgotten cultures.

The youth absorbed knowledge so quickly and thoroughly that his overseers felt confident that, with his help, the chances of their fantastic plan's success would be increased a thousand-fold.

The diligent Evoquitus was permitted free access to Anama's vast library, which contained the greatest extant resources for the necessarily intensive study of numerous aspects of both wizardry and the sciences. Only a few isolated bookshelves were deemed inappropriate for the youth, the contents thereof dealing specifically with necromancy, the black arts and the newfound means of traversing time. He would be taught the secret of time travel only after he had completed his apprenticeship, but the other subjects were considered far too improper and possibly even temptingly dangerous for casual exploration. For those reasons, certain volumes were declared off-limits to the boy.

In time, Anama inadvertently discovered that Evoquitus periodically defied his prohibition against consulting the forbidden tomes. He remained silent, however, convinced such infractions of the rules were due to the boy's natural curiosity. He assured himself that his charge would come to recognize the repulsive nature of the darker side of sorcery. Aside from this single indiscretion, Anama was both delighted and astonished at his charge's amazing ability to comprehend and retain seemingly endless amounts of the most complicated material.

As Evoquitus approached and attained manhood, Anama could not help but notice the increasing magnificence of the young man's physical appearance. He admired the way the pale perfection of Evoquitus' svelte form seemed to glow in direct contrast to the blue-black hair that heavily adorned his head before casually radiating down the center of his lean chest and flowing out onto his arms, legs and firm buttocks. His dark, penetrating eyes, far too commanding for one so young, were as discomfortingly mesmerizing as they were alluring. It had become Evoquitus' habit to bathe daily in a nearby river, and whenever passersby caught sight of his naked figure emerging from the waters, they paused to speculate as to the identity of this nude Adonis.

Despite all this, Evoquitus' self-esteem remained low, a fact that Anama found worrisome. Such extreme humility could eventually lead to a misguided need to prove himself worthy through the misuse of supernormal abilities. Only time would tell.

Anama reluctantly recognized the burgeoning of a most unexpected emotion within himself. Aside from the great pride he took in his apprentice, over time his attraction and fondness for the boy grew, eventually fermenting into full-blown love. This realization became the source of intense trepidation for Anama. As a teacher, it was his duty to maintain an aloof but supportive attitude toward the charge and nothing more. An inner struggle ensued, one that would later prove disastrous to both. The teacher determined it vital that he conceal his feelings at all cost, for he was more than aware that even in optimal circumstances an intensely attractive, bright and desirable youth such as Evoquitus had become could never return the affections of one as old and worn as he. He did his best to reject such feelings for his charge, not only as the appropriate thing to do but as a means of protecting himself from the pain of certain rejection.

The years passed quickly until the time arrived when the Six deemed Evoquitus' principal education complete. Now all that remained was the final, definitive test; Evoquitus must prove himself capable of utilizing his new power wisely in the absence of supervision of any kind. Evoquitus was compelled to take leave of his mentors for two years, during which time all communication with the Six was strictly forbidden. At the end of the allotted time, it was agreed, Anama would seek out his student and personally assess his actions during the preceding two years. He would then return to his comrades with a report for his comrades' further consideration and final determination. Should it prove that their student had comported himself in a responsible manner, Evoquitus would then be adjudged their equal and worthy of acceptance into the fold.

Thus the adult Evoquitus took leave of the rolling green hills and pastureland he had come to love so well, using his newfound freedom to search for a place familiar to him only from his dreams.

Evoquitus found Barootha to be a small, sleepy village nestled in a valley located between a giant stone outcropping and a dangerously unapproachable sea cove just a few miles inland from the northern-most shore of Zothique. Something about this seemingly unimportant, isolated community of farmers and herdsmen deeply appealed to Evoquitus' soul.

As the verdant hills and vales of Barootha were cradled between the shadow of a great rough-stone massif and the sea, the people of Barootha had maintained total isolation and the resultant freedom from the threat posed by those who would otherwise subjugate them. The looming barrier of the threateningly high and flat-topped mesa acted as a barrier to prevent any inland invasion, and the devastating force of the stormy sea sheltered littoral Barootha from attacks launched by sea.

The nearly vertical cliffs of the awesome massif had changed but little since the cataclysmic moment it first burst forth from the molten depths of primal Earth. The great precipice had never been fully scaled or explored to any real extent as the Baroothians shunned the peak, sensing something intrinsically unnatural and intimidating about the titanic boulder.

Yet, it was to the north, to Barootha's great outcropping of stone that Evoquitus was drawn. His dreams revealed a secret path by which he might safely attain the village and pass through it to reach the precise spot described so clearly in his dreams.

The urge to create a spectacle as he passed through the streets of Barootha proved irresistible to the newly empowered sorcerer. He thus freely exercised his magical abilities during his march to Barootha, utilizing freely the necromantic secrets he had unscrupulously attained from his master's library. He gathered a gruesome entourage of grisly zombies and a terrifying bestiary of long-extinct monstrosities as he traversed a circuitous route on the way to his final destination.

The townspeople of Barootha hid when word of an approaching party of invaders reached them, although most could not resist the temptation to peek through drawn curtains as a dark-haired man traversed the town, vanward of a freakish assemblage of unsettlingly weird beings. The handsome invader sat proudly astride what appeared to be a grotesque curiosity culled from the denizens of some antediluvian hell in the form of a giant turtle-like creature bereft of flesh, the greater portion of its body concealed beneath an armored shell of exposed bone. Immediately behind the leader and his bleating transport trudged a rigor-stiffened troupe of gruesome zombies in attendance, their leathered skin and dry bones draped with the shreds of kingly robes. A host of bizarre and unruly beasts resurrected from extinction struggled to keep pace with the zombie herdsmen. The lumbering parade passed directly through and beyond the town without stopping.

The few stalwart Baroothians who dared follow the cryptically grotesque company of ghouls secreted themselves behind foliated roosts hastily fashioned from sapling boughs and shrubbery that they might spy upon the intruders as they approached the inclined foothill marking the base of the great massif. Abruptly, the leader turned and bid his tumultuous followers retreat. The animate corpses withdrew, ordering the rest of the ungainly assemblage to move back.

A commotion momentarily erupted when a throng of resentful sabertoothed tigers growled and spat threateningly as a skeletal flock of giant, plumeladen dinorni and epionrni, prehistoric ancestors of the ostrich and rhea, pressed too close. Disruption spread as a stubborn trio of massive, lumbering glyptodons was beaten into bellowing submission by a number of whip-bearing zombie masters. Both the tigers and the calcified anomalies were also subdued by the lash, the glyptodons limiting their diminished display of resentment to intermittently slamming their mace-like tails of mineralized bone into their disgruntled skeletal companions.

The concealed Baroothians watched as the regal stranger dismounted his remarkable steed and trod the shallow ravine separating him from the towering wall of solid rock. He raised both arms in mock embrace of the gargantuan mount before directing a series of incredibly shrill vocables toward the landscape before him. The screams of the Baroothian onlookers melded with the mewling chorus of the beastly herd as the sorcerer's hideous keening increased in intensity. All of the queer creatures were greatly affected by the sounds and a few collapsed, the piercing tones rendering them incapable of further resurrection.

As the stupefied farm folk struggled to cover their ears, the ground beneath them quivered and shook. Some of the spies took flight, convinced some long-imprisoned giant was furiously hammering his way toward freedom through the ground beneath their feet. A huge fissure suddenly appeared near the center of the massif, the rough fracture quickly widening in the wake of an enormous pressure accruing within the mountain.

The opening erupted in a spew of white-hot boulders and molten lava, spilling down the sheer cliff into the valley below. Miraculously, the burning barrage parted just before engulfing Evoquitus' nefarious crew, separating into two infernal rivers which poured safely into the sea. The few Baroothians still keeping watch remained frozen in disbelief as the caller's incomprehensible incantations continued, next fashioning the smaller of the lava flows into a spiraling stairway extending from the gaping fissure high on the cliff face all the way to the valley floor below. Thin rivulets of superheated bedrock twisted and entwined to create fabulously convoluted filigree and arabesques across much of the mountain's surface.

At the further behest of the conjurer, dozens of seething-hot, demonic figures twisted free of glowing pools of bubbling lava, each figure more ghastly than its predecessor. These molten beings scaled the slippery heights until, having reached an unaltered area above the freshly created opening, they pummeled the vertical surface with hardening paws to slice a narrow perch for themselves in the form of a band that encircled the entire massif. They stationed themselves upon the precarious ledge they had created, fixing their cooling bodies in a variety of strikingly dramatic and intricate poses in blasphemous caricature of the Greek and Roman reliefs of antiquity.

THE BLACK MASSIF

Having completed the transmogrification of the massif, the richly-garbed Evoquitus paused to inspect that which he had accomplished. Well aware of his unseen audience, he parted his lips slightly, reveling in sardonic satisfaction.

Motioning for his servitors to follow, he mounted the burning hot solidifying lava steps. His gruesome bestiary responded immediately, mindlessly unaware of effects the searing heat of the newly-formed inflicted upon their bare bones. The mesmerized herd marched in single file up the stair, undaunted by the fact that, with each step they ground the disarticulated bones of their fallen brethren to dust as they lumbered up the steps. At intervals, pairs of disconcerting creatures remained behind, establishing themselves as immobile guardians on the landings leading to the main entrance to the sorcerer's abode. Having attained the entry, the rest of the profane troupe passed through the portal into the infernal void of the hollowed-out massif.

Beyond the view of the prying watchers, Evoquitus spent the next week reshaping the massif's interior into a virtual honeycomb of chambers and storerooms, all of which were interconnected via serpentine tunnels. Like Jehovah, the mythical god of centuries past, on the seventh day Evoquitus finally rested, satisfied with that which he had accomplished.

The frightened and confused Baroothians debated long and hard as to the prudence of sending emissaries to greet the still-unidentified sorcerer in hope of establishing a friendly relationship and divine his intentions toward Barootha, be they malign or benign. Given his grand arrival had caused no real harm to anyone, they eventually concluded that a small delegation should be dispatched to welcome the powerful mage. By means of secret ballot, three prominent citizens were chosen to undertake the venture.

Lest their intentions be misconstrued, each of the three members of the delegation bore gifts for presentation to the mysterious stranger. As Barootha possessed no precious metals, jewels, or other priceless treasures, the gifts consisted of delicately carved wooden figures, tapestries of finely spun linen, gaily painted pottery and other handmade fineries. Such hand-made offerings were the most valuable items the villagers had to offer. Within a week, the delegation bid farewell to their well-wishing comrades before setting foot upon the twisted stone path leading to the high entrance to the sorcerer's fortress.

The progress of the unarmed ambassadors was decidedly hampered by the disparaging and all-but-unmanageable dispositions of the mules required to bear the ominous weight of the gifts up such a steep incline. Despite the pairs of petrified chimeric guardians set at intervals along the way, the pilgrims faltered only when the heads of the two huge saber-toothed tigers that guarded the apex of the treacherous stairway blatantly turned to observe the approaching visitors. Despite their fearful unease, the trio persisted.

When they reached the top, they found themselves confronting an enormous, intricately-carved ebony-wood door. One of the three gingerly raised the heavy golden dragonhead that served as a knocker and dropped it, allowing it to slam against the wood.

The awesome door yielded, slowly retreating inward. Two nearly fleshless cadavers appeared and silently bowed, indicating the trio should enter. One of the exotic doormen took charge of the gift-bearing mules while the other led the shivering Baroothians through the winding confusion of the dark labyrinth to a great hallway that culminated in an impressively large chamber. The previously faint illumination of torches set in cressets along the walls suddenly rose to blinding brilliance, directing the visitor's attention to a raised platform at the far end of the high-vaulted chamber. Set atop the platform was a lone, raven-haired figure seated upon a magnificently bejeweled throne.

The enigmatic lord rose to welcome his guests, bidding them approach his person. He introduced himself politely, his warmly soothing manner somewhat allaying the fears of his obsequious guests. The three ambassadors began to relax only when Evoquitus descended to their level and led them into a less ostentatious room where a friendly discussion ensued over refreshments.

Evoquitus explained he had no interest in instituting rule over the district. The only real interaction he desired with the locals was that they provide him with supplies for which they would be well paid. Beyond this, he made it clear that his privacy must be strictly and absolutely respected.

He thanked them for the gifts they had brought and burdened the mules in return with a number of far more valuable gifts. A mutual agreement had been reached and, having established Evoquitus' benevolent attitude toward them, the Baroothians heaved a sigh of relief. Soon thereafter, they took leave of the enigmatic sorcerer, anxious to share the promising news with the rest of the townfolk.

With Evoquitus' departure, Anama had rejoined his five compatriots in their ongoing efforts to refine the scheme to abort the impending apocalypse. Nonetheless, rumors of his young apprentice still occasionally reached his ears.

Word of Evoquitus' grandiose arrival in Barootha caused Anama only minor apprehension. Such a tawdry public performance, he realized, was to be

expected from one so young. Surely Evoquitus had merely found the opportunity to display his newly acquired wizardly powers an irresistible temptation. Beyond the childishly frivolous showmanship of the occasion, the only aspect that truly bothered the elder mage was the necromantic nature of Evoquitus' company; how dare he so blatantly utilize the necromantic knowledge he had pilfered from Anama's library? The master sorcerer could only pray that the novelty of resurrecting the long dead would soon wear thin. Should Evoquitus fail to live up to the standards of the Six, there could be no hope of saving mankind.

Anama's faith appeared to be borne out by reports of the benign, even friendly, relations his former charge established with the Baroothians. In every instance of official contact with the dweller in the massif, the Baroothians overwhelmingly approved of the respectful treatment afforded them.

In the wake of his initial relations with the Baroothians, further news of Evoquitus' activities became extremely scarce. He was occasionally observed enjoying leisurely strolls through the valley's lush wooded areas, always in the company of just one other person, most often another male. Without exception, these companions were described as exceedingly attractive and exotically attired. No one recognized any of Evoquitus' companions, and introductions were never offered despite the cordiality exhibited by the wizard during any brief encounters with the locals.

As the months passed without further report of any negative nature, Anama grew increasingly confident that his protégé would soon be prepared to take his rightful place among the group.

When two years had elapsed, Anama traveled directly to Barootha and, without delay, ascended the stairway of Evoquitus' impressively elaborate stone retreat. Although optimistic for the most part, he still harbored a certain trepidation in his heart. After all, everything, *literally everything*, depended on the outcome of this meeting.

At the apex of the twisted stairway, Anama paused momentarily before employing the bizarre knocker against the gigantic door. Before he could knock, the great wooden barrier slowly opened, and Anama watched as an animated skeleton struggled to maneuver the heavy burden. Having achieved its task, the mindless automaton bowed awkwardly and stepped back, indicating the visitor was expected and welcome.

Assuming the grotesque apparition was incapable of speech, Anama stepped boldly from the brilliant sunlight of day into a gloomy passage without addressing the doorman. Darkness enveloped the aged sorcerer, demanding his eyes adjust to the dimly lit interior of a disheveled, expansive hallway. The bony guide stumbled ahead, negotiating with difficulty not only the rough-hewn texture of the passage but the disordered mass of vitrines and clutter stacked and crammed haphazardly against the walls and into every available space.

Anama followed closely, making note of the pitch-black maws of darkness he assumed led to a multitude of rooms attached to the main hall. A thick blanket of dust covered the jumble of display cases so completely that he could not discern the nature of their contents in passing.

Taking momentary advantage of the slowness of his guide, Anama approached a vitrine at random. He wiped away enough grime to allow him a peek at the contents. According to the label, the case he had chosen contained the crown jewels of Great Britain. The adjacent cases contained other fantastic treasures, including the precious religious icons of a hodgepodge of long-lost cultures.

Realizing his cadaverous pilot had outdistanced him, Anama hurried to catch up. The animated cadaver was nowhere to be found, thus the aged sorcerer continued on alone in the direction of a distant illumination. Coming upon the source of the light, he stumbled into an expansive chamber. The chamber fit the description provided by the Baroothian ambassadors except that it was no longer an empty post-volcanic hollow containing only a throne. Now it was filled with beautifully framed paintings, tapestries, bas-reliefs, statues and all manner of other wondrous artwork. As he gawked at the fantastic contents of what could only be compared to a massive museum, Anama was startled from his reverie by a familiar voice calling his name.

"Anama, my master and friend! You have come to me just as promised. I have anxiously awaited your arrival," boomed the voice.

The old wizard responded with a request for more light, that he might better view his host. At this, a hundred torches burst to life all around the grand chamber, the dazzling glare causing him to wince. When his vision cleared, he saw Evoquitus standing before him, his arms outstretched in greeting. The pair embraced for a few moments, then Anama pulled away that he might better assess his former student's appearance.

Apart from the relative paleness of his complexion, Evoquitus was even more astonishingly handsome than Anama remembered. He looked quite dashing in his knee-high leather boots, loose tan trousers and half-open white shirt.

"Well, what do you think? Have I changed so much in two years?"

"The short, trim beard suits you well," Anama admitted, "in fact, you look very well indeed."

The younger man accepted the compliments with a hearty laugh. "You flatter me, old friend," he said. "It is wonderful to see you! I'm very happy to see you are in such good health as well."

Recalling his manners, Evoquitus bid his guest be seated, indicating a luxurious set of table and chairs that Anama adjudged to be from one of Louis XVI's palaces. Two necromantic denizens of the massif scuttled in and out with refreshments and a tempting array of viands. Although Anama and his host shared a glass of wine, the old master found it difficult to keep his mind on the niceties of conversation in the midst of such intimidatingly splendid and crowded surroundings. Unable to restrain himself longer, he finally asked, "Tell me, Evoquitus, what is the nature of this extraordinary abode you have made for yourself?"

His host, welcoming the opportunity to explain, proceeded to point out one masterpiece after another, agitatedly detailing the provenance of each, his voice echoing throughout the breadth of the enormous chamber. Many of the paintings, carved figures, frescoes and ceramic styles were familiar to the aged guest. As the speaker rattled on enthusiastically, he seemed oblivious to the growing change in the listener's demeanor.

Indicating a twenty-five foot colossal stone figure of an androgynously-shaped pharaoh wearing the double crown of ancient Upper and Lower Egypt, Evoquitus proudly declared, "And this special beauty is the only intact sample of nearly a hundred blasphemous images the eighteen-year-old Pharaoh Akhenaten defiantly erected in the long-destroyed temple of Aten at Karnak." Turning, he pointed, "Just down the hall, you'll find the solid gold sarcophagus and funerary mask of his young son, Tutankhamun, stationed next to the Berlin bust of Akhenaten's hauntingly beautiful queen, the infamous Nefertiti."

He continued excitedly, describing the difference between two giant sculptures of human-headed winged bulls guarding either side of the chamber entry, explaining that one was Assyrian, the other Persian.

"Come," Evoquitus enthusiastically called out, "I'll give you the grand tour. Within these walls reside the most glorious art ever created. I've collected treasures from all over the world, everything from the horrendous statue of the Aztec snake goddess Coatlicue, numerous intricately-carved Mayan stelae, and the finest examples of Scythian gold to the platinum crowns fashioned for the heads of Atlantean kings! One room contains nothing but amazing friezes plucked from the freshly-built Parthenon. One intact frieze in itself represents a single brilliantly painted scene extending more than five hundred feet in length! I've even obtained a number of wonders created by horrific alien races that controlled the Earth eons before man began his slow evolutionary rise from apelike creatures."

He grinned, gesturing to indicate the whole of the massif, "It's all here, carefully preserved in an all but endless series of catacombs. The most splendid objects d'art ever created are right here, safe within the confines of my fortress."

An atavistic fear began to race through the fabric of Anama's mind. Exerting great self-control, he interrupted his overly ecstatic host. "All of these things are, as you say, clearly precious and wonderful beyond definition," he said calmly. "I have seen pictures of many of them in the world's greatest historical records, yet I also seem to recall that the majority of these treasures were either lost, badly damaged or completely destroyed in antiquity. If these are the originals, how can they be here and all in such pristine condition?"

The younger man fell silent, suddenly finding it difficult to look his teacher in the eye.

After a time, he responded in a stammering, shyly apologetic tone. "You of all people are aware of my high esteem for beautifully crafted things and my all-consuming passion to preserve them. I couldn't bear their being damaged or lost and ruined forever, so I, well, collected as many as I could, the very best of the best, and I have brought them here where they will forever be spared the ravages of time and wanton destruction of ignorance."

When he looked up, it seemed Anama was peering directly into his very soul. Judging from the expression on his well-lined face, Anama did not approve of what he was hearing.

"Not only did you pilfer the secret of negotiating time from the forbidden tomes of your friends and benefactors, but you then proceeded to violate the paramount obligation imposed upon anyone who would dare use that knowledge responsibly," the mage chastised his companion.

Anama allowed a moment to pass, praying the deep implications of his words might be absorbed by his protégé. He felt like Agamemnon demanding Paris comprehend the full effect of the abduction of Helen, the difference being, in this instance, that Evoquitus gambled not with the fate of a city but of an entire world.

Evoquitus attempted to defend himself. "I admit I learned the secret of time travel without your approbation. I felt I was doing wrong at the time but I also felt compelled. As to defying the prohibition against tampering with the past, my motivations were never of a selfish nature. The world is already doomed, so how could anything I do possibly make things worse?"

Thoroughly disgusted, Anama grumbled, "You are a fool, Evoquitus, and I see now that we, as your teachers, have been equally foolish in our optimism. We have spent years carefully sifting through the past in a fruitless search for the catalyst that has caused the Sun's premature demise. Not for an instant did it occur to us that we would eventually become our own executioners. By nurturing and encouraging the magnificent creature that you have become, we have unwittingly created the very instrument of our ultimate destruction."

Evoquitus stared uncomprehendingly at the speaker.

Exasperated, Anama barked, "Use your head, man! The problem was not in the past at all, but in our present and the future. In spite of our good intentions, we were unwittingly constructing the very device of our own destruction — *you!*"

It seemed Evoquitus still did not understand.

"When you interfered with the past, you defied the laws of nature and thus undermined the very principles that maintain order in the universe. Each additional violation served to widen the irreparable rent you made in time until, eventually, our sun fell through the gap. Had we not provided you the means to do this, none of this would have occurred — the Sun would have continued to function predictably for another five billion years." He leaned closer to his audience for emphasis. "You know very well that time is cyclic. We may not know much about the working of time, but we do know that when one travels back in time, even the most minute change will dramatically and unpredictably affect the future, the effects expanding exponentially through the centuries!"

As understanding dawned on Evoquitus, he stopped grinding his knuckles against the sides of his head and slammed his open palms onto the surface of the table. "Assuming all this is true, I put it to you that this precious world of yours does not deserve to continue. You and the others persist in deceiving yourselves with your idealistic dream that mankind had the latent potential to evolve into some kind of wondrous superior being. You blindly ignore the fact that the human species has repeatedly failed to prove its intrinsic goodness throughout of millions of years. Doesn't that tell you something? No matter how much we learn about ourselves and the world around us, we insist on repeating the same unforgivable mistakes endlessly, inflicting war upon our own kind, committing unimaginable atrocities, and mindlessly destroying anything and everything around us, including the very environment that makes life possible. Nothing changes from century to century apart from the scope and intensity of the horrors we create.

"Even with the tremendous reduction of our numbers, we still we insist on cultivating the errors of our ancestors. A few elite still dominate the masses that they might exploit the helpless and send them off to certain death in an insane quest for ever more power. You've seen what remains of the world's once great cities; you've witnessed firsthand the verminous condition to which humanity has reduced itself. What will it take for you to realize that after all is said and done, it matters little whether we annihilate ourselves now or in some future time? Look at the what is left of the world right now. Odds are that, given another decade or two, those few who manage to survive will be reduced to predatory beasts, roaming the countryside like a pack of ravenous wild dogs, mindlessly pillaging the remaining communities and slaughtering each other until everyone and everything worthwhile is dead."

Evoquitus leaned forward intently, continuing in a voice that reflected sincerity and conviction. "It's true, I had no right to steal your secrets. Had it not been for you and the others, I would either still be rotting in Quilac or I would be dead. Believe me, I am not ungrateful for all that you have done for me.

"But you must know as well as I do that your plan to refuel the Sun is destined to fail. A thousand sorcerers possessing powers equal to your own could not succeed, so what chance do just seven of us have? None!"

Anama could only nod mournfully, acknowledging the impossibility of the task at last. "It was all we had," he whispered. "We could not just surrender to the void without a struggle."

"It was a noble gesture," Evoquitus assured his friend, "a most commendable gesture, but that's all it was. You would not have listened to me had I confronted you with the truth before this, so I took it upon myself to rescue whatever I could of humanity's truly worthwhile creations, that these things might survive to represent our species' noble attempts to rise above its base nature.

"I have discovered the means to make this massif impregnable. It will remain intact, absolutely impervious to the decimating force that threatens to obliterate everything else in the solar system. In fact, the blast of infernal heat itself will serve to seal the massif and launch it like a rocket into the vastness of space.

"There is still time to do more, much more. Together we could create a number of safe havens like this one, that we might rescue the great writings, musical compositions, and cinematic and photographic works of mankind and more. Think of it, man! Imagine the salvation of those things that represent the very best and noble aspects of humanity! Isn't that preferable to leaving nothing behind? If nothing of value remains, then we might just as well never have existed."

Anama shook his head. "But not enough time remains to collect the things you suggest."

"For those who possess the key to the past," Evoquitus offered confidently, "an infinite amount of time is available. If necessary, we could simply avoid the solar catastrophe by seeking shelter in the past."

The older man rose and began pacing back and forth as he tried to assimilate Evoquitus' bold suggestions. What he proposed defied every precept upheld by the Six. How could this young novice perceive things so differently and, more importantly, was he right? Before allowing Evoquitus to proceed any further, it was essential that Anama present Evoquitus' case to the others. There could be no margin for error in the dire situation in which they now found themselves; any decision to change course now must be the result of the unanimous decision of the Six. The others might perceive some flaw in Evoquitus' plan that he had missed.

"You must realize I cannot simply agree to your plan," Anama replied matter-of-factly. "I may represent the others, but I can neither consent to nor condemn the drastic change of plan you advise without consulting my compatriots. You can be sure, however, that I will present your ideas to them immediately that we might thoroughly evaluate the concept and its possible ramifications. I will then return and present you with our final decision."

Satisfied that he had finally gotten through to his former master, Evoquitus nodded his consent to this arrangement.

"However," added Anama, "as you were initiated in the art of sorcery under my tutelage, I am responsible for you. Therefore, until I return, I am obliged to relieve you of all supernormal abilities that I may be absolutely sure you are incapable of proceeding any further on your own. Until a student achieves full status as a mage, his teacher posseses the right and the power to revoke your powers, and I do so now. In light of the circumstances, I doubt you have any real objection to this." Before the shocked Evoquitus could respond, Anama added, "I am sorry, but this is the only way and, be assured, I shall act expediently. In addition, you must give me your solemn word that you will not leave the massif before my return."

The initial look of outrage slowly drained from Evoquitus' face; he knew he had no choice but to acquiesce his superior's wishes. It would only be for a few days before his powers would be restored, then he and the others could continue the great work together. He harbored no doubt they would perceive the validity of his plan. In the meantime, there was naught to do but consent and, like a defrocked priest, patiently await the decision of the hierarchy.

THE BLACK MASSIF

* * *

Evoquitus wandered through the vast expanses of his museum fortress, confident that the Six would decry the wisdom of his plan. He had expected his teacher's initial condemnation, but he had been surprised at how easily he had convinced Anama that his was the more logical and practical means to deal with the inevitable total destruction of the solar system. Curiously, he had felt certain all along that he would win Anama's approval. The very fact that Anama and the others had chosen him, above all others, for a decade-long tutelage under the most learned living sorcerers only served to reinforce his conviction that the events of his life were all predetermined.

Quite unexpectedly, however, Evoquitus realized that, if anyone had ever shown him love, it had been Anama. Further consideration made him realize that the deep feelings he harbored for his master approached the level of love. Unlike everyone else in Evoquitus' life, Anama treated him as a person rather than a tool. With Anama and the others by his side, he could finally assume the role destiny had ordained for him as the ultimate guardian of beauty.

Still, he found it irritating that he could no longer force his resurrected servants to do his bidding. One by one those over which he held sway had crumbled to dust, finally achieving their eternal release. Feeling lonely within his titanic fortress, Evoquitus yearned for Anama's speedy return.

He took comfort, however, in the knowledge that, despite the demise of all his uncouth attendants and the haunting silence of the halls and endless chambers of his prison, he was not truly alone, for Anama had not received a full accounting of the contents of Evoquitus' treasures by any means.

News of the most disturbing type awaited Anama on the occasion of his reunion with his fellow magi. Their most recent calculations indicated that the Sun had all but expended its fuel supply already. Any attempt to rekindle the star and thereby salvage its dependent worlds was now out of the question; all would perish within three weeks or less. Anama's comrades were at a total loss as to the cause of this secondary acceleration. In light of this shocking revelation, Anama was compelled to reevaluate Evoquitus' alternate proposal before presenting it to his peers.

The group was astounded by their unspoken leader's account. An extended discussion concerning the responsibility for the impending disaster resulted, but in the end, all were compelled to accept Anama's theory, laying the blame on their headstrong apprentice while admitting to their own lack of foresight as well. Further consideration of the matter was deigned futile as nothing could be done to avert the inevitable with so little time remaining.

Anama proceeded to delineate Evoquitus' suggestion that storehouses of knowledge similar to the one already created could be devised to preserve man's other meritous accomplishments. The proposal prompted a heated assessment of the advantages and disadvantages of such a challenging last-minute undertaking.

In the end, however, the Six concurred in declining to participate in what they viewed as a most dangerous course. As appealing as the conservation of humanity's redeeming accomplishments might be, the benefits of such were greatly outweighed by the unpredictable repercussions that would surely result should the time-space continuum be disrupted by a further massive assault upon the past. They dared not challenge the ultimate stability of the rest of the universe for this seemingly selfish purpose.

It was also decided that Evoquitus would be permitted to continue his own plan so long as he refrained from any further ventures into the past.

Anama, unable to refute the group's decisions, acquiesced to their wishes before departing the following morning to relay the news of the fraternity's judgment to the waiting Evoquitus.

Upon once again attaining the lofty entrance to Evoquitus' opulent mansion, Anama entered without attempting to summon the doorman. Too well he knew the reanimated servants of his young apprentice would not have survived the withdrawal of the necromantic energies that endowed them with a semblance of life. The shattered remains of the prehistoric guardians he had encountered as he ascended the formidable stairway were ready proof of that.

The heavy wooden door gave way to his touch. Facing the nocturnal darkness of Evoquitus' retreat for a second time, Anama used his powers to illuminate the murky hallway that he might more easily and quickly navigate the circuitous path through the disheveled mass of vitrines for the last time.

He forged his way forward, toward the grand vaulted chamber where Evoquitus surely awaited him with fervid anticipation.

Reaching the chamber's threshold, the wizened traveler hailed his beloved student. When no response was forthcoming, he shouted Evoquitus' name repeatedly into the spectral silence of the huge chamber. He still received no answer. Evoquitus had given his word that he would remain within the confines of the massif until Anama returned, so Anama felt sure that he must be somewhere within the dank fortress. He began to fear something sinister had taken place during his absence, though he could not imagine what it might be.

For the next few hours, Anama systematically searched the honeycomb of rooms and corridors in vain. Finally, he retreated to the central chamber, hoping to discern some clue as to his student's whereabouts. There he came upon the missing sorcerer's personal diary lying open upon a large wooden roll-top desk of ancient Shaker design. Due to the mysterious absence of the author, Anama did not hesitate to read the contents of the handwritten volume.

The diary contained a detailed record of not only the events of the previous two years but of Evoquitus' emotional and intellectual reactions to those events. Each entry contributed to the extremely intimate portrait of author's inner essence. From the very start, Evoquitus' own words depicted him as a man who considered himself inadequate and of little value other than as a tool for others to use to their own ends. The unusual circumstances of his upbringing had taken a more terrible toll on the boy than Anama realized, to the extent that Evoquitus viewed himself as an incomplete being who had never been given the opportunity to understand what it meant to be a fully self-realized person. He saw himself as a commodity or tool of those who prevented him from experiencing any true social interaction.

The reader was intensely moved by Evoquitus' desperate plight and his desperate need for even the slightest intimacy or sign of respect from those around him. He discovered at an early age that with tremendous effort he could satisfy those who controlled him, yet their acceptance depended not upon him but upon the results of his actions. He saw himself as a complete non-entity, isolated and separate from the very world in which he dwelled. His was an intolerably lonely existence in which he considered himself a solitary and unlovable individual.

The old mage berated himself for his utter lack of sensitivity to the feelings of his apprentice and beloved friend. Only at that moment did it occur to him that Evoquitus rarely, if ever, laughed aloud or smiled openly and spontaneously. Anama berated himself for being so self-involved in his role as the all-knowing instructor that he failed to notice the isolation and emotional pain harbored by one so near and dear to him.

Evoquitus' diary went on to describe the only avenue Evoquitus believed could lead to redemption — his discovery that there were rare things of beauty in what he otherwise considered a foul and ugly world. For the first time in his life, he dared consider there might be a worthwhile meaning to existence and that he was destined to play the key role in its realization. The remainder of the diary shocked the reader as he recognized the scribblings represented a meticulous account of Evoquitus' unwitting descent into madness.

The diary became a detailed record of Evoquitus' solitary efforts to seek out and deliver the most beautiful things the past had to offer. He retrieved these ancient treasures and brought them into his own time with total disregard for the unpredictable ramifications he knew would be the end result of irresponsible disruption of chronological events.

Later entries revealed that Evoquitus harbored an even stronger subconscious drive, one his benefactors had foolishly neglected to take into account. Although twenty-six years of age, Evoquitus had never had the slightest opportunity to express or experience his own sexuality. Understandably, he felt compelled to explore the strange cravings he found so impossible to resist. As he continued to read, Anama was reminded that he had earlier identified Evoquitus with Paris; only now did he come to realize the terrible veracity of that comparison.

After retrieving a number of precious objects from various eras and locations in the past, it occurred to Evoquitus that he should acquire at least some token of the fabled wealth of Troy. Timing his arrival well before the city's fall, he too was struck by the unrivaled beauty of the infamous Lady Helen. Finding her irresistible, he used his powers to magically cause her to become infatuated with him to the extent that he convinced her to accompany him upon his return to that which was, for her, the distant future. Having isolated her within the desolately eerie interior of his massif, Evoquitus eagerly indulged in the surrendering of his virginity to such a marvelous creature.

Having remained chaste well into adulthood, Evoquitus was greatly dismayed to find the sexual experience, famed for its miraculous joy and rapture, failed to meet his expectations. With each successive coupling with his stunningly breathtaking lover, his disillusionment grew stronger.

As a further deterrent to his passion, Evoquitus realized the journey into the future had mysteriously drained the infamous Helen's mind of all thought beyond the perpetual lust and craving for intimacy he had implanted within her.

Anama sighed loudly. Had the boy read his entire collection of treatises relating to time travel, he would have understood it is impossible to bring but a duplicate of living persons to the future. Early attempts to do so proved such replicas were naught but impermanent automatons devoid of all ability to think beyond the most primal levels. While inanimate objects had been transported through time without detectable alternation of that object, only a little was actually known about the resulting effects of transporting human duplicates from one time to another.

It seemed Helen's tireless advances eventually became so annoying to

Evoquitus that he deemed the situation intolerable. In a moment of extreme frustration, he magically rendered her incapable of movement. She became frozen in place, suspended between life and death and immune to the process of aging. She would remain in that condition until he chose to release her. In time, he began to view her as but a splendid icon, another acquisition for his burgeoning collection of beautiful things.

Unaware that his Helen was but a copy of the original, the distraught sorcerer spent a great deal of time trying to fathom the cause of the diminished mental capacity Helen had incurred due to her transportation through time. Frustrated, he eventually concluded the problem was the result of some inadvertent error on his part, some minute miscalculation in his manipulation of time. He did not discover the truth until he retraced his steps through time. When he returned to Troy, he was astonished to find the original, wholly intact Helen still there in the ancient past. He felt as if a great weight had been lifted from his shoulders, for now he knew he had not actually harmed the real Helen. Unfortunately, this realization granted him the freedom to commit further abductions without suffering a guilty conscience.

Still, he continued to ponder the sexual disappointment he had experienced with Helen. Maybe, he thought, it had been a mistake to choose a woman as worldly and experienced as she for his initial sexual encounter. He concluded a novice like himself would be a wiser choice. Helen had repeatedly praised his sexual prowess, but she could hardly do otherwise due to the spell of infatuation he had cast over her senses. Her lavish endorsements of his physical qualities and sexual abilities thus were not enough to reassure him; he needed further proof that he was at least an adequate lover. His own self-doubt, he realized, might well be the underlying reason sex had not as yet lived up to his expectations.

With increasing anxiety, Anama read on, increasingly concerned about the consequences of his student's deranged conduct. It came as no surprise that Evoquitus wasted little time magically enticing a lovely, nubile maiden of Bronze Age Greece into the future, then into his bed. The results once again proved disappointing. The poor girl's innocence failed to affect Evoquitus' sexual enjoyment. Anama was not surprised when the diary disclosed that within a very short time, the frustrated Evoquitus placed the immobile girl next to Helen's deathly-still form in a special gallery he created deep within the nethermost depths of the massif. Each of the mannequin-like figures was poised with care atop its own individual stone plinth bearing an inscription identifying the sedentary occupant by name as well as her original time and place of origin.

Undaunted, Evoquitus resumed his assemblage of inanimate artistic treasures, relentlessly raiding the great storehouses, temples and palaces of the pharaohs, the Greeks, the Roman emperors, the priest-kings of the Maya, Azteca and Inca cultures, and many others. He chose Minoan Crete as his next destination as he hoped to acquire a fine specimen of the brilliantly colored, lively frescos of that period as well as a few ivory and inlaid gold images of the Cretan snake goddess, Herpete. This trip would culminate in a particularly revealing experience for the unsuspecting sorcerer.

Once in the Cretan capital of Knossos, Evoquitus easily managed to locate and transport some of the items he had set out to find. With a flick of the wrist and a few mumbled words, each of the chosen items disappeared in time and space. Finding the Minoan culture much to his liking, he delayed the return to his own time that he might undertake a short excursion to Phaistos, another large metropolis on the island. It was in Phaistos, while attending an exhibition of the sport of bull-jumping, that Evoquitus became infatuated with a champion acrobat.

At this point, Anama was not surprised to read that the object of Evoquitus' unbridled desire was a slender, twenty-one-year-old male acrobat named Arkas.

By applying the very same incantations used to bewitch Helen and her successor, Evoquitus spirited Arkas into the future. To the kidnapper's astonishment, he experienced the elusive state of mental and physical ecstasy with the copper-skinned, doe-eyed Cretan that had previously eluded him; it was an experience beyond anything he imagined possible. To his utter despair, however, Arkas's mind proved as vulnerable to the rigors of transport as his the minds of his predecessors. Thus, despite the intense physical satisfaction attained with Arkas, the athlete's constant, urgent craving for bodily contact with his wizardly lover eventually became so tiresome to Evoquitus that he felt compelled to add Arkas to his growing collection of human statues.

Having finally found the key to true sexual gratification, the lustful sorcerer thereafter ignored women in favor of one male after another, luring each into his inescapable web before whisking him away to the confines of the massif. He set out to find the most comely heroes of history and even legend; not all of these proved to be actual persons, and of those he actually did manage to locate, only a few met his high standards. The sorcerer grew ever more frustrated as each new conquest inevitably became a tiresome pest after a time, including the Greek hero of heroes, the massively-built demi-god called Hercules.

Although Evoquitus periodically abandoned his exclusive quest for sexual pleasure to resume the harvest of artistic treasures, he was always on the lookout for men he deemed outstandingly attractive for one reason or another. His taste varied greatly within weeks, as he enjoyed an ever-widening variety of men of different age and race. He thought it odd that something as simple as the way a fellow smiled or carried himself could prove sufficient to capture Evoquitus' interest. It mattered little whom he chose in the long run, however, for no extreme of physical beauty could compensate for his lovers' incapacity for anything beyond the desperate and obsessive demand for physical contact with Evoquitus. Despite the application of innumerable spells to prevent or cure the depletion of consciousness in his lovers, no remedy was found. Although disheartened, Evoquitus was forced to accept this inevitable consequence as, ironically, even his magical powers could not relieve him of the inescapable addiction to sexual gratification he had acquired.

From time to time, pleasant memories of one of his former lovers would cause him to release his hold over that particular captive that he might, for a time, attempt to recapture the initial joy of the sexual experience with that person. Such futile attempts to relive the past always proved less than satisfying, thus it was not long before the temporarily rejuvenated subject resumed the rigid pose of his assigned station.

The number of immobile occupants comprising Evoquitus' gallery grew exponentially; Anama estimated the total at nearly one hundred, but he could not be sure based solely on the text of the diary. It seemed that Evoquitus had determined it wise to keep secret his special gallery, rightfully convinced that Anama would disapprove of every aspect of his student's sexual and/or romantic pursuits, let alone the blasphemous collection.

The final entry in Evoquitus' diary was naught but speculation as to Anama's reaction to the drastic measures his student planned to propose in opposition to the agenda the Six had so carefully contrived.

The wizened old mage closed the book and sat quietly for some time, solemnly contemplating the situation and the repercussions of Evoquitus' perverse actions. It occurred to him that the massif now bore the character of a tomb, similar to the stone-hewn burrows that housed the treasure of the great pharaohs of ancient Egypt. The gloom and silence suddenly became suffocating as his thoughts increasing invoked a terrible fear that gripped the old mage's heart like a vice.

Anama's brooding reverie ceased as a sudden clangor caught his attention. Someone or something stirred in the very bowels of the massif. He fought to overcome the instinct to turn and flee the terrible place without further exploration, but he could not leave without knowing what had become of the man he loved. He forced himself to rise and reluctantly set about the task of finding a path to the hidden gallery described in the diary. It came to him that the answer might lie in the slight but incongruous movement he had noticed as he passed a lavish tapestry on the far wall of the central chamber. The rustle of the cloth might reveal a concealed access the deepest bowels of the massif.

Returning to that chamber, he carefully inspected the lavishly-woven masterpiece, and closer scrutiny quickly confirmed his suspicions. The woven image depicted a woodland setting in which a number of goat-legged satyrs were apparently enjoying a homosexual romp. Battling a growing dread, he shoved aside the heavy embroidery and reluctantly began to descend the crude, stone stair that lay behind the covering. Lest he stumble, he caused parallel streams of light to adorn the length of the narrow, downward-spiraling path before him.

The claustrophobic tunnel wound endlessly downward, penetrating the bedrock for what seemed like miles. Although Anama detected no sounds other than those of his own making, his olfactory senses protested the noxious smell that became more potent as he proceeded. It was an odor he immediately recognized as the acrid stench of death.

The passage came to an abrupt end before a large bronze door, the surface of which was molded to depict a bevy of nudes, both male and female, engaged in various sexual practices. The door stood slightly ajar and easily gave way to Anama's touch. As he entered the pitch-black sanctum, his hand brushed against an oversized lock; it was dangling loosely, open with the key lodged in the hole. Whoever had unlocked the door had neglected to lock it again upon exit if, in fact, he had left at all.

He paused momentarily before proceeding. His stomach lurched at the sickening fetor permeating the atmosphere of the room he felt compelled to enter. He braced himself for the worst, sure he was about to encounter an unavoidable horror of unknown nature. A terrible sense of dread tortured his brain. He strode slowly forward, dispelling the darkness of the area ahead reluctantly.

Within a few feet he encountered the first of a series of niches lining the walls on either side of an expansive chamber. Each niche contained a low square plinth topped by the convex molding of a somewhat smaller torus of identical stone. He spied the word "Helen" where it had been carefully cut into the outer face of the plinth; "Troy" and ancient date appeared immediately beneath the name, as could be expected. The niche itself was unoccupied.

He wandered past several other empty niches without pausing to read the inscriptions, anxiety about to rip the heart from his body. Having left the niches behind, he was startled to suddenly find himself confronting a great crowd of people. All of them were completely naked, and all save one were men, although another female might well be concealed amidst their number. None of the people paid the slightest attention either to Anama or the light he focused upon them. The stream of nude figures, undoubtedly Evoquitus' bevy of mindless lovers, trudged round and round the room, their overall path describing a circular pattern revolving around an empty area. They frequently bumped into each other, and those who fell flopped helplessly upon the floor like stranded fish, ignored by the others.

Anama rose up on his toes in an effort to see over the heads of the naked zombies and into the central space. Something caught his eye, causing him to lunge forward, rudely shoving the dull-eyed nudes aside in an effort to reach the target central area. When he finally attained his goal, his worst fears were confirmed. He covered his eyes and ran, stumbling and howling like a maniac, as if the fleeing all the devils of Hell.

At the foot of the stairway, he collapsed. He unleashed a torrent of sobs and curses that echoed the length of the stairs before fading in the chamber above. He damned his own soul, blaming himself for the unspeakable tragedy he had just witnessed. If only he had not deprived Evoquitus of his powers, this thing could not have happened.

The scenario, as he imagined it, played out repeatedly in his mind. Frustration and loneliness had surely driven Evoquitus to seek the companionship of one of his captive former lovers. What a shock it must have been when, upon entering his secret gallery, he discovered them waiting for him. By revoking his powers, Anama had unknowingly released all of Evoquitus' collection at once. They surely flung themselves upon him, driven by the rampant lust Evoquitus had instilled in them.

Anama visualized the desperate multitude grabbing, clawing, and clutching the object of their desire. They would have raped him repeatedly, mindlessly, each ruthlessly fighting for his or her chance. Evoquitus, unable to defend himself against the throng, was overwhelmed by a seething, ravaging mass of uncontrollable zombies. In heated, mindless frenzy, they tore at his body, each slavering for direct physical contact until, eventually, his perfect body was ripped apart. In time, the murderous lovers failed to recognize the cold, still, dismembered corpse as the object of their craving. How long, Anama wondered, how many days had they stood there, gathered around the ruined form of Evoquitus, staring blankly at his bloody remains? Deprived of a goal, their minds had surely short-circuited, rendering them capable of little further function. He felt certain they would maintain their silent, uncomprehending vigil until they died, one by one, of starvation and dehydration.

For what seemed like hours, Anama was totally incapable of the slightest further thought or action. He lay down upon the cold stone of the stairs, the shock of the unbearably painful scene leaving his mind mercifully numb.

A muscle spasm in response to the painful position of his collapse, caused Anama to rise instantly, slamming his head against the wall. His self-awareness slowly returned as a result of the pain, and he slowly dragged himself to his feet. Summoning every ounce of inner strength, he repressed his subjective feelings in favor of the immediate duty he was obligated to perform.

He forced himself back into the grim gallery of death. Little, if anything, had changed during his lapse into unbridled grief; the eerie glow of the light he had conjured continued to illuminate the disgusting scene.

"Get back," he screamed with impatient disgust at the imbecilic idlers, "all of you! Return to the stations to which you were assigned!"

The befuddled herd of vagrant forms passively obeyed, shuffling back to their appropriate niches without as much as a glance toward the issuer of the order.

When all were in place, their cold bodies posed according to Evoquitus' original arrangement, the great sorcerer again addressed the group. "I command you to remain where you are in perpetuity, ageless and unchanging forever, just as your master would wish."

A tortured grimace marred his face as he returned to the bloody vestiges of his lost and tortured love. His stomach churned uncontrollably as he stretched both arms out before him. He recited the verbal components of a spell he otherwise would never have dared to use. In violation of the sacred oath he had taken more than a century earlier, he called upon the dark, forbidden forces, compelling them to aid him in his solitary mournful task.

Slowly, almost imperceptibly at first, the shattered flesh stirred within the innumerable small pools of smeared blood scattered across the floor before him, suddenly animated in necromantic response to Anama's spell. In time, the ravaged shreds came together to reconstruct Evoquitus' original, flawless form. When the transition was complete, Anama wept over the restored beauty of the handsome corpse as he bent to lift the limp body up in his arms. Unhindered by the dead weight of his charge, Anama clutched the burden close to his breast. He then strode to the only unoccupied and unlabelled niche. He transferred the still form to the stand, then gently, lovingly, arranged the limbs, head and torso into a proudly magnificent pose.

Retreating a few steps, Anama rested his eyes upon Evoquitus' restored glory for the last time as he stepped onto the platform's base. He carefully embraced his dead comrade. "I can do no more for you, my friend," he whispered sadly, "for that I am sorry.

"You represent the ultimate beauty you strove so diligently to preserve. Should some alien race one day happen upon this place, they will surely recognize the wonder of your singularly flawless countenance, though it be dead and cold for many millennia. Would that I had not been so blinded by your beauty that I failed to perceive the latent child within you, the child who never received the nurturing required to attain true understanding and maturity. Deprived of love, you desperately searched blindly for some way to express your needs. Your inborn craving for love and understanding ultimately found only distorted release, but bereft of guidance, you cannot be blamed either for the mistakes you made or the crimes you committed."

Having said all he could, the hoary wizard turned, leaving the confinement of the unique gallery behind for a final ascent of the stairway. Twice he stumbled on the rough stone edges before attaining the upper chamber, his vision blurred by irrepressible tears of regret.

The inconsolable mage abandoned the treasure-laden mountain, sealing its entrance behind him. As he slowly retreated to the valley below, he caused the masonry of the stairway to dissipate, that the curious villagers might be not be tempted to intrude upon the peaceful solemnity of the towering mausoleum.

There was no need, upon his return, for Anama to explain anything to his five compatriots regarding the tragic outcome of his fateful journey. The pain was all too obviously etched into the old man's face.

During the three remaining weeks, the Six spent much of their time together, bearing their mutual love and overwhelming sense of failure in stolid silence.

When the end finally came, the Earth and its sister planets were overtaken and consumed in silence, swiftly and mercilessly, in a searing, all-consuming blast of solar hellfire many thousands of times hotter than the blast of a crematorium. Neither the hand of any god nor guardian angel interceded at the last moment to prevent the ultimate holocaust.

All was reduced to less than ash in an instant. The radioactive remnants of an entire solar system slowly surrendered to the infinitely weakened force of the dark, shrunken mass that had so freely radiated life-giving heat and light.

The only survivor of the cosmic disaster was a small, irregularly-shaped boulder. Though its outer surface had been scorched to the hue of pitch, its contents remained intact due to the unbreakable force of Evoquitus' miraculous spell. No longer a captive of the dead star, the black massif slowly drifted out into the cold unexplored depths of limitless space, the final legacy of man and only remaining proof that humanity had ever existed at all.◆

-Dedicated to the Memory of the Incomparable Hannes Bok

The Tale of Toad Loop

So you want this old codger to tell you about Pritchy Kwik and the goin's-ons out at Toad Loop, do you? 'Though forty years is a mighty long time, I remember it clear as a bell. Mind you, there's none can give a more accurate account 'cos I eye-witnessed the better part of the whole she-bang. There were those that differed with me on a couple of the finer points of events, but I was there and ain't spinnin' no fool's yarn. I got proof positive of my words if you still harbor any doubts after, and I'll show you. Let me give you some background, then we can get to the meat of the matter.

When Mazrah Mulltree first showed up here in Madland County, I was sixteen years old. You wouldn't have recognized me; I was a strappin' lad livin' down on my daddy's farm. It's hard to believe now, but back then, the girls were crazy for me.

Mazrah seemed an okay feller at first. He right away bought up a good-sized piece of land which for years had laid idle. Word was he plunked down full payment in ingots of solid gold, though I didn't see it myself.

I asked him once why he'd left back East. He said he'd had a fallin' out with a relative, Captain Marsh, who more or less ran his hometown of Innsmouth. Mazrah up and left when he and this Marsh feller didn't see eye-to-eye.

The property he bought was mostly good pasture land, not wantin' for water. One part was wooded-over, though, down where the Mad River curved all the way around. The river wasn't much more than a trickle at that point, yet by looping around, it made an island we called Toad Loop. Nobody knew it then, but the Loop was the reason Mazrah chose that particular piece of land in the first place.

Well, sir, there was a lot of clearin' needed doin' before plantin' season, so Mazrah hired himself a bunch of us locals to help out with the clearin', cuttin', and stump-guttin'. We built him a one-story catslide house, two-story barn, hog pen, and chicken coop, so he'd be in shape for Spring. Hiram Kline, Martin's daddy, dug the hole for the outhouse.

Though the house wasn't far from it at all, ol' Mazrah never allowed us near the Loop itself. It wasn't like the waters was any danger or nothin', 'cos like I said, the river'd dwindled to a creek by then.

So everything went along just fine for a couple years, though folks felt

Mazrah kept to himself too much. He up and courted Asaph Kwik's youngest girl, Pritchy, who was considered a good catch by most. She wasn't the prettiest girl around, though her curly white-blond hair was much admired. Mazrah was a good lookin', though stern-faced, man and Pritchy fell for him right off. Next thing we heard was they was gettin' married. Even though Mazrah didn't attend church meetin's, old Asaph favored the wedding. If you ask me, he hoped some of them gold ingots were still tucked away somewheres. It wasn't long, though, before Asaph learned he wasn't so welcome at his son-in-law's, though it gnawed his gut somethin' awful.

The couple kept to themselves exclusive 'cept for Mazrah's monthly supply trips to town. On rare occasion, Pritchy'd call on her folks, but Asaph said she looked kind of peaked and down in the mouth, like she'd lost her spark, rather than like a blushin' bride. He had to admit, however, that never once did a bad word pass her lips either about Mazrah or his treatment of her. 'Ventually though, Asaph and Mazrah got in a big blow up and Mazrah forbid Pritchy's folks to visit. Pritchy was stuck in the middle and when she chose to stand by her man's wishes, Asaph up and disowned her, sorry to say.

The first sign of other trouble came about three years after the weddin'. Folks reported weird glowin's up in the night sky directly above Toad Loop, glowin's brighter than a harvest moon. And at April's end, Quent Swiggart swore he seen a big circle of brightness, round as a dinner plate, floatin' over the island about level with the tops of the trees. Now, mind you, this was decades before anybody claimed to see flying saucers.

Most didn't take it all that much to heart. It was only logic that Mazrah would clean up the Loop sooner or later, and the lights was thought to be stump-burnin' fires reflected on the night fog or clouds. Still, there were some who whispered about the dangers of tinkerin' with the Circle.

The Circle wasn't nothin' but six rough pillars of limestone, each a foot thick and nearly tall and wide as a man. Though the better part of the island was flatter than a pancake, it raised up right in the middle to a hump 'round which the stones roosted like fenceposts. None ever knew their purpose or who put them there in the first place. The Injuns claimed the Circle was built for some kind of unearthly critter that come down from the sky on occasion. Toadaggwa, they called it, sayin' it put the stones to questionable uses at certain times of the year. Truth is, they were scared shitless of the place without really knowing why. They gave the Loop the widest possible berth, swearin' the stones were the works of demons here long before any of the tribes. None of the whites confessed to belief in such savage superstitions, yet we all steered clear of the Loop just like the redskins did.

THE TALE OF TOAD LOOP

The crap first hit the fan when some school boys claimed they heard weird singin' and chantin' comin' from the Loop. Their curiosity got the better of them 'til they went and got themselves an eyeful — of Mazrah and Pritchy blatherin' a raft of gobbledygook while cavortin' naked as jay birds betwixt the Circle stones. Word of such carryin's-ons spread and set tongues a-waggin'. It soured most folks on Mazrah, so's they steered clear of him when he came to town after, though he paid 'em no never mind. The younguns was warned to stop cuttin' didoes anywhere near the Mazrah's land.

Things quieted down after a time, mostly 'cos there was little to be done otherwise. Hell's fire, nobody was gettin' hurt by such carryin'-on, and Madland County done away with witch laws decades ago.

It was that durn Simmons kid, Steve was his name, that kept things buzzin' by rattlin' on about how the Circle was all fixed up with the fallen stones raised and tilted ones straightened. He carried on about holes the size of a man's fist havin' been bored through the stones about a foot from the top for ropes to be tied off and strung to the Circle's middle. Such things worried them that listened.

It all might've just all blown over if it weren't for that Simmons kid, who was a smart aleck bully of a redhead as I remember him. He went and dared three of his cronies to hike out to the Loop with him, promisin' 'em a gander at Pritchy in her altogether. Least that's what he spouted later, though if you ask me, he was hopin' to catch sight of Pritchy and her man doin' things a lot more vulgar than naked dancin'. Whatever the call, however, them boys sure as hell got more than they bargained for when they accepted that dare!

They waited 'til after dark on Halloween as most likely for festivities. Once they waded the creek and were on the island proper, they swore it was rainin' real hard, which struck the Sheriff as mighty peculiar when he heard it later, 'cos he recalled it being clear as a bell that whole night.

The way they told it, the four of them hove up through the mud to hide behind a crop of cat tails about ten yards from the stones. They kept just back from the light of the bonfires Mazrah had lit at the foot of each stone in spite of the rain. What little they could make out didn't make much sense to the gawkers, but it sure as hell stopped them dead in their tracks.

Pritchy was nowhere in sight, though Mazrah stood out clear in the drizzle, standin' clingin' onto a rope for dear life. The oglers couldn't determine right off just what he was strainin' to keep ahold of, just that it was bound up in the ropes running from holes in the stones. Their ears told them that whatever he'd snagged was madder than a hornet; though it screeched and bellered loud

Daniel Alan Ross '99

enough to make a body deaf, they couldn't get a gander at it 'til Mazrah finally stepped aside, allowin' the light to shine on his catch direct.

Well, them boys was like to die of fright upon seein' what Mazrah'd snared! One fainted right off. The others claimed they saw a giant toad, ten foot long and taller than a man, sloshin' in the mud, tryin' to free itself of the ropes. That's hard to swallow, but they swore to the truth of it on the *Bible*. They said it had a mane of long black hair trailin' down its back and didn't croak like a toad, but let fly with screams and roars the likes of which nothin' could compare.

Up in the sky above all the commotion, they claimed a big, glowin' hole was floatin'. They said it looked like an upside down twister or a cyclone with a light inside its spinnin' innards, only there wasn't no wind like accompanies a regular twister.

All of a sudden the great toad reared up on its hindquarters, like to jump, but the ropes held it fast to earth. It cut loose with a stream of what Steve swore were words in some nasty-soundin' foreign language. Whatever it was, it had an effect.

Frogs by the hundreds poured down from the whirlin' hole, peltin' Mazrah like a plague straight from the *Bible*. They slammed into him or plopped down on the ground only to bust wide open like gut balloons! I'll hazard it was a hell of a mess!

Old Mazrah, well, he slipped in the muck 'til he lost footin' and fell flat on his back. He lost hold of the rope in fallin', givin' the toad an opening. That rope must have been the key, 'cos the toad snapped the other ropes once Mazrah lost his grip.

The toad turned and reared up right quick on Mazrah, pinnin' him down in the mud. They said a look of pure evil joy came over its bloated face, it's eyes shinin' all red, cuttin' through the rain and dark like fire brands.

The damn thing bent down and wrapped its big ol' black tongue around Mazrah, then sucked him up like a bug! Half his body dangled out the side of its mouth for a bit, thrashin' and floppin' up and down like a raggedy doll in agony, while the toad just squatted there, lookin' for all the world like it was fast asleep. Then, with one quick jerk of its head, it snapped up the rest of Mazrah and gobbled him whole! Must have been awful sickenin'!

Well, them boys took off at a clip, 'cept for Steve, who was so scared he couldn't budge. The way he told it later, the toad let out another stream of them weird word-noises to bring the lip of the cyclone down low enough for it to jump inside. The hole raised up, closed in on itself, and disappeared, just like it hadn't never been there at all.

With that, Simmons found his legs and skedaddled at such a pace that he nearly trampled his buddies in passing them up. He made a bee line straight for home.

Now, keep in mind that I can't vouch for any of that part 'cos I wasn't there in person. 'Though it defies belief, wait 'til you hear the rest before making your mind up final.

Anyways, Steve's daddy was waitin' up for him, and as you can imagine, he was madder than a stick! But when the kid came in soaked to the skin and scared half to death, the old man backed off. He listened to the boy's tale, then marched right over to the Sheriff's. The Sheriff wasn't all the way convinced it wasn't a case of high jinks, but he fetched old Doc Jefferys nonetheless, and together they high-tailed it out in the Doc's cutter to take a look.

They run into heavy mud as soon as they crossed to the island and saw the ground 'round the Circle was rife with frog guts, broke rope, and the ashes of several fires. There wasn't much in the way of tracks left in the drying mud, but they could make out where somethin' had been dragged from the Circle up towards the Mulltree farm. The trail led 'em right up and into the house.

Turned out it was Pritchy's pitiful path they was followin', where she'd crawled and dragged herself through the mud. She was in real bad shape, but Doc fixed her up. Problem was she couldn't seem to talk — she was in shock as Doc put it — so she couldn't say what happened. Mazrah was nowhere to be seen, which added more credence to Steve's story. The Sheriff eventually went home, leavin' Doc there for the night in case Mazrah didn't show. He never did.

The Sheriff had talks with the other boys and their families after that, and asked them to keep to themselves 'til he got Pritchy's side of the story, but that didn't last long.

Doc took supplies out to Pritchy on a regular basis after and even got one of the neighbors, Oly — that's short for Olivia — Johnson, to look in on her daily. But despite all, Pritchy's mind didn't heal up in tune with her body. Whatever'd happened must've been more than she could bear, causing her mind to just close up shop permanent. When she finally started talking, she didn't make much more sense than a child, and she never did get any memory back.

A month or so later, Doc realized Pritchy was in a motherly way, which didn't bode well what with her no longer havin' a man around. I think old Doc felt sort of fatherly toward poor Pritchy; he kept a careful watch over her for the rest of her pregnancy like one'd only do for a daughter of his own. He paid Oly to help care for Pritchy the whole time while providin' food supplies himself. Pritchy'd set her mind on havin' herself a little girl, so Doc bought her a pretty little doll that was all dressed up fancy like a princess for when the baby arrived.

When Pritchy's time finally come, Oly fetched Doc herself, but as she told later, she refused to stay and help with the birthin'. She claimed Pritchy'd been heavin' up seaweed and foam, which scared Oly silly. So Doc sent her home, knowin' she wouldn't be any help while in such a state.

Nobody ever saw Doc alive again after that. It appears sometime near dawn, he slipped an envelope under the door of the Sheriff's office, then went home direct and shot himself dead. He put a 12-gauge to his head and, well, that's all she wrote! Ain't that a fine howdy-do?

Unbeknownst to Doc, the Sheriff was out of town, though, and the deputy didn't feel he should read the letter since it was marked "personal" for the Sheriff. So he just cleaned up the mess over at Doc's and waited for the Sheriff to get back.

A week later, I come into town and heard a bit of what had happened. I'd known Pritchy all through grammar school, though we was never close, so I couldn't allow for her being all alone out there with a brand new youngun. I loaded some food goods in my wagon and headed out to see how she was copin'.

I s'pose you could say the situation hit home with me. When I was just five, my own mother died givin' birth to my sister Marcella. When we lost Marcella too, a few days later, it hit me so hard that I wasn't right for months. 'Though there was nothin' could've been done, I felt I should've done more to save little Marcella at least, like I'd let her down. So when I heard about Pritchy and her new baby, it struck a close chord.

I knew somethin' was wrong as soon as I passed the barn and saw livestock strewn out on the ground like they'd been slaughtered, the dead bones picked clean as a whistle. The Simmonses were my neighbors, and Angus had told me some of what his son said about a monster toad. I got to admit to sweatin' a mite more than usual recalling that story while standing there in the yard lookin' at them bones.

When nobody answered my knock, it was plain somethin' was wrong. The door was part way open, so I let myself in, callin' out so Pritchy'd know who it was. The baby was whimpering somewhere in the back part of the house, which took some of the edge off my nerves, at least at first.

The minute I pushed the door wide, the most sickenin' smell I've ever known hit me right in the face. It was enough to gag a maggot! I right quick stuffed a hanky over my nose, hoping I could keep my lunch. I swear it was gawdawful!

The curtains were all drawn tight in the sittin' room, so I found myself stumblin' through in only half-light. The furniture was all smashed and tossed ever'which ways, which gave another real sickenin' pull to the pit of my gut.

I came upon what was left of Pritchy in the bedroom. Lord, what a hellish sight! It was obvious she'd been dead for days, with half of her layin' draped off the side of the bed. The way her arms and legs was splayed-out all a-kilter, it looked like she'd exploded from the inside out. Before I could cover her up with one of the bloody sheets — and I ain't proud of this — the sight and the smell got me so bad that I barely made it outside before gettin' sicker than a dog. It must have been fifteen minutes before I could drag myself back in there, and only then 'cos I heard the baby squallin' somewhere towards the back of the house.

I still felt mighty queasy, but I just had to find that child. So I went 'round to the back of the house, feelin' a mite too unsteady to go inside again.

When I opened the back door, somethin' about my own size shot out of nowhere and busted ass 'round the corner of the house towards the barn. It must have been hiding in the spring room off the kitchen. Damn thing was so quick I hardly got a decent look at it, but I did note it was trailing a blue blanket from somethin' it was totin'. I tried to fool myself into believin' it'd been a young bear or great big ol' dog, but I knew it was somethin' a lot worse. And I knew too that it had the baby 'cos the cryin' sounds was now comin' from out by the barn.

I'm ashamed to admit I took my time chasin' after it. I wasn't about to stroll right into whatever might be lurkin' 'round that bend, so I strode clear of the house to get a good look before goin' any further.

There wasn't nothin' waiting there, so I figured it must've gone on into the barn to hide. I wasn't too all-fired inclined to traipse in after it, but I kept hearin' cryin', this time from the barn. I knew I'd have to bite the bullet sooner or later, and I feared later'd be too late.

All I could figure was that the Simmons boy's toad must've come back. Seein' somethin' like that could well cause a body to suicide, though Doc had never been the type to leave a helpless mother and child alone. I guessed the toad had ate the livestock in the yard, then went for what was in the house. After tearin' poor Pritchy up, it must have been full, or maybe it had other plans for the little one. Regardless, I was bound and determined nothin' bad was goin' to happen to that child.

The barn stood quiet as a stone inside. I should note the stink didn't trail from the house into the barn. And all I could hear was the squeakin' of the plank boards as I stepped, and believe you me, I was scared plumb shitless.

Being that time of year, the barn was chock full of hay, and that meant scores of hidin' places. The best places to hide were in the loft, where it'd be dark and hot as hell what with all that fresh-cut and packed hay generatin' a shitload of heat up there.

So I hove up my courage and climbed the wood ladder I'd nailed to a support beam while workin' on the barn just three years before. The sun was settin' and, what with failing light and hay dust, it wasn't an easy search. By the time I got to the back of the loft, all I had to go by was a few pencil lines of light comin' in between the boards of the walls. Lucky for me, I managed to find a workin' lantern, otherwise I might have fallen through the trap door down twenty feet or more from the loft to the cattle stalls below; probably would've broke my damn neck in the process.

Mazrah'd known enough to allow tunnels through the baled hay for ventilation, so I ended up pokin' my head down a bunch of dark holes while listening for any kind of noise anywhere around me. Considerin' the bales were stacked twenty high, there were lots of tunnels. When my ears caught some whimperin' noises, I crawled through a dark square of tunnel right to the heart of the hay pile to look for its source. Breathin' wasn't any too easy in there and, on top of that, I had to keep movin' for fear of catching the hay afire with my lantern.

After crawling straight towards the back of the barn for a while. I came to an empty space that by all rights shouldn't have been there. I held the lantern up high and saw a scene I could hardly accept!

I can see it in my head just as clear as glass even now. Lord Almighty, I never seen the likes of such a thing! It must have been ten, twelve feet from top to bottom and at least fifteen feet deep and long. It brought to mind a mud dauber's nest, hanging there from the back wall of the barn like that.

The more I looked at that conglomeration of mud and hay, the more it 'minded me of a mud dauber nest; a wasp nest hangs free, but this thing didn't. From where I was standin', I counted three rows of cells, six to a row, tunnelin' up and inside at an angle. The entrance hole to each cell looked big enough for a man to crawl through, but I wasn't about to find out! Like I said, I ain't never seen nothin' to compare.

I parked my lamp on the end of a pitchfork I'd found propped up against the wall and shoved it up into the holes one at a time, figurin' I'd find out what was inside without puttin' myself at risk. All 'cept the last hole held a chicken that looked dead, though they was still breathing. Next to 'em lay a group of what appeared to be frog eggs like one'd see in a pond; the difference bein', these were bigger than basket balls. They were all wrapped in some sort of gut sacks, and things was movin' around inside 'em. In the final cell I recognized Old Champ, a good ol' neighbor dog, layin' there in place of a chicken. It was terrible troublin' to me.

I soon realized I hadn't been far off comparin' the nest to a mud dauber's. You see, daubers look just like regular wasps, but they sting bugs instead of people, even when they're pissed off. The sting knocks the bugs senseless so the daubers can stuff 'em in the cells of their nest with new-laid eggs. The par'lyzed bugs get eaten by the newborn daubers, and I had an idea that was to be the fate of the chickens and Old Champ alike. It gave me a nightmare vision to think of such vicious critters scatterin' all over creation!

I looked real hard for a place where the nest builder might be hidin', and before too long I located two big holes in the hay, one on either side, about ten feet from the nest. The bales'd been broke apart around each hole, then patted down to hide the openings. I've seen toads doin' that very thing in order to have two or three escape routes from their burrows. I piled a couple hay bales over each of those holes to block them up, then crawled back out to the main floor of the loft. Then I plugged the hole I'd come out of and climbed back downstairs again.

Sure enough, the bales on the main floor had been stacked up from floor to ceiling in order to hide a tunnel of mud stretchin' down the wall from above. I guessed the critter's lair must be secreted in the hay 'neath the nest somewheres.

After scoutin' around outside a bit, I found where a hole come out under the barn. With the inside escape routes blocked up, the only way out had to be down the side of the barn and out that hole.

I figured I'd scare the bastard out by tossin' rocks up against the barn wall. I might have come up with a better plan in time, but the sun was settin' and pretty soon I'd have only the light of my lantern betwixt me and that hole. I threw a bunch of rocks and waited with fork in hand to see what commenced.

When I heard the baby cryin' like the dickens, I breathed easier, knowin' the little feller or gal hadn't been stung as yet. Some loud thumps followed, along with a sound like somethin' scurryin' full chisel down the inner wall of the barn. The baby's squalls changed to more of a whimpering, and it struck me all of a sudden that there could be more than one of them monsters lurkin' in there. But it was a bit late for worrying about that.

After a time, somethin' poked its head up the hole and crawled out real slow, clutchin' a blanketed bundle to its breast. When it sniffed at the lantern, I got my first good look at it.

THE TALE OF TOAD LOOP

It appeared to be a great bloated toad, but the size of a grown man and nowhere near so big as the Simmons boy reported. Its kisser was plug ugly and put me in mind of a bat. The skin was all warty like a toad, and I was surprised to see the bumps made some kind of weird design on its back. For a bonus, it had a light coat of curly, white-blond fur streamin' from its head down over the design. Rearin' up on all-fours, it stumbled towards me on its hind legs like a drunken sailor! Its waddle blowed up ever' now and then like a bullfrog's, but I couldn't make out if it made any sound 'cos the baby seemed to gurgle and coo whenever the wattle deflated.

My skin was crawlin', but none of the rest of me could've moved. When the toad was about seven, eight feet from me, I raised my fork up ready to strike, but Toadaggwa, or whatever it was, was too fast for me.

A pitch black snake of a tongue shot out its mouth and, before I knew it, the fork was snatched from my grip and I was knocked face down in the dirt. The toad slammed down on top of me. I rolled over quick to grab it by the neck, but the loose leathery waddle under its chin wouldn't allow for no real choke hold. We wrestled and thrashed back and forth for quite a spell, with me staring into its half-closed scarlet eyes most of the time.

I must've been bleedin' like a stuck pig from gettin' bit all over a whole raft of times — it had a mean set of teeth for a toad! It held me down fast with its stubby foretoes, and I felt its ice cold breath on my face when it finally stung me with the tip of its tongue. I was later told it had a sack of poison growing on each side of it where shoulders should have been. When the feeling started drainin' from my body, I was convinced I was a goner for sure.

Then the whole world exploded in deafening thunder! I thought I'd come to Final Judgment! But the thing I'd been strugglin' with fell off me and some-how I overcome the poison in me enough to run at top speed to grab the baby. Ever' part of me was screaming from pain, but I snatched the bundle up and kept going as best I could go in my feeble condition.

I ran like a madman 'til the world turned black and caved in on me. De-spite it all, though, I somehow made sure my little charge was safe. When the Sheriff caught up with me, he said I was singin' a lullaby to what I cradled in my arms. As it turned out, what I'd read as thunder was actually the blast of the Sheriff's shotgun as he blowed that monster back to Hell!

For a time after, I wasn't right in the head at all, and I'm willin' to admit to it. I was half dead from shock and toad poison, yet they still had to knock me out before they could take the baby away from me.

I spent close to six months in the hospital, then I was brought here. I owe my life to the Sheriff, I don't deny, but he's long dead now and, damn his soul, it's his lying that's kept me locked up here ever since.

Even the Sheriff had trouble acceptin' the contents of Doc's note, least ways at first. He'd just got back to town and read the note when he heard I was on my way out to see about Pritchy. In the note, Doc declared Toadaggwa was the real sire of Pritchy's child, Mazrah havin' planned it that way without her knowing. It was the awfulness of the coupling, Doc claimed, that blanked out her mind.

The note contended Pritchy'd been beyond help when Doc left as the half-human baby'd not been *born* so much as it'd *eaten* its way out of her. Doc didn't have it in him to kill the child even then, so he charged the Sheriff to do it for him. Doc wrote that it was more than he was capable of handlin', so he decided to end it all.

Hopin' to head off any panic among the locals, the official tale the Sheriff gave out afterward was that Pritchy had caught some terrible, fatal disease from Mazrah, and Doc had kept it secret from ever'body including Oly, even after Mazrah died of it. Pritchy died from the disease after a stillbirth, then when the Doc realized he was infected too, he shot himself. It was a hundred percent bullshit, but it was easier to swallow than the truth, so folks accepted it without question.

The only other person who knew the truth was the Sheriff's deputy 'cos he helped burn the house, the barn, and all their contents "to prevent the spread of infection." You can't tell me the neighbors didn't suspect somethin' more though, since a week later they hammered the Circle's stones to powder and dammed the river up so it didn't loop around no more.

I never did figure what possessed the Sheriff to get me labelled insane so's I'd be kept in this nut house for the rest of my life. Nor can I see these head shrinkers believin' monsters could beget offspring with a human woman. Even if such were possible, how could they give credence to any tale of a baby that growed to six feet in under a week? It don't make no sense unless they're the ones who's crazy!

I sure as hell ain't idiot enough to get myself all but ruined for no doll, but that's what the Sheriff claimed I did! Hell, that thing butchered my looks so bad my face is only fit to scare snakes now! Would I allow that to happen over a doll? A man'd have to be insane to do such a thing!

I can see from your face there's need for that proof I promised, solid proof that can't be ignored. I got it, or rather her, right here. Now, can you look at this pretty little baby here and still tell me Pritchy birthed some half-breed monster. I've been takin' care of her since that very day, and there ain't no-body can convince me she ain't a real live, flesh and blood baby!

THE TALE OF TOAD LOOP

Ain't she just an angel all dressed up in her pretty little princess outfit? And she's never once been a bit of bother or noise in all these years. Bless her tiny soul, little Marcella here's been the best sister a boy like me could ever hope for!◈

-Dedicated to the memory of Robert Bloch

When the Stars Are Ripe

"And the angels, all pallid and wan,
Uprising, unveiling, affirm
That the play is the tragedy 'Man,'
And its hero the Conqueror Worm."

— Edgar Allan Poe

"Ernest, you are the only person with whom I can discuss my special research," my host, Porter Worthy, declared unexpectedly. "Should I venture to tell anyone else what I've been delving into lately, I'd be dismissed as a fool or a madman, and God forbid the Board should hear rumors of my 'unconventional' theories."

I sat in a comfortable overstuffed chair in the home of a man who had been my best friend since our freshman year at the University of Pennsylvania. Our friendship had endured despite differing lifestyles and fields of interests. Porter's fascination with paleontology eventually led to his becoming a full-time instructor of same at Arkham State University, whereas I taught cultural anthropology at larger Miskatonic University in the same town. The bond that kept us together all those years was a mutual interest in esoteric, even Fortean theories considered preposterous by the mainstream scientific community.

The source of our steadfast trust in each other was twofold. According to Porter, I had saved his life one night when the two of us were set upon by five hooligans. We were both somewhat inebriated at the time, but my training in the art of self-defense turned the tide for us, enabling me to disarm two of the knife-bearing attackers before scaring off the lot. Porter never forgot the debt he felt he owed me for that night.

Two years later, he proved his worth to me after inadvertently catching me in a rather compromising position — in bed with another male student. After a dumbfounded moment, Porter had simply said, "Sorry for the intrusion, Ernest; I'll see you in class tomorrow," as he scurried from the room. He spared me the scandal and embarrassment that surely would have resulted had he told anyone about the incident, thereby leaving me indebted to his discretion.

So I listened, nearly 14 years later, as Porter related the details of his latest brainstorm, never imagining that I would soon share my friend's enthusiasm for ideas the mainstream scientific community would consider implausible at best.

Porter went on to tell me his interest had recently been aroused by the discoveries of a cave geologist, Dr. John Holbrook of Southeast Missouri State University. Holbrook's team had drilled some sixty feet into the earth to explore hitherto inaccessible passages of Mammoth Cave's 350-mile complex. There they found what resembled the gnarled roots of ancient stone trees. Holbrook recognized the massive branchlike tangles as the petrified burrow tunnels of some unknown organism that had thrived in the area during the Paleozoic Era, some 350 million years ago. The organisms had dug through the muddy subterranean soil which over time had changed into limestone hundreds of feet thick; the burrows themselves had filled with a much harder mineral called chert. When an underground river cut through the district, carbonic acid in the water easily dissolved the limestone, scooping out miles of interlocking subterranean chambers. The chert, however, resistant to the weathering effects of the carbonic acid, remained intact, exposed as weirdly twisted, tendril-like constructs jutting up from the cave floor.

Samples of the burrow contents were sliced in cross-section, sanded down and mounted on glass slides for further investigation. Microscopic study revealed the crystallized remnants of feces and seed pods used to shore up the sides of the burrows, but no remains of the burrowers themselves were found. Holbrook tentatively ascribed the burrows to prehistoric worms or shallow-ocean shrimp, despite the fact that no such creatures were known to exist until some 100 million years later.

Excited by the prospect of being the first to identify these curious antediluvian organisms, Porter subsequently scanned an endless number of scientific journals worldwide, both old and new, in search of similar finds. His investigations turned up a fair number of instances describing what appeared to be comparable artifacts, although all were subsequently misidentified as odd geologic formations rather than the byproducts of living organisms and, therefore, were dismissed as mere curiosities. These examples were, without exception, encountered deep underground in natural caverns and in limestone chambers attached to cenotes, the huge sink holes created when a subterranean water flow eats away enough subsurface limestone to cause the land above to collapse. The fossil burrows ranged in size from roughly a few inches in diameter, like those identified in Mammoth Cave, to specimens documented in Yucatan that exceeded a meter in diameter. Judging from the depths at which the burrows were reported, it appeared the unidentified organism, assuming all or most of the burrows could be credited to a single species, had increased in size with the passage of time, the Yucatan examples being the largest as well as the most recent, dated at less than 30,000 years old.

"The burrowers seem to have grown as they neared the surface, and it seems likely they survived into the era of man," Porter hypothesized. "Which leads me to speculate that they encountered ancient humans at some point." Proof of this, he felt sure, could be found in the myths and legends of early cultures. Yet, on his own, he had failed to uncover mention of anything that would even remotely corroborate his theory. There were, of course, hundreds of tales of giant serpents and worms spread throughout the legendry of innumerable cultures, such as the marine serpents sent by Neptune to destroy the Trojan priest Laocoon and his sons, Apollo's battle with Python at Delphi, Fafnir of Scandinavia, the West African Voodoo god Da (Danbhalah-Wedo in the New World), Thor's stalemate with Midgard, and even the giant eel of the Polynesian Maui, but none of these were said to live beneath the earth in colonies, as the evidence indicates the burrowers did. Only the Nagas of Indonesia were said to have congregated in large numbers, but they were depicted as surface dwellers for the most part and thereby did not fit the essential criteria.

In frustration, Porter turned to me for aid; he sought my expertise and knew I, due to my specialized field of research, was one of the very few who had access to Miskatonic University's library of rare and forbidden ancient texts.

"Of course I will help you, Porter," I responded. "I'd have suggested it myself if you hadn't beat me to it. Out of curiosity, I've read a bit of some of the better-known volumes they have locked away at the library, the notorious *Necronomicon*, the *Cultes des Goules*, the Borellus' texts, and even the infamous *Biblia Sinistre*. I've not pursued their contents in depth, but I'll see what I can come up with at the very first opportunity," I assured him.

I promised to let him know the moment I came across anything that sounded promising. As it turned out, nearly four months slipped by before I found enough free time to look into the matter, but once I did, I became totally engrossed in the project. Five weeks later, I contacted Porter, telling him I had come across something that might very well apply to his situation. We agreed to meet that same evening.

It was not until after dinner that we retired to his library for our discussion.

"Have you stumbled come across the name Shub-Niggurath or Niggrath in your studies?" I asked as my opener.

"No, I haven't," Porter responded without hesitation.

I would have been surprised if he had.

"Well, Shub-Niggurath has become the focus of my research," I told him. "It seems this Shub-Niggurath, or simply Niggrath as the term is modified in the *Biblia Sinistre*, is said to be some sort of alien entity pervasive throughout the universe. 'It,' or more frequently 'she,' is also known as 'The Black Goat of the Woods with a Thousand Young,' obviously a reference to fertility.

"One source describes Shub, as I like to abbreviate the name, as a mass of black goat hooves and tendrils spilling forth from a noxious cloud, while an equally reliable source depicts it as a black tree-like entity with animated branches and roots."

I paused to study the face of my one-man audience as he sipped his wine distractedly, his curiosity not as yet aroused.

"Despite the aforementioned characterizations," I continued, "Shub is classed as a subterranean burrower, dwelling deep within the interior of the Earth, which accounts for it rarely being encountered by human observers."

Porter finally discarded his nonchalant aire. He leaned forward on the edge of his chair and whispered 'Shub-Niggurath' to himself repeatedly before encouraging me to go on with my story.

"Now, I hope you will bear in mind that a key element in folklore of this kind is often gross exaggeration of the truth, for the details relating to Shub become rather fantastic at times," I added.

Impatiently, Porter waved me on.

"The fragment of the *Book of Azathoth* I consulted claims Shub's home lies beneath the surface of a distant star called Yaddith, but the *Biblia Sinistre*, the contents of which were culled from a number of ancient tomes no longer in existence, tells a rather different story. I might add that the library holds Joseph Curwen's handwritten copy of that rarest of volumes, the *only* copy containing his copious marginal notations." It was obvious the name meant nothing to my friend, so I proceeded to share the little information I had about the man.

"Joseph Curwen, a notorious American alchemist of the late 17th century, strove to interpret the ancient lore at his disposal in a scientific light, being himself a well-read and educated man for his time. From what initially appears to be little more than a confusion of excepts, he came up with the hypothesis that the term Shub-Niggurath is in fact the collective label for a species of alien organisms rather than simply the name of a godlike supernatural entity. After all, the Hebrew '-ath' suffix is plural."

Despite his now-intense interest, I hesitated to reveal more of Curwen's theory as it doubtlessly would put the scientist in Porter off if not presented carefully, just as it had put me off at first.

"Now, I should warn you that Curwen ran with this species idea, taking it to quite extreme lengths, so I must ask you to bear with me for a moment as I feel obligated to present the whole picture. You're patience will be rewarded," I assured him. Taking a deep breath, I plunged right into the thick of it.

"Curwen came to believe this species had a physiology completely foreign to anything known then or now ... because it existed long before the birth of our galaxy, it's anatomy being so nearly perfect that it has resisted evolutionary change for billions of years." I paused a moment, then continued before Porter could stop me. "He was convinced these creatures were impervious to the effects of extreme heat, cold and pressure far beyond anything we can imagine. Their numbers were actually distributed throughout the universe by cosmic calamities such as the Big Bang."

Unable to restrain himself, Porter objected, "Good Lord, Ernest! This man was obviously making this all up as he went along. I need something tangible, something I can relate to as a scientist."

"For the moment, I ask you to simply listen to what I'm telling you. Whether or not you reject certain aspects of what Curwen has to say is irrelevant should the rest shed new light upon your research.

"As for the scientist in you, I might add that, without any doubt whatsoever, Curwen possessed a thorough grasp of all the concepts involved in the Theory of Relativity more than two hundred years before Einstein formulated it. I can prove that, if you'd like."

Still skeptical, Porter remained politely silent.

"Although vague as to the specific source of whole blocks of information, Curwen stated with certainty that members of the species have inhabited and continue to inhabit the core of every world in the universe and have done so since the time those worlds were created, Earth being no exception."

Squirming uncomfortably in his seat, Porter stopped me once more. "This is quite fascinating, I'm sure, Ernest, but what makes you think any of this relates to my interests?"

I leafed through my notes to produce a page of thin tissue paper upon which I had carefully traced two illustrations from Curwen's manuscript. Handing them to Porter, I said, "I'd have to say this page was the real clincher."

My friend's jaw immediately dropped with amazement. Awed, he whispered the word "incredible" as he studied the drawings

Pleased at his reaction, I indicated the higher figure on the page. "Odd looking creature, isn't it? One might even call it unique." Pointing, I added, "At first, it struck me as just a huge eyeless grub with a black, leathery exterior, but then I read Curwen's accompanying notes. He was convinced the creature's perception of its environment is limited to an ever-altering set of vibratory images received through tiny receptors that run the entire length of its torso. The frontal extensions are retractable tendrils, twelve in number, that comprise fully a third of the body. These appendages shoot forth in rapid-fire succession with enough intensity to drive their arrow-like metallic tips through solid rock, allowing the worm, if one may call it that, to propel itself right through such impediments, especially stone as malleable as limestone, with relative ease. At their base, the tendrils surround and conceal a nasty parrot-like beak, similar to that of certain types of squid. This beak serves to crush the dirt and stone fragments so they may then be consumed."

Porter's amazed silence urged me on. "In the lower drawing, the Shub is shown as it appears free of the restrictions of the burrow. The upright stance of the main body segment and the resulting splaying of tendrils make it easy to understand the reference to it having a tree-like appearance, don't you think?"

Porter nodded dumbly in agreement.

"And, though I may be stretching a point, the metal tips on the drooping tendrils could easily account for the reports of its having 'hooved feet.'"

"Does this Curwen fellow say anything about its size, growth cycle, longevity or reproduction?" Porter asked breathlessly.

"Oddly enough, he makes no mention of the method of reproduction, although he claims the species' numbers are legion. He had the impression that they are all but immortal, their size being the only obvious indication of their age. However, the largest one he ever saw ..."

My friend jerked nearly out of his seat at my words. "The largest *he saw*? You mean he actually encountered a living specimen?" Porter shrieked.

I admit, at that point I was thoroughly enjoying my companion's newfound enthusiasm.

"Why, yes," I responded, "he saw a whole room full of the queer things in a chamber beneath an abandoned church in some small town in Massachusetts, Innsmouth I believe was its name. He visited the leader/high priest of a cult there that worshipped the Shub worms as the minions of Dagon, a deity I've managed to trace all the way back to ancient Phoenicia.

"The worms Curwen saw were young ones, less than two feet in diameter. However, the priest informed him that he had personally seen older worms that were nearly six feet in diameter and some twenty feet long. He claimed their growth rate changed over time due to environmental and other, less-tangible factors."

Scanning through my notes, Porter inquired about a particular section I had copied down verbatim. "What's this about the Shubs all someday rising to the surface at once 'when the stars are ripe' in order to reveal man's ultimate place in the scheme of things?" he inquired.

"Oh, that," I said. "Keep in mind that alchemists are usually also occultists, which would account for many of the embellishments Curwen added to an otherwise valid manuscript. He declared mankind would reach its zenith with the coming of the worms but doesn't really explain the connection between the two events, aside from the mention of the timing. This is all supposed to come about 'when the stars are ripe.' I've run across the phrase 'when the stars are right' several times in other references, so I think it is safe to assume that the use of the word 'ripe' in place of 'right' constitutes an unintentional error on Curwen's part. Quite honestly, I must admit that I've disregarded that entire part of Curwen's monograph."

"When did you say this Curwen lived?" Porter asked.

"Born 1662, died 1771," I answered.

"My God, he lived for one hundred and ten years! That's quite an age even for now, let alone back in those times. Maybe he did know something we don't," he joked.

I left the drawings and my notes with Porter that night for further review, then bid him a fond good evening, feeling a bit smug at the impression I had made with my research. Only later was I to realize how intensely Porter studied the notes I left behind, especially those relating to Curwen's hints that the worms are benevolent creatures destined to one day herald a golden age for all of humanity.

I was not to see or hear from him again until he phoned me at the university nearly two months later.

"Ernest, you're coming on a trip with me," Porter excitedly announced when he called," to the Yucatan Peninsula."

Once calmed, he informed me that he had received a tip from an archaeologist friend working in Mexico that led him to believe that actual surviving specimens of the Shub worm had been spotted but not yet documented in central Yucatan, not far from the post-classic Mayan ruin of Chichen Itza. His archaeologist friend had spoken first-hand to three local Indians who explained that the inner cliff face of a huge cenote near a small village had dropped off and fallen into the waters below during a recent earth tremor, exposing a series of large tunnel-like burrows in the extant limestone wall. The friend's informants claimed they had lowered themselves on ropes to the very edge of the tunnels where they were frightened nearly half to death by the sight of giant black worms moving about within the newly-exposed cavity.

Porter was hardly able to contain his excitement. We had to leave as soon as possible, he insisted, and I was the only person he trusted to accompany him. Coming from a wealthy family, Porter offered to make all the arrangements and cover all my expenses. I had nothing scheduled at the university for that quarter, so I accepted his fervid invitation. To tell the truth, I was not convinced we would find Curwen's Shub worms, but I feel there was a chance we might discover a new species of some kind, and that alone would made the trip worthwhile.

There is no need for me to document our preparations or even the details of the journey itself. Suffice it to say, we arrived in the small town of Qonnoco one week later, eager to reach the site. Porter hired as guides and helpers two of the locals who identified themselves as his friend's informants. I should mention that, along with climbing, photographic and specimen collecting equipment, I insisted we both be adequately armed. Aside from the dangers of entering unexplored territory, I did not fully trust the local people themselves. I had read about epigrapher Peter Matthews' near fatal encounter with a mob of misdirected vigilantes in the Chiapas area of Mexico in mid-1997, and I had no intention of exposing Porter and myself to a similar situation without some sort of protection.

We reached the cenote early the next afternoon after hacking our way through an insanely hot, humid and insect-laden stretch of jungle. Peering over its edge, we could clearly see the massive corner of the freshly fallen slab of limestone that jutted up from the dark, slime-covered pool at the bottom of the well-like aperture. The newly-exposed side of the cenote reminded me of nothing more than a toy with which I had been fascinated as a child, an ant 'farm' that allowed me to observe the insects in a cross-sected simulation of their natural habitat.

Our superstitious guides steadfastly refused to do more than secure the ropes with which Porter and I lowered ourselves from the lip of the circular opening. The vertical inner walls of the well receded quickly, leaving us suspended in mid-air. We climbed hand-over-hand down ropes for thirty or more feet before swinging back and forth in order to catapult ourselves into the dark cavity before us. I confess that I felt considerable discomfort, even fear, as I gazed into that pitch-black honeycomb of tunnels. Porter, on the other hand, struck me as being almost too eager to plunge into the shadowed unknown.

I felt a certain relief as my feet touched solid ground again, the powerful beam of my battery-powered lantern revealing a twisting labyrinth of huge empty burrows before me, as if I were staring down the abandoned path of an ancient subway line that stretched off into inky nothingness. Both my companion and I were immediately struck by the uniformity of the interlocking shafts, all of which were perfectly rounded and, to our best measurement, approximately ten feet in diameter. I could not imagine a creature large enough to dig such passages, yet it was unlikely that the weathering effect of flowing waters could carve with such steady uniformity. An uncanny silence, reminiscent of an abandoned tomb, haunted the empty, otherworldly terrain. The air was reasonably fresh, at least, tainted only by the humid heat, the smell of wet limestone and an unidentified odor I associated with the rotting contents of a compost pile.

The floors of the shafts proved remarkably free of any debris that might have provided some clue as to what type of creature dwelled there. Not incidentally, there were no indications that the shadows hid any of the normal cave-dwelling life forms we had expected to find; the terrain itself struck us as completely and unnaturally dead. Additionally, the tunnel walls were entirely coated from top to bottom with a gelatinous slime that made walking a veritable challenge, for it clung to our boots and was as slippery as any lubricant.

The tunnels branched off here and there in a most haphazard manner, connecting one to the other on all sides and sloping both up and downhill without warning. We had to take care least we stumble into holes that abruptly opened in our path, holes that continued right on up through the ceiling at various angles. We were both aware that we would have to rely on Porter's uncanny sense of direction to find our way back to the entrance as, typically, I became hopelessly confused after only a few turns.

I had decided not to inform Porter that I suffer from claustrophobia, and as we traversed the limestone maze I gained confidence that I could contain any mild feelings of discomfort I might experience. I would simply distract myself by taking endless flash photos.

We wandered further into the cliffside for what seemed like an eternity as Porter made note of endless observations or called out the information for me to jot down. Eventually he suggested we pick up the pace of our explorations in anticipation of an encounter with a 'live' specimen, whether it be the expected Shub worm or something else entirely. I, on the other hand, secretly wished the creators of such a weird habitat were long dead or had at least fled the vulnerability created by the recent rockslide.

Directly, Porter whispered that I should stand still and remain perfectly silent. I complied in deference to the imperative tone of his voice. Fear knotted my gut as I too heard a noise, as if something large were scraping against the rough walls of an adjacent tunnel, a noise that sent chills down my spine. Porter remained transfixed with fascination.

I tried to give voice to my fear, but Porter hissed, "There, in the tunnel next to this one ... something's coming this way!"

He quickly stumbled to just inside the opening of the indicated passage, pausing there to listen and aim his beam toward the direction of what had become a roar. I finally came to my senses enough to call out before running over and grabbing Porter by the arm, barely snatching him from the path of whatever was approaching at a furious pace.

Just seconds later, we were both thrown backward against the tunnel walls by the tremendous force of the dark leviathan's passing, its canvas-rough skin whizzing awkwardly past us. Neither of us were prepared for the sight of a behemoth whose bulging segments sagged through the opening into our tunnel, one after another, expanding and contracting with a peristaltic movement that propelled the enormous bulk along its earthen trail at a goodly speed. Although the ubiquitous slime surely acted as a lubricant, we were still stunned that such a giant could move with such ease. Had I not snatched Porter back at the last instant, he undoubtedly would have been dragged along the corridor by the titan, crushed into an unrecognizable pulp spread along the curved interior of the shaft. As he realized this fact, I saw real terror steal across his features.

To my utter amazement, all of Porter's previous courage totally evaporated in an instant, causing him to bolt and run headlong down the tunnel away from me. I set out after him, amazed he could maintain his balance without slipping on the dangerously slick flooring. As we ran, a second gargantuan beast came thundering down a parallel shaft like an infernal engine. Porter screamed as it passed near him, which provided me with new hope that I was not about to lose track of him.

By the time I finally did catch up with him, I felt compelled to try and bolster the man's confidence for both our sakes. I grabbed and held him tightly, shouting that I too was frightened but that we could leave now, having found more than enough proof to confirm the existence of either colossal Shub worms or something equally spectacular.

Unfortunately, I held onto him as I spoke, so when he slipped in the slime, we both tumbled to the ground, one on top of the other, sliding and rolling until we were covered with earth and disgusting goo. Porter was the first to manage to stand again, and as he helped me to my feet, I insisted we reverse our path and return to the university where we might organize a real research team to study our tremendous discovery. Porter slowly calmed. Once he caught his breath, he sobbed, "But, Ernest, I ... I've lost all sense of direction. I was fine, I knew exactly where we were until ... until those things ... Oh, God, I never anticipated such enormity!"

I assured him that we would be fine once he composed himself, although, in all honesty, I really disbelieved my own words. Yet I could not blame him for having turned tail and run; I might have done exactly the same had he not beaten me to it.

"I've let you down, Ernest, let us both down and maybe ... maybe even led us to our deaths," he moaned. "So full of myself, so intent on making a name for myself. How could I be so selfish, so damnably foolish?"

I let him go on, somehow sure that he needed to rid himself of self pity before going on. But, as I watched, his mood dramatically changed once again.

"Oh, what is wrong with me?" he blurted out. "There's nothing to be afraid of! The Shub worms are benevolent toward mankind, Curwen all but said it himself."

Dumbfounded by his instant transformation, I asked him what he meant.

"You read, even copied down Curwen's words. Surely you must have realized what he was hinting at?" Seeing my blank expression, he continued. "Curwen implied the worms are guardians of sorts, awaiting the time when mankind is ready to receive whatever knowledge it is that they hold, the knowledge that will show man his true worth and value in the cosmos. It was all there; all it took was a bit of reading between the lines."

"And so?" I inquired dubiously.

Still choking back the tears, he said, "We have nothing to fear from the worms. Don't you see? And to think I was terrified of them, convinced we were going to die." His laugh struck me as somewhat maniacal, I did not like the look in his eyes, and his words made little sense to me.

It was becoming more apparent by the moment that Porter had fallen into some kind of shock as he was spouting nonsense. Nothing short of sheer desperation could have driven him to believe Curwen's fantasies about the messianic potential of the worms. The only option open to me was to take charge of the situation and humor my befuddled companion, even encourage him in his delusions should it become necessary, at least until we managed to reach safety. Once back in familiar surroundings, I told myself, Porter would surely regain his normal mindframe.

"It's really ironic, you know," he added, grinning. "Here I am shivering and crying like a frightened school girl, while you remain steady as a rock. Isn't the stereotype that the heterosexual is supposed to be macho rather than the homosexual?"

I could not help but smile. Maybe there was still a chance that we could make it out of the hellhole alive.

We did our utmost to make a rational assessment of our location but produced little by way of results. We concluded that we would have to head in what we hoped was the direction opposite the path the worms had taken. Porter was fairly sure they had been headed south, the same general direction we had traveled, so we set out upon a northerly path as determined by our compass.

As we trudged on, I was not particularly encouraged to notice the batteries in my lantern were giving out. To cover my increasing edginess, I adamantly charged Porter several times to keep his loaded rifle in preparedness.

The endless twists and turns of a tunneling devoid of landmarks confounded our struggle to stay on course. We forgot our despair, however, when we encountered a gaping aperture twice the girth of anything we had as yet encountered.

By that time, we were both dependent upon the feeble glimmer of Porter's lantern, by which he lit the path immediately in front of us. Just a few cautious steps beyond the great opening, he raised an arm to halt my further advance. Following his gaze, I saw that the path ended suddenly just a few feet further on. Without a word of warning, Porter switched off the lantern.

As my eyes adjusted to the new depth of darkness, I perceived hundreds of pinpoints of light in the void. It was as though we were poised atop a high hill overlooking a star-studded sky.

Nearly overcome with awe, Porter whispered, "Ernest, we've come to the end of the world." Only much later would I realize the ironic truth of his words.

I remembered reading of archaic theories which claimed the Earth was a series of hollow shells, layered like an onion with worlds within worlds, the underside of each layering providing a firmament for the layer below. I had to drive those thoughts from of my mind along with the vertigo I felt at being suspended in darkness above what truly resembled the vastness of outer space.

Presently, Porter asked if the lights were really stars, to which I replied, after a moment, "Stars don't make the sort of noise I'm hearing." We both listened as a subtle rustling sound gradually increased in volume, became more of a shuffling, as if dozens of very large objects were being dragged across the earthen floor.

All at once, a group of brighter, star-like points of light appeared out of nowhere, just a few yards away from us. After a few moments, they rose up high above our vantage, then blinked out of sight. Whatever they were, they were much too close for comfort. These new lights were accompanied by the wheezing tones of large amounts of air being repeatedly forced in and out of a colossal bellows, or such was the image that came to mind. Porter and I dropped to the ground at the sound and lay quite still, half out of our wits with terror. It provided little relief when, from just a few feet beyond and below our position, something the size of an elephant heaved loudly before dragging its carcass dully over the ground and away from us. Only after it gained some distance did we feel free to breathe easily once again.

"What, in the name of God, was that?" I croaked.

"I don't know," Porter replied, "and I don't want to know. Not anymore."

Yet, we could not just lie there in the dark forever.

"Give me your lantern," I said. "We can't deal with anything until we know what it is. I've got to see what's out there."

I crawled carefully to the furthest point of the ledge before switching on the light. Taking a deep breath to steady myself, I aimed the powerful beam directly into the blackness. What I saw there further stunned me. If we had not come to the end of the world, as Porter had suggested, we were at least perched on the brink of insanity.

As far as was visible in the dim illumination of the lantern, I beheld an unearthly primeval wood of ancient, leafless trees crowded tightly together across a level expanse of cavern floor. The thicket seemed to float in the surrounding nothingness, the distant walls and ceiling lost to sight in the encroaching darkness. Tiny, pale blue points of brightness, like decorative Christmas lights, dotted the upper trunk and boughs of each tree. The irrationality of the scene left me feeling totally disoriented.

Finally, Porter crawled up next to me. He pointed out that the trees, in particular their sprawling, gray-tipped branches, were moving, as if swaying in the grip of an otherworldly breeze beyond our own senses.

"Those aren't trees, Ernest," he whispered. "Remember Curwen's drawing of the worms and how they looked with their upper third lifted to an upright position? That's what we're seeing right now, although I can't account for the lights that dot their forms." His voice sounded almost too controlled to be natural, but I had to agree with him, the 'trees' were identical to Curwen's sketch of a Shub worm freed of its burrow. I cannot describe how it affected

me to actually witness an impossibility come true, yet there they were, nearly a hundred of them, just a short distance ahead. It hardly comforted me to realize the creatures we were seeing had attained a length of at least thirty feet, each being about ten feet in diameter.

We watched in fearful fascination for some time, hoping to determine what the beasts were doing. Now and then, when the lights on their bole-like bodies brightened in intensity, the creatures emitted a deep, plangent cry, similar to that of a cow in dire distress. The unsettling chorus of grunts was repeated incessantly for several minutes before ending abruptly.

The creatures, we knew, were devoid of vision, so Porter held the lantern while I observed the mewling individuals more closely through binoculars. The lights were, in fact, small, bubble-like eruptions on the upper torsos of the worms, just below the spot where the tendril extensions attached to the body. Upon attainment of an intense luminosity, the bubbles burst one at a time, releasing a blue phosphorescent gas that hung like a cloud in the air around the body; the resultant odor was noxious indeed. Moments later, a flood of pencil-thin snakes of flesh, none more than five or six inches long, belched out from the burst bubble, only to tumble down the larger creature's side and onto the ground. They lay still only for a moment before beginning to writhe and thrash wildly. Their disgusting motion ceased only when they attached themselves to the nether regions of the parental torso or, failing that, to the body of another worm in close proximity. Once attached, they gave the impression of being the animated roots of the host 'tree.' Porter and I took turns studying the curious reproductive ritual as it was so unlike any other of which we were aware.

Each of the eldritch beasts gave birth to hundreds of offspring which, once appended to a parent's 'tail,' bestowed a centipedal look upon the bizarre giant. We could no longer doubt but that we had made an extremely important scientific discovery.

I suppose I am partially to blame for the horror that followed, as, in all the excitement, I neglected to fully take my friend's disturbed mental state into consideration; we were both totally caught up in an enthusiasm that is, I imagine, peculiar to men of science. I can offer no other excuse for raising only a half-hearted objection to Porter's subsequent actions.

First, he startled me by jumping to his feet and clapping his hands loudly several times.

"Are you mad?" I hissed through clenched teeth.

Smiling confidently, Porter squatted down beside my prone form. "I had to find out for certain whether the Shubs are deaf as well as blind. I believe their total lack of reaction to my clapping demonstrates the veracity of that hypothesis."

I did not breathe easily again until I had surveyed the herd of worms lumbering on the plain below. As far as I could determine, none had reacted to Porter's outburst. Despite the seeming correctness of his deduction, however, I voiced strong yet futile objections to the plan he then described to me.

"There's an incline over to the left that provides easy access to the cavern floor," he declared as he rummaged through his backpack. "And if you'll notice, the Shub 'cow' nearest that spot has moved on, abandoning several spawn that failed to attach themselves before it moved away, so ..." He paused a moment to ply a glass specimen jar from the pack.

"So," he continued, "I'm going to climb down and snatch one of the little ones as a specimen. Then," he said, "I suggest we get the hell out of here as fast as we can."

I admit, I was more delighted than suspicious at what I interpreted as his miraculous recovery; his terror apparently had vanished as quickly as it had manifested.

"I'll only be a minute and you, being my brave protector, can cover me with your rifle." Noting my look of burgeoning concern, he anticipated my objections with, "No one will believe us without the undeniable proof a specimen provides, man. You know that!"

I glanced at the camera strapped to my shoulder, but he further announced, "Even photos of the herd will be questioned should we fail to produce a 'live' sample. They'll claim we faked them, using some trick technique or other." He smiled smugly at my inability to refute his words.

Porter suggested I retain the lantern. I was to light his way and thus allow him the freedom to use both hands as he scurried up and down the ledge. I nodded my agreement, but reminded him to keep his loaded rifle handy at all times. Looking back, I doubt that anything I might have said at that time could have deterred him from achieving his goal. Before I could say anything further, he was on his way.

I took great care to keep the light focused upon Porter and the ground immediately before him. Periodically, I asked him to stop momentarily while I made a cursory check on the Shub worms, making certain none had noted his presence.

He easily reached the intended area. The newborns worms had slowed their movements once the adults had vacated the area. Their sluggishness made it easy for Porter to successfully scoop one of the tiny worm spawn into the jar. Instead of returning immediately, however, he stayed where he was long enough to carefully place the now-occupied specimen jar securely within his pack.

Unnerved by Porter's nonchalance, I called out, pleading with him to hurry. A brazen grin was his only response as he slowly reclimbed the ledge and returned to my position.

"See," he boasted, "nothing to worry about! I got us a beautiful specimen. We're going to be famous."

I deferred to his judgment and we congratulated each other heartily with back-slaps and mock award-giving, utterly oblivious to the fantastic backdrop to our foolish shenanigans.

All at once, Porter's expression dramatically altered and he began to moan, his body weaving back and forth as if he were about to faint.

"What is it?" I cried, suddenly panic-stricken.

"I don't know," he gurgled.

As I watched, he undid his belt, then thrust his pants down with such immediacy that he sat hard on the ground as he kicked them off. I had no idea what was going on, but he was shaking all over and uttering disconcerting sounds. Grabbing the lantern from my hand, he aimed its bright glow at his now-bare legs. I do not mind admitting that I was the first to scream.

I was unable to fully understand what I saw until much later, and I still wonder if Porter had any idea what was happening to him. My later experiments with the specimen have led me to believe the hide of the Shub worm is unbelievably tough, so tough that when the young attach themselves in search of nourishment, their minuscule beaks are only able to penetrate the adult's flesh with pinpoint incisions. Due to its delicate vulnerability, however, the hungry spawn are able to bite right through human skin and thereby feast upon the vital liquids and organs, even the bone structure, of the human body. Several of the needle-thin creatures must have done just that while Porter was occupied with the collection of his specimen, the resulting trauma revealed only when his legs were lit by the glow of the lantern.

The horror of that moment is truly beyond my ability to describe, and I cannot even begin to fathom the ungodly amount of pain poor Porter must have experienced. I could see, even in that dim light, four or five of those filthy little worms moving just beneath the surface of his pale skin, devouring blood and muscle tissue in their passing.

Once Porter saw the vermin were inside of him, he must have realized the threat to me, for he crawled away, shouting for me to keep back as his body writhed and pitched in agonized seizure. Somehow overcoming my terror and squeamishness, I made move toward my friend so as to help him in any way I could. Before I reached his thrashing form, he sat straight up, his face clearly visible to me in the full brilliance of the lantern. His eyes were stark-wide with anguish, and when he opened his mouth, either to speak or scream, I will never know which, he spit the decimated, worm-riddled remnants of his tongue and larynx into his lap. The worms must have already been at his brain, for his movement halted almost immediately and he was dead within just a few seconds.

I fought the urge to pass out, convinced it would mean my doom as well. Instead, I fired my rifle at the short black lines that crawled toward me from Porter's ruined form. I fired until the gun was empty, disbelieving the evidence of my own eyes — the damnable things were impervious to the effect of the discharged bullets. In desperation, I grabbed the backpack that Porter had thrown aside in his misery and beat at the minuscule abominations, knocking them away and off the ledge, down into the darkness of the cavern with its equally awful occupants.

Finding myself alone in that madhouse of death and unconscionable monstrosity, I temporarily lost my reason. Seeing the backpack as the only weapon of value, I clutched at it and the lantern before running as fast as possible from the site. My memory of what followed remains a claustrophobic nightmare of confusion ending only when I found myself desperately trying to keep my head above the surface of the dark waters of the cenote. Three days had passed since we had entered the tunnels; I must have wandered those chambers for many long hours, locked in the thralldom of madness.

Our guides had long since given us up for dead, so it was only by chance that my cries were heard by anyone. A small child proved the means of my salvation; in disobedience of her mother, little Maria came to pray to the gods of the well, asking that her parents might somehow afford a fancy doll she had seen in a store window in a nearby town the day before. Risking punishment, she reported my presence in the waters, and within the hour I was rescued. Needless to say, I later made sure little Maria received not only the desired doll but many other gifts as well.

The necessary reports were made to the local police, who seemed unconcerned as to the circumstances of Porter's demise. They obviously felt the world was better off with one less *gringo* in it. Nevertheless, I told them only what they expected to hear, that Porter had fallen down a deep shaft in the tunnels and his body was thus unrecoverable, the same story I was to tell again and again upon returning home to Massachusetts.

ANCIENT EXHUMATIONS +2

*   *
   *

Only now, nearly a year after the trip to Yucatan, have I come to realize the full treachery of Curwen's implied promise that the Shub-Niggurath will rise *en masse* to the surface that humanity might attain its glorious apex. I find myself recalling, too, Porter's naive belief, based on the copies I made of Curwen's lies, that the worms are benevolent beings that mean no harm. I would publish my findings, offering the photos and, of course, the specimen as proof, but to what end? Even if the world should heed my dire warning, nothing can stop that which is inevitable.

After exhaustive testing of the specimen Porter obtained at such high price, I have concluded the worms are indeed virtually indestructible. Even this young spawn's biology thrives on deadly poison, and its flesh cannot effectively be crushed or penetrated with sharp instruments or bullets. As Curwen, whom I now recognize as less a scientist than a foul necromancer, related, the worms are immune to every extreme of temperature and pressure. Even highly lethal doses of radiation fail to affect the thing adversely. What chance can man possibly have when millions upon millions of invulnerable behemoths simultaneously emerge from the depths everywhere across the globe?

Further study of the Shub legend in certain rare volumes overlooked in my earlier research has instilled in me a most frightening and unsettling view of the universe in which we live. I have concluded the Shub-Niggurath are nothing less than cosmic scavengers bent on completely devouring any form of sentient life that dares aspire to evolutionary enlightenment. Thus, when the stars are "ripe," the worms will rise to demonstrate mankind's true significance in the universe as fodder for the feasting of worms.✦

The Paladin of Worms

"I, who am dead, must guide him here below ..."
— Dante's INFERNO - XXVII, 49

They were greeted at the door by a reserved but hospitable gentleman. He expressed no undue surprise at their unexpected appearance.

"Reverend Peterson, Sheriff McKinny, come in out of this disgraceful afternoon heat!"

The visitors, on an official rather than a social visit, entered the old but well-maintained Georgian farmhouse of Richard Walraven, a distinguished, forty-year-old high school teacher. He held the screen door open for the pair as they strode into his home. Once inside the parlor, Walraven warmed to his guests. "Please, gentlemen, sit down and make yourselves comfortable. And excuse me while I put the kettle on for tea. Reverend," Walraven fussed, "you might want to try that slat-backed rocker to your right. It's of Shaker design, nearly a hundred years old and most comfortable. As one gets older, comfort becomes so important, wouldn't you say? Sheriff, the leather chair next to the good Reverend should suit you quite well." Satisfied his advice would be taken, Walraven shuffled off to the kitchen where the visitors could hear him toss wood into the cast iron stove and fill the kettle from a hand pump.

Reverend Peterson had never been inside the Walraven farmhouse before, but he was well aware that it was the oldest residence in the county. The polished puncheon floor, here and there littered with hand-hooked throwrugs of muted, tasteful colors, the crude but solid antique furniture, and glass-chimnied hurricane lamps appealed to his fondness for the old-fashioned. Every inch of the room bore blatant testimony to the heroic Europeans who had braved the wilds to bring the Lord and civilized ways to a heathen land. He recalled hearing that the walls of the original structure, a cabin, had been built by Adodiah Walraven from massive, handcut logs bound together with pitch. Although those old logs were no longer visible, having long ago been covered over as the house was updated and enlarged, still the place retained an atmosphere of hardy dignity he found lacking in modern constructions. The homes built in the last decade, since 1920, lacked the solid, enduring workmanship of structures from before the turn of this or the previous century. Even the room's musty odor of age made him feel somehow at home.

"I don't often have guests, so you must forgive my lack of tidiness," Walraven apologized as he reentered the spotless parlor, then seated himself opposite his visitors in a large wing chair decorated with hand-crocheted doilies. "I've paid little attention to niceties since my wife passed away; it isn't easy keeping up with a full-time job when one also owns such a large farm. I've had to forego the corn and wheat crops in recent years just to keep up, and I still have to hire outside help."

The Sheriff cleared his throat, having decided it was time to state the reason for his and the Reverend's presence. "Mr. Walraven, me and the Reverend here, why we're here on account of ..."

Walraven interrupted, "I know why you are here, Sheriff. You see, I've been expecting you. You're here to inquire after my hired hand, Luke." Before the officer could say anything further, Walraven arose in response to the whistle of the teakettle, excused himself, and scurried off to the kitchen once more. He returned moments later, bearing an old fashioned, bone china tea set on a tray.

Walraven poured a cup for each, informing the Reverend that the tea was "store tea, not that spice wood or yarb stuff for which most people settle."

As Walraven fiddled with the tea set, the impatient Sheriff asked politely, "Supposing you're right, Mr. Walraven, that we are here to see about Luke. What would you say in that case?"

The host adopted what the Sheriff perceived as a feigned gravity in his voice. "Luke hasn't been into town for supplies or even to the beer garden for his usual nightcap for several days, so it is certainly understandable that his friends should be concerned about him."

"That's right, sir. We were hoping to have a word with him, so we can put folks' fears to rest," added the solemn official.

"I fear it is my sad duty to inform you gentlemen that poor Luke has met with tragedy. He is dead," Walraven announced without emotion.

The visitors rose from their seats in unison at the shocking news of young Luke's demise. Madland County was a small, close-knit area of rural Ohio, so news that one of its better-liked young citizens had died was the last thing the pair expected to hear.

"Please sit down, gentlemen!" admonished the schoolmaster. "You act as if I were a madman confessing to heinous murder! Luke's death was, in fact, no accident, but I assure you that it was not I who killed him."

"What happened and where's the body," the portly Sheriff stiffly demanded.

Walraven sighed. "In due course, Sheriff."

Frowning, the Sheriff insisted he be shown the body immediately.

The thin, wiry Walraven arose from the chair before responding. "The body is not on the immediate premises, but I shall lead you to it presently, if you insist. First, however, I must answer the first half of your question. I will satisfy your demands in that order and that order only."

The Sheriff raised his bulky torso from his seat and struck a threateningly officious pose. The Walravens had long had a reputation for sticking to themselves and wanting to be left alone, but this was too much. "Now you listen here, bub ...." he commanded.

The frail, elderly Reverend carefully rose from the rocker, placing his tiny form between the two stalwart men.

"Gentlemen, please!" piped the clergyman. "I'm sure Mr. Walraven has an excellent reason for this delay if only we allow him the opportunity to explain."

Against his better judgment, the lawman reluctantly conceded to the preacher's judgment. The Reverend was used to dealing with confessions, he thought to himself, so for the time being he would defer to the church. It would not look good if he overreacted to Walraven's peculiar behavior, especially if it turned out the teacher really was not in any way to blame for Luke's death. Maybe the parson too had picked up the inconsistencies in Walraven's demeanor, like the way he seemed relaxed and in control one moment, then edgy and nervous the next. He hoped the man did not turn out to be some kind of dangerous nut case. He kept to himself outside his classes, as the Walravens had for decades, so how could one know what to expect of the man?

The Sheriff slowly calmed, sighed resignedly and resumed his seat. Reverend Peterson, obviously relieved, sat back down as well.

"Thank you kindly, Reverend. I don't mean to be obstinate." He put his hand to his furrowed brow and, covering his eyes, added softly, "It is just that I, well, have not been quite myself of late."

Before his listeners could ponder their host's newfound solemnity, they found themselves sharing the distinct impression that Walraven was actually slyly chuckling. Dropping his hand and straightening his posture, he addressed them further.

"Really, Sheriff, there's no need for a confrontation. It is just that my thoughts become somewhat disjointed when I get agitated. I do apologize if I seem uncooperative, for that is not my intent." He reached out a trembling hand for a sip of tea.

"I ask only that you humor, for a short while, a shaken man." he whispered. "I assure you I will answer any and all of your questions, but first, it is absolutely necessary that I be allowed to provide background information that, although it may at first seem irrelevant, is quite essential to your understanding of this — to use your word, Sheriff — "case?"

Walraven turned his attention toward the window behind and to his right, then, as if searching for something very important, he ogled the yard outside. After nearly a full minute, he relaxed, returning to a conversational position in his chair. He smiled at his guests as if nothing untoward had occurred.

"About three weeks ago, Luke reported a shortage among the cattle. As I'm sure you are aware, Sheriff, like all the other cattle owners in Madland County, I'd lost a few head during the previous months; this time several were missing. While searching for them, Luke came upon an area where large gouts of blood had been spilled. He found no actual carcasses, however. More and more of my cows turned up missing during the following days and, each time, he found similar stains in that same area of pasture, near a small, seemingly natural opening at the base of a limestone crag which overhangs the creek. The area I'm talking about is in plain sight of the house, actually."

The listeners maintained their uneasy silence as he continued, "My grandfather dubbed that particular opening the Death Hole many years ago. It once had an Indian name but he considered the appellation too burdensome to remember. He attributed the Hole to Amerinds of the Hopewell or Adena Mound Builder cultures, which flourished here long before even the Shawnee arrived around 1730. You may not know this, Reverend, not being from this area, but the vestiges of the Mound Builders can still be seen all over the southern half of Ohio, at Fort Ancient, Serpent Mound, and various other artificial mounds and pyramidal earthworks."

The Sheriff sighed, only to receive a reprimanding glare from the Reverend at his side. The lawman resented the unspoken rebuke but still feigned rapt attendance to the words of, to his mind, a speaker who, in spite of his robust middle-age build, struck him as rather prissy. He made a mental note to have a few off-the-record chats with some of Walraven's male students, just in case the man was a pervert. He dwelled on the mental image of the teacher fooling around with a naked young boy in the showers after gym class but quickly drove it from his mind when he realized he was becoming aroused.

"My forebears," he heard Walraven say, "maintained excellent relations with the native population, which caused them to be ostracized by the other settlers, as is well-documented in the county histories. What the others didn't realize was that my twice-great grandfather, Adodiah Walraven, had his eye on this tract of land from the start, despite the fact that the Shawnee deemed it sacred territory. The old rascal struck a bargain with them; in exchange for continued access to the land for the tribal leaders and shamans, Adodiah was granted the use of approximately 200 acres of the richest land in the state. You see, he convinced the chief and head shaman that the tribe's only means of preserving any hold over this sacred site of theirs was to allow him token possession of it. Should they refuse his offer, Adodiah explained, sooner or later the other whites would lay claim to the land and take it, by force if necessary. As part of the deal, Adodiah was made privy to the tribe's most sacred traditions, all of which centered around the hidden entrance to a massive underground gallery said to rival Ohio Caverns and Kentucky's Mammoth Cave in size. This cavern was the centuries-old burial place of the Indians, and Adodiah was the only outsider ever to be entrusted with the knowledge of its whereabouts."

Walraven poured more tea for himself and his guests, peered intently out the window at the yard, then picked up the story where he had left off, his increasingly odd behavior leading his listeners to doubt his sanity.

"The earliest tribes buried their dead in artificial earthen mounds, which proved unwise in light of the looting tendencies of the European settlers who arrived here in the early part of the eighteenth century. Later, the cavern complex became the repository of the dead, offering the bodies safe sanctuary from not only scavenging animals, but also from the deliberate desecration of whites. The bodies were wrapped in several layers of animal hide, then tied in a seated position with forehead resting upon upraised knees, before being interred with ceremony within the cavern. One can only imagine the number of corpses that accumulated in those dark depths over the decades."

Sheriff McKinny fidgeted in his seat, openly displaying his frustration at the recounting of what he considered superfluous history, as Walraven continued his narration undaunted. "My family immigrated here in 1789," he offered, then, "I believe it was not until sometime in the mid-1800s that your clan arrived in Madland County, Sheriff. Still, you must be familiar with local lore concerning legions of dead warriors moldering beneath the valley of the Mad River until the day of Dar."

Without waiting for a response, Walraven turned to Reverend Peterson, explaining that, "On the day of Dar, it's said, a gruesome army of warriors, actually giant corpse woms, will rise up and sweep the white invaders from Madland County and the surrounding areas. Mothers often still frighten their naughty children with the story, its immediacy proving more effective than vague tales of bugaboos and bogey men."

"Ridiculous. Just old wives' tales," grunted the insular Sheriff.

Walraven ignored the lawman's scoff. "With one epidemic after another, including everything from diphtheria and small pox to chicken pox, death swept through the native population of this area after the arrival of the Europeans; untold thousands were wiped out within a matter of a few short years. Yet the diseased corpses were entombed along with the rest in the cavern as Indian tradition strictly forbade the burning of bodies."

After pausing momentarily, Walraven proudly spouted, "And that cavern's corridors run directly beneath this very house."

He further told them, "The Indian population eventually dwindled to nothing, the few survivors seeming to just disappear forever into the deep woods. My father came across only three Indians in his entire life, while I have only encountered one. I was a mere child at the time, and although he observed me for some time, he took flight the instant I tried to approach him. It was as if I terrified him. I suppose his reaction was understandable for, when it comes right down to it, once the Wyandots had been shipped further west in 1843, we whites proceeded to exterminate the Native Americans who remained in the area, although here in Ohio we did our killing with more subtlety than was done elsewhere."

He smiled at his guests' unease. They obviously had heard tales of the land-greedy early settlers purposely giving disease-riddled blankets to the Indians.

"The people around here refuse to give credence to the tales of the cavern and the Indian curse I mentioned. Yet, as you may have noticed, they avoid my property like the plague. You couldn't pay any of the old-timers to come anywhere near the creek area of my pastureland, which is one of the reasons Luke was so very valuable to me. Being from out-of-state, he'd never heard any of the legends and therefore had no fear of either my family or of my land."

The Sheriff stood up. "I'm sorry, Reverend, but I've had enough of this man's wool gathering," he firmly announced. "Either I find out this instant what happened to Luke or, Mr. Walraven, I'm going to haul your butt off to jail. You can spin your spook tales to the judge tomorrow morning."

Before Walraven could react, the Reverend held one hand up in the air. "If you will be good enough to excuse us, ah, Richard, I'd like to speak to the Sheriff alone, outside, for a moment."

"Of course," Walraven acquiesced, "take your time. I'll be right here when you return."

The Reverend led the disgruntled Sheriff out of the room and through the front door.

"Look here, Reverend," the Sheriff complained, "I've got a job to do and I intend to do it, and that's all there is to it."

The Reverend stated his case calmly, almost patronizingly, pointing out the strange quirks in their host's demeanor as an indication that, should it prove he was in some way responsible for Luke's death, Walraven might be dangerous. Thus, he concluded, it would do no harm to humor the man a bit longer, and they might even get a confession out of him.

"I suppose you're right," said the Sheriff. "Given enough rope, he just might hang himself. I reckon you're the expert when it comes to confessions. But keep in mind it's getting late; the sun'll be going down shortly. I got other duties I could be tending to rather than sitting here listening to this feller rattle on and on, so let's cut it short as possible."

"Certainly, and thank you," the Reverend said. "I doubt you'll regret this decision. Now, let's get back before the situation becomes any more awkward than it already is."

As they reentered the parlor, Walraven said, "I apologize, gentlemen, for straying from the point. If you will be seated, I shall rectify that now."

The Sheriff sighed audibly as he resumed his seat next to the Reverend.

Walraven nodded. "Thank you, both of you. Now, when Luke alerted me to the blood spill and just where he'd found it, I told myself some animal, perhaps a large 'possum, wolverine or wild dog, had come to inhabit the Death Hole, savaging the livestock from the relative safety of that haven. Even I scoffed at the tales of Naaqwatta and his army of vermin, so I had no particular fear of the Hole."

The Reverend asked, "Who or what is this Naa-whatta you just mentioned?"

"That's the name the Indians gave to the earth spirit they believed dwelled within the cavern," Walraven answered. "As he was supposed to someday lead the army of corpse worms against the whites, my grandfather dubbed him the Paladin of Worms. Tradition claimed the Paladin had been here long before the first tribe set foot in this territory."

"Oh," uttered the Reverend, "please go on."

Walraven nodded before going on, "Luke and I decided to check the Hole. It wasn't a trip we relished, not in this terrible heat, but we roughed our way there through all the overgrown, chigger- and mosquito-ridden terrain. That's a part of the meadow the cattle avoid, so the weeds and brambles have grown wild and, in some spots, as high as a horse's back. And there are sinkholes to be avoided where it's marshy as well, which makes for slow going. Still, I had to see for myself whether the bloodstains really led right up to the Hole.

"I should explain for your benefit, Reverend, if the Sheriff will allow, that the county dammed the Mad River way upstream over fifty years ago, around 1880, creating a whole new drainage system through the local creeks. That caused the creek which flows across my property to make a sharp U-turn precisely below the Hole. At the turn, a deep and wide stagnant pool formed, which makes the Hole tough to reach. We could barely see it what with all the weeds since it is merely a crack in the lower recess of a steep embankment. Yet somehow I knew exactly where it lay."

A dreamlike quality crept into Walraven's voice as he droned on, "The Hole's downstream from where the old slaughterhouse used to be. I had that particular structure torn down years ago, but as a child, I once followed the crimson stream of blood that poured from its drains after a particularly large number of hogs and cattle had been butchered. I traced the bloody path all the way to the creek proper, where it stained the Hole's pool a forbidding scarlet. I can still recall the overwhelming odor of that grisly water. I don't mind telling you it spawned many a nightmare in me. Several times I cried out in the night, believing I was drowning in that sanguine pool while, above me, the mouth of the Hole laughed mockingly at my plight."

Falling silent for a time, lost in reverie, Walraven presently picked up where he had left off.

"Luke and I approached the pool from the opposite embankment after building ourselves a makeshift dam in hope of diverting as much water away from the pool as was possible. We did our best but still had to don rubber waders to navigate the dirty-brown, slime-covered water that remained. Luckily, I watched my step, trying to avoid scavenging crawdads on the bottom, otherwise I might have fallen. You see there's a dropoff just a short distance in, after which the water gets very deep in places. As is, the pool's surface came up to our chins. Luke worried about disturbing water moccasins as we waded, but neither of us saw any.

"The opening, although displaying signs of recent enlargement, was still a tight fit for us, but we squeezed through with rifles in hand, repressing not only our claustrophobic tendencies but a growing sense that we were entering a place of evil. The opening led to a space large enough for us to stand upright, but before we could light our kerosene lanterns, we were assaulted by a stench that made us both gag and return to the opening for what little relief it had to offer in the way of fresh air. I'd never experienced such a rotten, nauseating smell in my life, and I'd spent the greater portion of my youth around slaughterhouses."

Walraven leaned forward, speaking in low tones. "Minutes later, we steeled ourselves against the terrible odor, thrusting our lanterns in the face of the dank tunnel's pitchy blackness. We agreed to make fast work of our inspection that we might return to the open air as quickly as possible, away from the hot, humid atmosphere of the place. If only we'd turned and left right then, but ...." he shrugged, "we don't always choose the wiser paths in life, do we?"

As if relating a ghost story to a group gathered around a campfire at night, Walraven slowly proceeded. "Our eyes adjusted slowly to the diminished light as we followed the curve of a downsloping dirt shaft. After about thirty feet, the tunnel took a sharp turn to the left, to open onto an expanse of twice the capacity, the flooring now littered with loose and broken bones. Every imaginable type of wildlife was represented by the thick strew of bones — rabbits, 'possums, fish and even a few birds. It was the cattle skulls, however, that drew our attention. Luke pointed out that many of the still-pink bones had been gnawed and, in many cases, bitten right through. We began to wonder just what we were getting ourselves into."

Walraven paused for more than a minute, but when neither member of his audience said a word, he dove back into his tale.

"Further down the stifling hot tunnel, the root-riddled dirt walls abruptly gave way to solid bedrock shafts. Without realizing it, we were about to enter the legendary cavern itself. Still, we pressed on until we stood at the threshold of an expansive domelike chamber of such incalculable size that its perimeters were far beyond the poor definition provided by our lamps.

"The chamber floor was dotted with an array of fang-like stalagmites of what appeared to be pale limestone deposits, their numbers trailing off into the outer darkness of the gallery. Most of them peaked well over six feet above the floor. Luke whispered that they looked like teeth in the mouth of Hell.

"We were so busy trying to discern the details of what lay ahead that we neglected close observation of our more immediate surroundings. That changed instantly, however, when, after casually leaning against a wall, I gasped and flung myself away from the shadowed surface. When I raised my lantern to determine what it was that had felt so repulsive to the touch, I was appalled to see that the entire face of the wall was alive with a carpet-thick layer of countless thousands of writhing, swollen white maggots."

Recreating the scene in his mind, the Reverend shivered involuntarily. The Sheriff, on the other hand, had the disquieting notion that Walraven was studying their reactions.

"Luke retreated, thrusting his lamp upward to illuminate the area directly above us, only to catch his breath at what the glare of the lamp revealed. The ceiling was alive with a repugnant horde of squirming maggots clinging to each other for purchase. We were appalled at the unnatural size of their numbers, some being nearly a foot long and several inches wide. The undulating mass of the hateful creatures hung above us like an animate Damocles' sword. Nowhere could we discern even a patch of the underlying stone, it being totally obscured by the slimy scavengers. I assure you our stomachs were churning as we waked to the danger inherent in our position; any slight atmospheric disruption would certainly have dislodged an incalculable number of the unholy brood, and a downpour of the teeming crawlers would certainly have buried us alive."

He fell silent once again. The Sheriff, still suspicious, wondered if this was a ploy for dramatic effect.

"We threw up our arms in a feeble attempt to cover ourselves and ducked down, although such impromptu methods would have proven absolutely futile had the crawling obscenities let loose of their precarious perch."

"Good Lord!" cried the Reverend aloud.

Walraven smiled patronizingly at the pastor before commenting, "You might say that, Reverend."

"With unsteady steps, we inched our way toward the larger chamber, foolishly believing the higher ceiling there might provide us some degree of safety. Luke led that way as we crept forward, then he suddenly halted upon encountering the nearest of the stalagmites. His boot must have struck its base, for we were shocked to see the yellow-white outcropping sluggishly heave to one side and rise up before flopping onto its side with a dull thud. What we had taken for stalagmites were, in truth, titanic multi-segmented worms.

"As we recognized the truth of what lay all around us, we had to clamp our hands over our mouths to stifle our own cries. Neither of us dared move, fearing the slightest disturbance would alert the bloated giants to our presence. Like the maggots, this grotesque behemoth was likewise devoid of eyes, which led me to hypothesize that it might well rely upon vibrational sensitivity as its principal means of assessing its immediate environment. We gazed into the dark, limitless expanse of the cavern, unable to even estimate the number of living stalagmites with which we were confronted. I confess barely being able to remain upright as my mind began to darken and spin with the pulsing brilliance that presages a blackout; such an artificial escape would certainly have proven fatal."

Now it was the Reverend's turn to rise slightly from the rocker's seat and nervously peer out the window beyond Walraven. The sun was setting, staining the sky with brilliant, blood-red swaths of color. If anything was amiss in the yard, he could not detect it.

"We had no choice but to retrace our steps as unobtrusively as possible, that we might return the way we'd come. I recall giving silent thanks to the Almighty for the blindness of the vermin.

"Yet by stepping backward several yards, we inadvertently backed into a tunnel other than the one by which we had entered. We were unaware we'd erred until the wall to our right yawned open, revealing yet another mammoth recess. Our dizzied senses were confronted by an even more nightmarish scene, the chamber being overrun with another group of gigantic grave worms, their sizes ranging from that of a large dog up to that of a bull elephant. Our only relief lay in the realization that they appeared to be preoccupied, thus unaware of our close proximity, with the attendance of a platoon of rat-sized worms that roved indiscriminately and continuously over the surface of the larger worms' bodies, as if grooming or possibly freeing the deathly-pale hides of parasites.

"Somehow we retained a semblance of self-control in the midst of that unfathomably grotesque predicament — until we witnessed the next revelation, that is. As we spied upon the fearsome monsters, one of the largest of their number leisurely raised the forward end of its powerful form and swiveled slowly around. We held our breath as it seemed as if it were staring directly at the stones behind which we were concealed. The skin retracted back from the tip of what served the creature as a head, rolling back to uncover a huge and fearsome birdlike beak. The bulbous head tipped up and slightly back, its raw, hideous mouth gapping wide enough to easily swallow a man whole without effort. With blinding speed, the massive head lunged downward, up, then down once more, with each stroke devouring a dozen or more rat-sized worm attendants within its relentless, cannibalistic bite. At that precise moment, we recognized the true gravity of the threat posed by the mutant monstrosities.

"This new revelation proved more than Luke could bear. Overwhelmed with panic, he took flight. I chased after him, the light of my lantern casting grotesque images and shadow-demons across the breadth of the dark walls as I passed. Unable to overtake him, I was soon relieved to hear him cursing not far ahead. When I finally reached him, he had fallen and, to all appearances, had broken his right leg."

A subtle smile darted across the speaker's face, to the dismay of his listeners. They found themselves scooting back a bit in their seats, unconsciously distancing themselves a tad from the ominous narrator.

"Of course," Walraven went on, "the poor boy was hysterical with fear and pain. I had to forcibly clamp one hand over his mouth in order to silence him. I lied to him then, saying we were not far from the exit and safety. After swearing not to abandon him, I impressed him with the absolute necessity that he keep absolutely quiet. Once he calmed, we sat and listened for any audible indication that we were being pursued. We were relieved to hear nothing whatsoever.

Then, while helping my companion to his feet in the dim lantern glow, I was stunned to discern a most unwelcome development. To my utter horror, the tunnel ahead was completely blocked with worms, its expanse jammed with innumerable pale, sluggish bodies. They must have noiselessly pursued us, then amassed in a heap when our silence provided them no further trail to follow. Over Luke's shoulder, I watched their ugly heads dart to and fro in every direction, vainly searching for any indication of our whereabouts.

"I whispered to my befuddled friend that he should lean on me as we had to get moving, again reminding him that we dare not risk making the slightest sound. I feared he would cry out as he limped along upon his bad leg, but to my relief, he did not. I suppose he was too preoccupied with pain to note that we headed back the way we'd just come. Had he known the truth of our dire predicament, he would surely have given way to panic once more.

"I have no idea just how long we wandered through the maze-like corridors of that hell hole, the worms trailing our every step, though at a distance. We were forced to change course more than once due to our path being plugged with worms, but finally, after a torturous eternity, we stumbled upon the shaft that led to the outside world."

Walraven's voice dropped and he fell silent. The last rays of the setting sun streamed through the window as he rose to light two large hurricane lamps in opposing sides of the room. No one spoke as he undertook this task, although the Reverend unconsciously sighed aloud, relieved that the rest of the frightening tale would be related in a more brightly-lit setting.

As he resumed his seat, Walraven turned once more to glance out the window. He smiled for no obvious reason, then continued with his story.

"Where that tunnel divided into two distinct avenues, I could see bones far down the length of one shaft, bones exactly like those we'd encountered upon entering the Hole. I therefore tried to steer Luke in that direction, but he balked. Exhausted and half-crazed with shock, he suddenly lurched forward, thrusting me away from him with enough force to knock me down. When I got up and shone the light on my friend, I was surprised to see him standing, wildeyed, just a few feet away, his shotgun aimed directly at my face. Even worse, however, was the sight I beheld clearly defined behind him, a looming conglomerate of bobbing white appendages, their featureless heads nodding but a few feet beyond."

THE PALADIN OF WORMS

On pins and needles, the Reverend and Sheriff watched as Walraven buried his face in his hands, his anguished sigh giving portent of what was to come. Walraven's voice faltered as he went on. "All I can say is ... he must have seen the look on my face and followed my line of sight. The poor bastard, he turned and, in terror lost his balance. He tumbled, screaming, right into that living wall of pallid, ravenous flesh. The filthy things swarmed all over him instantly, battling amongst themselves for the choicest morsels. All this happened so quickly that, I swear, there was nothing at all that I could do to save poor Luke.

"I turned and ran, fleeing down the tunnel I knew to be the route to a saner world. I crashed through the boneyard in a crazed frenzy and fumbled my way through the aperture of the Hole. There being no ledge on the embankment, I fell headlong into the stagnant water below. I let loose of my lantern and, in the darkness, nearly drowned as I struggled, unable to gain any purchase upon the slippery, slime-covered bottom. Somehow I succeeded in righting myself, although barely able to distinguish up from down in the pitch darkness, and grappled for the shore, where I collapsed upon a bed of cold wet weeds and mud."

Taking a deep breath, Walraven declared, "I lay there face down in the muck for some time, shivering uncontrollably in my wet, filthy clothing, despite the summer warmth. It finally struck me that I had better drag myself back here to the house before I slipped into a dangerous state of shock.

"As I began to rise, I could feel something strange beneath me, a quivering. The next thing I knew, the earth below me undulated slightly, then convulsed. The slime covering my hands grew animated. I sat up and raised my hands to my face that I might discover what was under me. I could barely see at first, but as a cloud passed away from the face of the moon, I cried out in shock. My palms were engulfed in hundreds of wriggling maggots, the very ground beneath me being naught but a seething blanket of churning maggots! I jumped to my feet, brushing and brushing at the horrible things, but their numbers were far too great. They wriggled inside my clothing, in my shirt and pants. I can't describe the sickening experience of having thousands of vermin swarming all over your body. I have only the vaguest recollection of their reaching my face, dropping into my screaming mouth, and ... and ... then nothing. I must have fainted, my mind surrendering to the belief that I was being eaten alive."

The Reverend reached out to comfort the shaking Walraven, just as the Sheriff snidely asserted, "And yet you somehow managed to get yourself home all safe and sound. You must take us for fools."

"Now Sheriff, ...," begged the sympathetic Reverend.

The lawman stood up, assuming an officious pose. "Don't tell me you're buying any of this malarkey, Reverend, 'cos I sure as hell ain't! Either he's a ringtailed liar or, more likely, he's crazier 'n a bedbug!"

The parson looked at Walraven imploringly, then back at the Sheriff before lowering his head.

"I thought not," the Sheriff sputtered. Turning to Walraven, he demanded, "You're gonna lead us to Luke's body right now, mister — no more excuses."

Walraven displayed no sign of being intimidated.

"I regret to inform you, Sheriff, but I cannot lead you to the body tonight. Use your common sense for a moment. You may dismiss all I've related to you here, but beyond that, you know full well one can only maneuver the pasture safely in daylight. It's a virtual swamp, filled with sinkholes, snakes and muck. Do you really want to go traipsing across terrain like that in the dark?"

Unwilling to admit outright that it would actually be quite foolish to navigate the marshy terrain in the dark, the Sheriff plodded to the front door and, closing only the screen door behind him, marched out to the big open front porch. Standing there alone, with a cool evening breeze brushing across his face, he stared into the distance. He deemed it vital that he remain in control of this situation. Something did not feel right about all this, not right at all, and he dared not let Walraven get the best of him. He stood for several minutes, pondering the forest canopy that Walraven had permitted to encroach threateningly near the house. Avoiding the crystal clarity of the sky above, he focused upon the hazy light that marked the Haagenbaugh farm, suddenly so far to the northeast. The only distraction was the weird serenade of crickets and frogs emerging from the nighted void, the endless loop of their convoluted cries striking him as totally alien to the familiar world. A shiver raced along his spine, causing his entire body to quake. The old timers would say someone had just walked over his grave.

"They're out there, Sheriff, waiting," Walraven tauntingly called from inside the house.

"That cuts it," the officer grumbled under his breath. He turned and strode back into the parlor.

"It may well be that we gotta wait 'til morning before taking a good look at this Death Hole of yours, assuming there is such a place, but nothing's gonna keep me from looking around these premises right now."

In an intrusively high-pitched voice, the Reverend timidly proffered, "Without a warrant, you can't do that ... can you?"

Raising a lantern, the Sheriff ignored the remark. He further goaded

Walraven with, "Are you gonna aim me toward Luke's room or do I have to find it on my own?"

"Go to the end of the hall there, then past my bedroom and up the stairs," the still-seated Walraven coldly replied. "Luke's door is the first on the right once you've reached the landing."

The Sheriff frowned. "Good enough. Now I expect you two to wait right here. Reverend, I'd appreciate it if you'd give a holler if our friend here decides to go anywhere. 'Til I get back, he ain't to move, not even if he says he has to use the outhouse."

The demure Reverend nodded his silent assent.

Walraven smiled broadly. "I promise to stay put," he said with a hint of sarcasm not lost on the lawman.

Neither man spoke during the Sheriff's absence. The clergyman was obviously at a complete loss for words due to the awkwardness of the situation. His companion seemed to fix his attention once more on the blackness beyond the window.

The Sheriff soon returned, reporting that, aside from Luke's clothing and belongings still being in his room, he had spotted nothing suspicious in the course of his search. He concluded with, "Still, I got no choice other than to haul you down to the station for more questioning. If it's like you say and Luke is dead, then we'll find out in the morning and try to sort all this out then. I'll have some of the boys check out this cavern you claim you were in; we'll just see what they do or don't find there."

His announcement elicited no reaction, so he motioned for Walraven to rise. The Reverend started to object when the Sheriff handcuffed his prisoner, then thought better of it.

Relenting a bit, the lawman turned to the Reverend. "This ain't what I had planned, you know that, Reverend, but I gotta do my duty as I see fit. I'm going to pull the car up to the porch, and I want you and Walraven to come out and stand on the porch in the meantime so I can keep an eye on my prisoner."

A moment later, the pair were on the porch, watching the Sheriff's light diminish into the darkness of the yard as best they could. Their view was partially obscured by the peeling trunk and low-slung limbs of an ancient cedar tree that stood just ten feet from their roost.

They heard the car door slam, saw the headlights blink on, and heard the engine start. As the car pulled into sight, the clergyman sighed with relief and stepped forward, nearly overturning the lantern at his feet.

The lamplight eerily illuminated the lowest branches of the huge cedar as the Sheriff exited the car, having parked some five yards from where the others waited on the porch. When he had crossed half of that distance, he slowed his pace, then stopped to look up. He tried to determine the source of an odd rustling disturbance emanating from the upper boughs of the tree.

"Must be a raccoon up there," he assured the waiting pair.

As if on cue, three milk-white appendages, each as big around as a man and at least eight feet long, dropped nearly to the ground before him, their far ends lost amongst the cluster of leafy foliage from which they had come. Startled, the Sheriff drew back, his hand now at the holster on his hip.

The strange, featureless forms bobbed up and down like yo-yos, their motion diminishing with each subsequent bounce. As they came to rest, looking rather foolishly like enormously thick ropes, the Sheriff inched forward for a closer look at one of them.

"Don't!" the frightened Reverend whispered aloud.

The lawman cocked his head to one side. Unexpectedly, he grinned broadly, chuckled and turned to his human audience. "Nice try, Walraven, you had me going there for a minute," he said. Next, he reached out to touch one of the pale, taffy-like extensions, adding, "If this is some kind prank you and Luke are pulling, I swear I'll have both your heads."

At his touch, the lower end of the swollen hanger drew back, retracting several inches. The sight emboldened the officer as it reminded him of a shriveling penis, until, that is, that same end twisted upward abruptly to direct its now-blunt tip at his face.

Immediately, the tip unfurled like a gigantic flower blossoming at extraordinary speed. The Sheriff only had time to moan, "Well, I'll be a son of a ...," before the petals rolled back to allow a terrible parrot beak to emerge. The beak's upper and lower halves yawned nearly two feet apart. The snakelike apparition shot forth at lightening speed to envelop the dumbstruck policeman's entire head. With a sickening crack the beak's jaws clamped tightly shut, slicing through the Sheriff's spinal column with ease. The dangling horror seemed to wither as it retreated, unhindered by the pumpkin-sized lump in its throat. Along with its two ropy companions, it shot back and withdrew upward, vanishing into the unlit bulk of the tree's foliage. They were gone before the headless torso teetered forward and toppled lifelessly to the ground.

Suddenly looking far older than his age, the stunned Reverend stood frozen in place, paralyzed with disbelief, his hands clutching his shock-ridden face so intently that his fingers were nearly imbedded in the flesh.

Walraven casually turned to the minister, offering, "Have you noticed the frogs and their compatriots have fallen silent." He seemed totally unperturbed by the violent slaying that had taken place right in front of him.

Very slowly, the incredulous Reverend lowered his clawing hands. Turning to Walraven, he inquired in weighted tones, "Who ... are you?"

A sardonic smile crept across the teacher's face. "So you've finally realized I'm not Richard Walraven, although I wear his body or, rather, what remains of it."

Sneering, the Reverend mumbled, "The story you told us, it was ...."

"Totally accurate to the point where Walraven passed out upon maggot bed. I related it precisely as he would have done."

"*What* are you?" screeched the distraught minister.

"I will answer your questions, but first I suggest we step back inside," Walraven remarked offhandedly. "We should be comfortable for our little chat."

The Reverend docilely complied with the request, despite the menace his companion offered. The two returned to the parlor and their respective seats, the Reverend steadfastly holding the lantern between them as if it were a charm to ward off the other's evil.

Walraven smiled. "You're frightened and confused, I know, and that's to be expected. Regardless, we can still have a nice, relaxed conversation as soon as you get a hold of yourself. Take a few deep breaths if you think that will help or maybe say a prayer. I promise you have nothing to fear from the worms. I am quite enjoying this little masquerade and I would like to continue our little *communion,* if you can forgive my play on words. I look upon this as an opportunity to study your species from a more intimate perspective."

It was not until Walraven — or whomever or whatever replaced him — left the room to brew a fresh batch of tea, that the minister was finally able to breathe freely once more. His sixty-five-year-old heart was pounding at an alarming rate. While sipping two subsequent cups of tea, he managed to regain some of his self-possession. The reassuring yellow glow provided by tallow candles now burning on the mantle provided a certain solace in itself. He longed for a gentle flame within the fireplace but could not bring himself to request it.

Finally, both men sat facing each other. Unable to bear the muted standoff, the minister summoned all his courage in order to speak. "And now, sir, if you would kindly answer my question — what in the name of God *are* you?"

A snide chuckle escaped the other's lips.

"In the name of God? And what name might that be? Better yet, to which god do you refer? I have seen countless gods and groupings of gods come and go in my time. In each instance, the devout proclaimed their deity or deities to be the only true supreme beings, still, before long every single one fell by the wayside, discarded like so much trash, forgotten — exactly as your god soon will be." He leaned forward, causing his companion to draw back instinctively. "On the other hand, I might well claim godhead myself, dear Reverend."

"Blasphemy," uttered the offended pastor.

The other continued undaunted, "No, not really. I am immortal, at least for your intents and purposes. Also, I came here from heaven in the beginning, when your world was but newly born. I am forced to admit that I was neither the first nor the most powerful of those of us who came here, but, unlike my more powerful compatriots, I managed to avoid the catastrophe that hurtled the most powerful into their present dormant state. Thus, I can boast that I have had more than a little influence upon the course of this planet's entire history.

"You might go so far as to recognize me as a farmer of sorts, like Walraven himself. The difference being the scale, for my herds consist, at times, of whole populations. Agreed, my sphere of influence has dwindled over the millennia, but I once held sway over vast multitudes and entire species, some sentient and some not, and empires that rose and fell long before anything remotely resembling your kind came to be."

Leaning back in his chair, he added, "Oh, now I've confused you, haven't I? I apologize. I keep forgetting your science knows nothing of the Old Ones in the frozen Antarctic wastes, the subterranean-dwelling men-serpents or any other of humanity's numerous predecessors."

The clergyman protested, saying, "Were these 'predecessors' of any import, we would know of them. We would have stumbled upon some sign of their existence, their cities fallen to ruins or some other evidence of their having been."

"Oh, my poor, ignorant Reverend, you haven't the slightest concept of how extremely limited is your knowledge of history! The others of which I speak *did indeed* exist. As for what they left behind, well, the artifacts of some of the mightiest cultures that have existed would prove far too alien for a mentality as narrow as man's to recognize in the unlikely event that you should stumble across them. The remnants of others lay entombed far beneath the earth's surface, and legacies of still others have long since been ground to naught, erased by the endless shifting of lands and glacial masses."

Unrelenting, the minister declared, "God gave the world to man and man alone, whom He made in His own image."

"Very well, then you must indeed agree that I am most godlike for, soon after I came here, I created an entirely new species of my own. Its members reflect, albeit in miniature form, every aspect of my early development until, in the end, each and every one perfectly duplicates my own physiology. They are all inferior to the original, yet I *did* create them in my own image, of my own flesh, and ... they have become legion."

"Oh, yes, the worms you spoke of earlier. Can I assume then, that your true form is that of some sort of worm like those depending from the tree outside?" begged the Reverend. Receiving no answer, he continued his prodding. "Maybe I could better understand if you were to explain what has become of the real Richard Walraven. Are you some kind of disembodied spirit inhabiting his physical form?"

Walraven poured himself a fresh cup of tea. "No, no, no! I'm not a spirit, disembodied or otherwise. I shall attempt to explain. Once here, I realized my form was proportionately impractical for the scale of this world, my body being what you would consider quite mammoth. Thus, I elected to create thousands of tiny, but otherwise nearly identical, versions of myself. I chose, however, not to disperse my consciousness within my spawn as such minute brains proved incapable of retaining information for but a short time, information gleaned from the minds and bodies of those my little ones have consumed. I devised a method, therefore, by which the thoughts of each were instantaneously transmitted to the central reservoir of my personal consciousness, where they are assimilated and retained.

"In this particular instance, admittedly a very special one, my warriors devoured Walraven from within after entering his body through variously accessible orifices. Thus the appearance of his outer form was preserved to allow for this most excellent impersonation. I thereby obtained the entire contents of his mind, right up to the very moment of his death. Thus have I recreated him from within after secreting my physical form within his skin."

The parson, taking into account the fact that his challenge regarding the other's true form had gone unanswered, began to doubt the truth of all he was being told. A means to defeat the demon might well be gleaned, he prayed, from what the demon chose to withhold from him. With silent prayer, he begged his maker for the insight and strength required to thwart this monster and abort its deadly plans.

"You see," the paladin went on, "being a *good* farmer, I interfere with my herds only when they go astray. The Shawnee faithfully keep my larder stocked with food in the form of their dead, as did the builders of mounds and countless cultures before them. The great Serpent Mound was, by the way, constructed by the Adena in my honor. Its form mimics the worm stage of my development. The so-called egg in the jaws of that effigy actually symbolizes my authority over a world that even they recognized as being round."

Ignoring his opponent's obvious hubris, the Reverend queried, "But didn't you say your influence embraces a limited area at present, not the world?"

Walraven smiled at his companion's flippant remark, his annoyance apparent. "That is correct, but only because I no longer desire to lord over great tracts of land." He paused momentarily as if lost in thought, then said, "Walraven's memory tells me you hail from somewhere in Arizona originally. Is that correct?"

Cautiously, the Reverend confirmed that fact.

"I am allied with he who holds tenure over that area. You may have heard the name of Yig whispered by those around you as you grew up. Yes, I see you are familiar with that most infamous Father of Serpents. He is even less tolerant of his charges than I; when those you call the Anasazi discovered the pleasures of cannibalism and thus neglected his minions, Yig eradicated them without mercy. That is our way, you see, our means of controlling the cattle should they displease or defy us.

"Returning to more immediate history, Walraven's ancestor, Adodiah, swore to uphold the tradition of pacifying my warriors with offerings of his own people's dead. He accepted that term in exchange for becoming the caretaker of this land and the caverns, yet he betrayed that trust by abandoning us who, to him, were already buried in the ground. Foolishly, he was convinced that we would simply die out; instead, we thrived. He underestimated the great horde of plague-ridden corpses that had accumulated in the cavern. Why, those corridors contained all but the last vestiges of the once proud Shawnee tribes of this territory. When those supplies were finally exhausted, we supplemented our diet with wild game and the occasional domestic beast. But now, as Walraven discovered, the larger worms turn on their smaller brethren for sustenance, and this is a practice I cannot long tolerate.

"They are *grave* worms after all, therefore they naturally prefer the taste of the moldering dead. Desperation, however, makes the consumption of the living a necessity in times like these. I might add that, having gotten to know you as I have, I feel I should direct my warriors to feast upon your very own congregation first, Reverend."

To mask his abject horror at this latest proposition, the clergyman posed the further question, "Then the day of Dar has nothing to do with your seeking revenge for the way we whites treated the Indians?"

Walraven scoffed, "Don't be foolish."

Angrily, the Reverend growled, "Do you really believe a bunch of maggots, even ones as big as those we saw outside, could bring this county to heel? Yes, there would certainly be casualties, but your so-called army wouldn't have a chance against guns, fire, explosives and all manner of weapons in our possession. Much has changed since the days of your Old Ones and snake men! I have no doubt that we will make short work of you and your pit worms."

Walraven laughed aloud. "How sure of himself my humble servant of god has suddenly become!" he shouted. "Had you been paying attention, you might have realized the worm is but one small phase in my development and, thus, in the development of my warriors. You are absolutely correct; worms are far too slow and conspicuous to successfully do battle with your kind. I have something far more insidious in store for you!"

Tiny beads of sweat had formed on the parson's forehead by the time the speaker elaborated.

"Surely you are familiar with the Black Plague to which nearly a third of Europe's population succumbed during the Middle Ages. Ah! I can see that you are catching on at last!"

"You intend to inflict some dread disease upon us by means of your minions?" stuttered the Reverend.

Nodding his affirmation, Walraven further stated, "Picture, if you can, tens of thousands of tiny messengers, nurtured on pox-riddled carrion for centuries, spreading death far and wide, messengers of form so ordinary as to hardly be noticed ... until it is too late, that is.

"You look surprised, Reverend. Have you never wondered at the mysterious, inexplicable disappearances of whole peoples recorded in your histories? The means vary from place to place and time to time, but my cohorts and I can claim responsibility in most of those cases. The majority of the victims weren't even aware an outside source was the intentional cause of the terrible misfortunes that befell them."

"Have you no pity for those you condemn to incalculable misery ... and hellish death?" begged the cleric.

Walraven's head turned from side to side as his negative response.

The Reverend fell silent, at a loss for words to either soften the devil's heart or refute his terrifying boast. The room and everything about him faded. His mind blurred, then seemed to refocus by its own volition, his total vulnerability giving way to a surreal vision of himself as a holy crusader, the blessed one chosen by God Himself to end this age-old blight upon creation.

In the meantime, Walraven rose, exalted that he had finally shaken the clergyman's faith in his god. "You still don't know me for who I really am, do you?" he taunted.

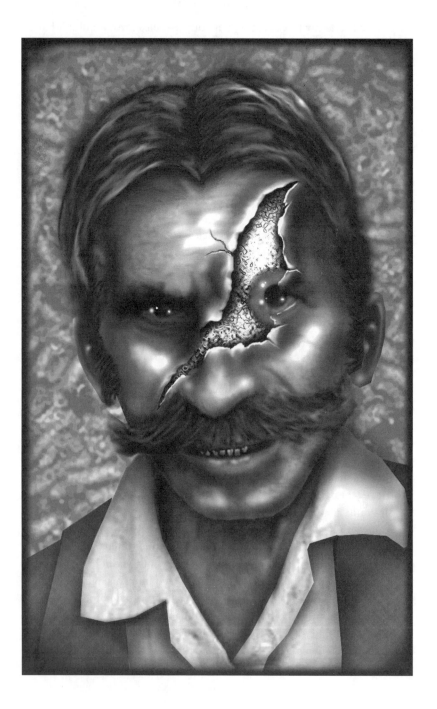

An unexpected sound from beyond the house caught the impersonator's attention, causing him to turn his back to his solemn companion.

Deeming this unexpected opportunity a sign from God, the Reverend rose as quietly as he could, tiptoed to the fireplace a few feet away, and grasped a heavy, wrought iron poker firmly in both hands. "I condemn thee to Hell!" he cried as he slammed the cold, black metal rod down with murderous intent upon his opponent's head.

At the force of the blow, Walraven staggered forward before turning fully about to confront his attacker. Blood spurted generously from a foot-long gash in the crown of his head, but the flow instantly subsided as Walraven regained control. Smiling sardonically, he whispered, "Your *Holy Bible* forbids man to gaze into the face of your god, least ye be blasted by its power."

The flesh of Walraven's face instantly cracked in a steady line from forehead to chin, then further still; the shriveling skin began dropping away in bloodless strips that reminded the dumbfounded minister of the dry parchment leaves of some ancient biblical text. Adroit hands stripped the clothing from the ribboning flesh as the hideous transformation continued.

The Reverend stepped back, falling into a chair. He fought desperately that his newfound resolve not give way to absolute horror at the sight of the human body literally unraveling before him in the yellowed glow of lamp light.

"I am your new god!" declared an echoing voice from somewhere within the disintegrating physique. The last shred of resemblance to anything human dropped away in a deteriorating gurgle. "Behold my face!"

The Reverend could only stare as the naked corpse reduced to naught but a hazy, undulating cloud of darkness, its contours flowing indefinably like a confined liquid. In a fruitless attempt to divert his gaze from the abomination, the parson lurched forward, only to stumble into the table that bore the nearest of the hurricane lanterns.

The table toppled over, flinging the glass chimnied lamp to the floor. As it shattered, a wash of kerosene and shards splashed across the rugs. The rugs instantly ignited and, in a blinding flash, a shower of flames cast about the room. The antique furnishings quickly caught fire. Despite the burgeoning inferno flaring all around, the Reverend remained defiantly transfixed upon the unholy, living shadow, the hapless victim of an enlivened gorgon.

His eyes widened with confused curiosity as the amorphous manifestation began to dissolve into wispy rivulets of browns and grays like tendrils of dark smoke that twisted and curled in upon themselves. These were extended toward him, beckoning him to come nearer. Only in those final moments before he bucked and ran screaming from the burning house into the starless night, did the holy man realize the truth of what he saw. Only then was he able to give name to the thing bent on the utter destruction of all who dared defy it. Well he knew its name and repeated it endlessly as hellish damnation overtook him.

A low hum breached the numbness of his senses, a nerve-shattering shrill sound that amplified a thousand times until the sound of a thousand tiny, buzzing horrors swarmed through his head. His screams could not prevent the groping of what felt like countless miniature limbs pawing at every exposed patch of his skin, their biting mouths ruthlessly attaching themselves to his face and hands. Still, he ran, unable to stop himself even when the filthy things flocked into his open mouth, drowning his final, helpless shrieks. More of the unseen tormentors tore at his eyes, scratching and digging their hideously alien bodies beneath his eyelids. Once inside, they chewed through the soft tissues, that they might fester within their victim's brain.

The flailing madman's gait began to slow once he had cleared the yard and burst into the fields beyond. In the end, the pathetic parson found some slight sanctuary in recitation of the jumbled confusion of prayers that swirled though the last vestiges of his fevered mind.

The following Sunday found the normally quiet rural community abuzz with the news of the awful tragedy that had struck the Walraven farm. Everyone for miles around had witnessed the brilliant illumination caused by the burning of the ancient farmhouse. Word that their children's high school teacher had gone berserk and murdered both his hired hand and Sheriff McKinny before attacking the community's beloved spiritual leader had shocked everyone. It was universally agreed that in being consumed in the subsequent conflagration, Walraven had met with divine justice in its most blatant form. No one would have believed such events possible had the details come from anyone other than Reverend Peterson himself, the only survivor.

Three days had passed and now, with the exception of those who were bedridden with an unusually harsh flu-like illness, the entire community had turned out for Sunday morning services at Peterson's church. They had heard that Peterson had emerged from it all without so much as a scratch, but folks wanted to see for themselves as well as show their support for the minister. With any luck, some hoped, his sermon might provide further details of Walraven's madness as an adjunct to the overall sermon which, according to the placard displayed on the sign outside, was peculiarly entitled, "The Lord of the Flies, He Dwelleth Within."◈

Self-Correcting Mechanism

> "Nature, having averted Her eyes for but an instant, stared aghast at the result of Her carelessness. For in that brief moment the means of Her undoing had come into existence."
>
> — unidentified Cathdenian philosopher

Deep within the Daleth-Vau star system, a gaudily-designed, globular metallic craft maintained its age-long silent sentry, unperturbed by the small Earthcraft presently keeping pace with it. The orbits of both ships lay far above a green-marbled world dubbed "Cathdeny" by its discoverer Clark Cathdeny, the Earthly astronomer who had charted the quadrants of the Daleth-Vau system using data transmitted back to Earth by an unmanned explorercraft. The data provided Cathdeny enough data to prove the "moon" orbiting the fourth planet was actually of artificial manufacture, undeniably the product of a highly-skilled, ultrahuman intelligence.

Within three months, the starship *Perception*, the smaller of the two vessels currently in orbit around Dr. Cathdeny's mysterious little planet, had been dispatched as Earth's ambassador to the newly discovered planet and the intelligent beings assumed to dwell there.

Chills flared through Captain Darius Khatami's lean form as he stared at arabesques adorning the surface of the artificial globe now limned against the blackness of space on the monitor in his cabin. Professor Galen Niles, standing next to him, noted the sudden shiver, then moved behind to wrap his arms protectively around the handsome Persian captain. "It's scary, isn't it?" he whispered directly into Khatami's ear as he felt his encircling limbs being caressed.

"More than I ever imagined. More than any of us could ever have imagined," replied Khatami. "I've dreamed of meeting another intelligent species all my life, and now it's about to happen — right here, and I'm in charge of the

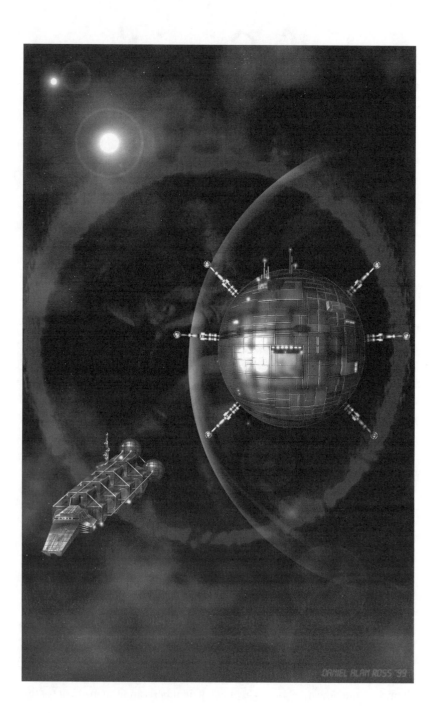

whole show. They say you should be careful what you wish for ...." He slowly closed his eyes and leaned back, resting his head upon Niles' chest. "I'm scared to death, though I hope you're the only one who knows it. Captains have to be fearless and in control at all times."

Although no known form of weaponry had been detected aboard the alien device, Khatami still worried that there had been no response to endless attempts at establishing radio contact with the satellite and its creators on the planet below. By all rights, the airwaves around the planet should be flooded with a cacophony of radio and television transmissions, short wave signals, and broadcasts of a thriving civilization. Yet nothing but silence came from beneath the thick cloud that blanketed the planet's surface. Radar maps of the landscape revealed thousands of metropolitan areas littering the planet's three huge continents, yet the ship's most sensitive equipment failed to register the slightest indication of the signal concentrations of energy that denote advanced technology. Were the aliens "playing 'possum" or were their ways beyond human understanding? Beings capable of placing an artificial satellite in orbit would certainly notice an unfamiliar craft invading their territory. Why didn't they communicate? He knew any unidentified craft approaching the Earth risked being blasted into oblivion by a net of autolasers, but Earth was very far away from this place, beyond even radio contact.

Aware of his lover's turmoil, Niles said, "If you weren't afraid, you'd have no business captaining this mission. It just shows you're human. You are a great captain!" He paused a moment, then added slyly, "And behind every great man stands ... another. Isn't that how the saying goes?"

Khatami chuckled, disengaged himself from Niles' gentle embrace, and twisted around to face his youthful companion. Raising both arms stiffly, he brought them to rest on Niles' shoulders with a smile. "Yes, I'm sure that's how it goes."

Great or not, Khatami still sometimes felt an urge to offer a silent prayer to Allah, a god he had abandoned years before, when he realized he could never reconcile his religious needs with his homosexuality. For years, he had repressed both of those inner needs, refusing to allow either control over his life. The battle had ended, however, the day he met Niles, a self-confident linguistics student who had surprised him with more than a fluency in Farsi. The ensuing relationship had brought an end to his frustration and attendant bouts of depression. Niles gave him the courage to recognize that his needs were natural, despite the opinion of the majority.

With time, Khatami had begun to realize he was "as normal as anyone else, only with better taste," as Niles put it. Khatami's family had disowned him when he had introduced them to his "lover," and friends had fallen by the wayside — but for the first time in his life, Khatami understood the meaning of self respect.

The vast majority of the military big brass consisted of heterosexuals who expressed their "open and unbiased attitude" by ridiculing homosexuals in private. Nonetheless, his career had progressed well, albeit slowly, based strictly on his merit in spite of the preference shown to more conventional officers. When he heard of his appointment to command the *Perception* for this most special of missions, his own incredulity far surpassed everyone else's.

He had been chosen from five candidates considered for the post by General Mark Anderson, a man who had been Khatami's roommate for four years during college. They had developed a strong bond of mutual respect and platonic affection that had endured throughout the years.

Anderson had flown all the way from Lunar Headquarters to discuss the appointment with Khatami on Mars Base. The General made it clear that their friendship had in no way influenced the decision; of the five candidates, only Khatami possessed the intuitive insight and sensitivity required for such a delicate situation.

Once Khatami had accepted the appointment, Anderson admitted he had recommended Niles be chosen to fill the position of linguist for the mission's science team; that, he confessed, had been a personal favor to his old college friend. Niles had accepted the assignment with his usual aplomb.

Khatami wished his own self-confidence matched Anderson's faith in him. The future of the human race might well lie in his hands, and every homosexual on the planet expected him to prove sexual preference has nothing to do with one's ability to perform well in a position of responsibility. He was constantly aware of that dual responsibility.

Niles roused him from his rumination.

"I should mention that by stonewalling those who voted to break into the alien satellite, you won the respect of every scientist on board, not that they'd admit it to your face. Now they see you as some kind of champion to their cause."

Niles' words brought a flood of remembered images to Khatami. It had been the first crisis of the mission, and he had vetoed his advisors' insistent demand that the alien satellite be "secured" as it posed a potential threat. Khatami had argued that common sense provided that any violation of alien property courted return hostile action, very possibly with weapons far superior to their own. He had ended the debate by emphatically stating that he would not permit any action that could be interpreted by the aliens as hostile.

SELF-CORRECTING MECHANISM

Niles found himself staring blankly at the satellite's image on the monitor, mumbling "You won't talk to us, so ready or not, we are coming to see you in person."

To Niles he said, "I still say it is entirely possible the aliens have tried to contact us. As far as they're concerned, our radio signals might be as primitive as a pair of tin cans on a string. Do they even recognize our attempts at contact?"

"You're probably right, but now you're really scaring me," Niles teased, reminded suddenly of how proud he was to be this man's lover.

Moments later they parted after a swift but affectionate embrace. The ship was leaving orbit, and each had to prepare for landing.

Radio contact was never established, and no one came to investigate their arrival, although they landed less than a kilometer from a medium-size city and within sight of an incredibly high mountain range that Niles jokingly referred to as "the Mountains of Madness" after a Lovecraftian horror novella.

Nothing about the alien world was as they had expected. The climate, atmosphere, and gravity of the new world proved to be within the bounds of human requirement, incredibly enough; radiation levels registered normal as well. The planet's ubiquitous golden cloudcover, they realized, served as a barrier, trapping heat and humidity beneath its umbrella to create a jungle paradise for the seemingly infinite variety of wildlife. The landing site itself presented a lush habitat of exotic trees and curiously bizarre plant life beneath a purled sky. None of the small, odd looking animals or insects appeared to threaten the humans, and three varieties of creatures were actually adopted by the crewmen as quite loveable pets, including one that looked very much like a house cat with reptilian scales. Protective clothing was not even deemed necessary when leaving the ship.

The more ideal the circumstances became, the more the Captain worried; he could not shake the feeling that they were trespassing in an alien Eden. Puzzled most by Cathdeny's environmental similarities to Earth, Khatami sought the advice of Dr. Nephram Chandra, the cultural anthropologist and supervisor of the expedition's scientific team. Khatami asked the Pakistani scientist if it were possible that higher life forms could evolve normally in an environment like this one.

Chandra curtly replied that he could not speculate on such an hypothesis as his definition of "normal" obviously differed greatly from Khatami's. It

seemed Niles had been mistaken — at least one member of the science team considered him something less than a champion.

Immediately after the landing, Khatami ordered three small unmanned robotic craft called "gnats" dispatched to compile a more detailed visual report on the planetary surface with special attention to the populated areas. The gnats were eventually to confirm a possibility that Khatami had dreaded from the moment it occurred to him — the gnats had been unable to locate any indication of a current population and none of the cities were currently inhabited. In all probability, there were no aliens left for the crew to meet.

On the second day of their stay on Cathdeny, the Captain gave the disappointed science team permission to leave the ship as long as they remained within sight of the vessel while collecting samples of flora and fauna. No problems were encountered, and involvement in the activities of the outing helped keep the morale of the participants from hitting rock bottom.

It was not until the third morning that Khatami and five of officers led a delegation of the scientists through the jungle and into the alien city. They hacked their way through dense undergrowth for hours before the heavy vegetation abruptly ended, giving way to a sandy area of several meters' width that surrounded the entire city. It almost seemed to the humans that the jungle had halted in its approach to the city, afraid or unwilling to barge into such an unnatural place. A type of parasitic vine had, however, crossed over the sandy no-man's-land and once inside, its endless tendrils had done their best to efface the factitious facades.

The awe and wonder experienced by the explorers as they wandered through the streets of the vine-draped necropolis was tempered by the realization that the actual opportunity to meet the alien creators of the weirdly magnificent city was lost to them forever.

The strange architectural structures looked as if they had been vacated centuries ago. They remained intact, however, indicating a voluntary abandonment rather flight from attack. The haunting mood of the place reminded Niles of the equally ancient and abandoned ruins of Copan, a majestic Mayan ceremonial center in the jungles of Earth; several of his fellow scientists concurred and they unanimously agreed to call the city "New Copan," at least until its native appellation could be discerned.

The architecture of New Copan did not, however, resemble that of its namesake. What they initially interpreted as skyscrapers populated a maze-like area of intertwined shafts that were bent and twisted at odd angles. The unordered reticulation of leaning near-obelisks bore no doors or windows recognizable to the humans, but rather were riddled with holes, as if a flock of giant woodpeckers had pecked countless holes in a forest of suspended causeways.

Murals and sculptures portrayed the former inhabitants of the city as a cross between a squid and a slug. A bulbous head with a pair of deep-set eyes topped a bulky mass of tentacular appendages, allowing the creatures to "stand" somewhat upright to a height of just over a meter. Apparently, the wet and viscous underside of the tentacles allowed them to adhere, slug-like, to any relatively flat surface, the suction making it possible for them to navigate the exterior walls of the tilting structures. They probably could even cling upside-down to the underside of the buildings' outer surfaces.

The peculiar architecture of New Copan made much more sense to the humans once they understood the basic physiology of the Cathdenians. The ubiquitous holes had provided entrances and exits for adherent aliens moving from one tangent edifice to another.

Khatami heard the scientists mumbling about the fascinating "cephaliza-tion" demonstrated by the alien form, which he knew meant the aliens' sense organs and brain were concentrated in the anterior section of the head. He actually understood quite a bit of the scientific jargon but thought it best not to betray such unexpected acumen.

Nowhere among the dusty, windswept streets did they find physical re-mains of the city's former occupants. This gave further credence to their ini-tial speculation that New Copan had lain empty for centuries. The metropolis bore none of the tell-tale signs of violence or plague; it was almost as if the entire population had just disappeared, leaving even personal possessions be-hind.

The most startling feature of the crumbling architecture was unquestion-ably the queer decor of the one-story domestic dwellings, which were only slightly smaller than human dwellings. Whereas every imaginable variety of stone, glass, metal, and even brick had been thoroughly exploited in the larger structures where strength and durability were of primary concern, the private dwellings were all constructed of a uniform material. This hard amber-like substance of perfect translucence was used to create domes; the painted inner surfaces providing the occupants with privacy in the confines of their homes. The domes themselves were identical in shape and size, undoubtedly created by molding a liquefied substance which later hardened. Before the substance fully solidified, however, the Cathdenians evidently had inserted various items into its two-thirds meter thickness to serve as individualizing decor for their homes. Gems, stones, and bits of organic life, often arranged in baffling pat-terns and designs, had been encased within the depths of the domes, and Khatami was appalled to discover the carcasses of animals that had been slaughtered for decorative purposes. Some of the animals were frozen in imitation of natural poses, while just the heads of other, more bizarre beasts were arranged in geometric designs that some long-dead Cathdenian must have considered attractive. All of the crewmen were shocked and repulsed at the aliens' flagrant disregard for other lifeforms, being reminded of Earthly trophy rooms of earlier decades. Further exploration would reveal rows of homes decorated with the butchered bodies of the affectionate cat-like creatures the crew members would come to love so much.

The alien technology had relied on geothermal power as its chief source of energy only, it was later learned, after natural fuels had been exhausted and the environment severely polluted. The ship's master engineer pointed out clusters of antennae used for wireless transmission, as well as a number of free energy receivers. He assured the Captain that much of the city's power system could easily be restored. Within a week, Khatami had that restoral accomplished to provide the necessary electricity for an on-site research facility.

The greatest discovery was made in the largest and most beautiful building in New Copan, a monolithic edifice perched in the exact center of town. Its more familiar cubic structure consisted of megalithic slabs of a polished marble equal to Carrara marble in quality. Its walls rose skyward to heights of over ten kilometers. The men dubbed it the "Archive" due to the archival treasure trove found within its more than one hundred rooms. Anyone entering one of those rooms automatically triggered a device that projected an animated holographic image into the center of the room. Each room's recording described a different phase of Cathdenian history, science, or culture, the overall repository constituting a audio-visual library of the alien culture. The majority of the holograms were sound recordings, although many were accompanied by delineating texts inscribed in both hieroglyphs and pictographs on tablets of argentine metal affixed to the walls. The interior walls and floors, fashioned from a material reminiscent of plexiglass, bore neither decoration nor furnishing beyond the inscribed tablets.

Niles, as linguist, had nearly forsaken all hope for a spoken alien language, but after sampling the holographic soundtracks, he identified the mellifluous clicking, whining, crying, and howling recorded thereon as a highly complicated form of interpersonal communication. Apparently the aliens had been capable of producing a wide range of ululations that delineated their peculiarly ritualistic language.

Even before returning to the ship, the various experts began planning the preservation of the libraric treasures. The irreplaceable information to be gleaned in every room of the Archive could be fed via Optical Holo Scanner into the *Perception's* complex computer system for later study and interpretation.

Within days, a research facility had been established in the confines of New Copan. Dr. Chandra supervised a team that funneled the holographic material directly into the ship's computer. Dr. Tara Devlin, a computer scientist, was assigned to create the software necessary for such a project; her previous experience with deciphering codes proved invaluable.

Although Captain Khatami fully expected to receive regular progress reports on the translation project, none had been forthcoming. He sought an update from Niles, only to learn that none of the participants in the translatory project were permitted access to the results. Niles could only confirm that although copies of all the holographic records now resided in the computer memory, only Dr. Chandra could access them, having doled the information out to the rest of the team in small, unrelated pieces. Niles offered to pay a visit to Dr. Devlin, Chandra's software whiz.

Dr. Devlin greeted Niles with an open, friendly smile. He had expected a female version of the laconic Chandra, but on the contrary, the pale young, platinum-haired Dr. Devlin turned out to be an eager conversationalist.

Unfortunately, she knew very little about the progress of the translation, having confined herself to the software work necessary for its implementation. She did think it odd that Niles had not been intimately involved in evaluating the alien linguistics. Her straightforward manner appealed to Niles, so he ventured to ask if she thought Chandra had excluded him from the project because of his differing lifestyle.

She did not seem to regard the question as extraordinary. "He definitely has problems dealing with unfamiliar social situations," she agreed, "but I assure you that yours is not the only situation unfamiliar to him. I can't believe he would permit his personal prejudices to affect his work though. He's not that much of a bigot!"

Niles laughed, relieved that she did not share Chandra's homophobia. He felt he should have gotten to know Devlin long ago. Still, he was glad he had kept his mouth shut after learning that Chandra and Devlin had been lovers for many years. It was difficult now to imagine the two of them together, and he wondered what qualities Devlin saw in the acerbic little man who had to be twenty years her senior.

Almost seeming to read his mind, she added, "You mustn't judge Chandra too harshly. He was raised to despise and distrust other people, so he's spent most of his life trying to avoid the world. Contact with other people has been difficult for him, especially now that his search for aliens has proven futile." She smiled. "He only agreed to join this expedition because he hoped he could find an intelligent species he'd like better than his own."

She paused thoughtfully before continuing. "Chandra's never known anyone gay, so you might consider remedying that situation; you may be surprised at the wonderful man he can be when his guard's down."

Again Niles laughed. "Wonderful man, huh? I'd be surprised, but I'm willing to give it a try."

A week later, the increasingly impatient Khatami directed Chandra to send him the translations to date, and was surprised to receive a three-hundred page report two days later. Along with the report was a request to meet with Khatami once he had read it. Chandra wanted to discuss "an unexpected aspect" of the findings, implying that it was of some importance. They met three days later.

Khatami greeted Chandra formally, intent on taking the initiative once they were both seated. "It is essential that this meeting be conducted free of the deprecatory attitude you've previously displayed; my choice of lifestyle in no way affects our meeting here today. Are we in agreement on this, Doctor?"

Chandra nodded solemnly, stating that many of his attitudes had been greatly altered in recent days. "But," he said, "we will get to that soon enough as it is."

Khatami told Chandra he had read the entire report, but he still had questions about the aliens.

"You've compiled an excellent overview of the alien anatomy, physiology, and social structure, but I felt the most vital issues were not addressed directly."

The attentive Chandra gestured for the Captain to continue.

"I need to know what happened here, Doctor. What sort of power wiped an entire species from the face of a planet without destroying everything else as well? The report assumes there were no survivors at all. What didn't they survive and how can you be sure there's not even one alien still extant? There's something you're not telling me."

For a moment they stared at each other in silence, each sizing up the other. Khatami suspected something was rotten in Cathdeny and only Chandra could tell him what it was. As commanding officer of the expedition, it was vital that he be aware of anything that affected the safety of those in his charge, not to mention the billions back on Earth.

"I can state with absolute confidence that no Cathdenians survive, which brings us to the very crux of the matter I wished to discuss with you. However, you must allow me to provide you with the necessary background," Chandra replied. "No one else is aware of what I am about to tell you.

"As stated in the analysis, we have achieved a generalized understanding of the Cathdenians, thanks to the detailed written, auditory, and visual records they left behind.

"That material has made it obvious that, apart from the obvious physiological differences between the Cathdenian and human species, which can be discounted as environmentally determined, the two species have much in common, to the degree of being nearly identical psychologically," Chandra continued. "The differentiation between the two is so insignificant as to suggest that the capacity for higher reasoning functions in a uniform manner regardless of physical circumstance."

The Captain interrupted, "We think alike. Could it be that both species share a common ancestor?"

"The odds against that are even more astronomical, Captain. It is appears that parallel evolution, at least in reference to intelligence, is demonstrated here. The thoughts and feelings of the Cathdenians differed from those of humans no more than yours differ from mine." Chandra smiled to indicate his amusement at the comparison.

"The Cathdenians shared our overall sensibilities, perceptions, and most importantly, our demeanor toward our environment." He paused until the import of his words was felt.

"Doctor, are you telling me that ...?" Khatami allowed his words to trail off.

Chandra nodded intently. "Yes, Captain, despite our obvious physical differences, the Cathdenians were virtually human and vice versa. Psychologically and emotionally, we and the Cathdenians have evolved along parallel lines. Not a very pleasant thought actually," he added.

Khatami motioned for him to continue.

"Unfortunately we share a dominant philosophical attitude with the Cathdenians. We both believe that our intelligence sets us apart and above the rest of Nature. Considering ourselves the pinnacle of evolution, we have dominated every other species on our planet, exactly as the Cathdenians did. They shared our total disregard for their environment as well. We have systematically subjugated, exploited, and obliterated every other life form, just as they did. We see ourselves as the crown of creation to which all else is subservient, existing only for our benefit."

Khatami caught himself leaning forward, totally absorbed in Chandra's explanations. As he eased himself back in his seat, he observed a momentary expression of pleasure on Chandra's face. At least, Khatami considered, he was not being buried in scientific jargon; maybe things were improving between the two men?

"And like us," Chandra continued, "they senselessly exploited their ecosphere, annihilating species after species until environmental havoc had been achieved. With their land depleted, their water and air polluted, they turned to technology for substitutes, but by that time they had rendered their planet uninhabitable."

Khatami mumbled, "Just as we have rendered the Earth nearly uninhabitable."

"In order to survive, the Cathdenians would have to abandon their own planet to seek sanctuary on other worlds — also as humanity has done."

"They all picked up and left the planet, just like that?" Khatami had a difficulty accepting that premise.

Chandra held up a hand to indicate the Captain had gotten ahead of him. "No, Captain. That is what they planned and would have accomplished had it not been for a major factor that is distinctly Cathdenian.

The scholar ran his fingers through what remained of his thinning hair. "The records describe a small group of highly gifted individuals who were elevated above the general population by their sincere dedication to rightness. Their entire existence was spent in the contemplation of deeper truths and the secret wisdom of Nature, much as Earth history claims our saints and mystics have done throughout the millennia.

"But unlike Earth's holy men, these beings abandoned themselves completely to the inner existence, allowing their bodies to age and die in their utter distraction. As their physical bodies perished, their individual consciousnesses melded into a spiritual Gestalt to which the Cathdenians paid their highest allegiance."

Chandra rose and paced the floor. He obviously felt the burden of the story he was imparting. Khatami waited patiently, unwilling to hurry the older man. Eventually, Chandra was able to continue, having carefully considered his next revelation.

"The Gestalt of purified consciousness was aghast at the decimation of an entire world. It encountered a cosmic dilemma: should such an unnaturally self-involved species be allowed to disseminate through the universe to violate an endless number of worlds? No justification was found, and rational thought was adjudged a mistake of Nature rather than its pinnacle."

Chandra sighed, seemingly exhausted by the intensity of involvement. The Captain had become equally concerned with the ramifications of such momentous disclosures.

"The Gestalt concluded that no species has the right to annihilate any other irresponsibly for self-serving reasons. It determined that all species are bound together, a living interdependent whole from which none may set itself apart. And so, ..."

Khatami interrupted, finishing his sentence for him. "And so the Gestalt was obligated to destroy that which it could not redeem. Am I right?" he asked.

Chandra nodded. "They were obligated to correct what they saw as an error of Nature, a malignant mutation that must be aborted before it could destroy all of Nature."

A sudden revelation caused Khatami to yell, "The satellite!"

"Yes, Captain, it was created to act as a self-correcting mechanism dedicated to protecting the universe from the pervasive evil inherent in any creature capable of reasoning self-awareness."

"None of the Cathdenians objected! No one told the Gestalt to go to hell as he packed his luggage for a long trip? No one?"

"No," Chandra insisted. "A semblance of responsibility had finally come over them, but unlike humans, they didn't ignore it or fight it. They united in their resolve to remove the terminal factor and to ensure such a disaster could never be repeated."

Frustrated with disbelief, Khatami pointed out that their acceptance of responsibility defined a change within the Cathdenians that belied any need for their destruction. They had changed.

"They knew themselves better than that," Chandra scoffed. "In a week, a month, a year, sooner or later they would have returned to their old ways and they accepted that fact.

"The satellite is attuned to detect the presence of certain chemicals in the brain that betray rational mental activity. At well-defined intervals every creature possessing a specific chemical combination would be incinerated regardless of its planetary location. The action would be instantaneous and painless; an intelligent species could never again gain a foothold should another evolutionary leap happen to occur. The Cathdenians vowed to make amends through voluntary self-extermination, in the hope that the planet could replenish itself thereafter, which it apparently has done."

Chandra suddenly chuckled to himself.

SELF-CORRECTING MECHANISM

Khatami asked to be let in on whatever was so amusing. When Chandra was able to regain control, he explained: "It amuses me that I was taught that homosexuals are the deviants, aberrations, and mistakes of Nature. It seems the joke was on me, for now I see that we are all mistakes of Nature! What a pompous ass I've been! I can only offer my sincerest apologies to you and your Professor Niles. All of us are the same, and if there is hope for one, there must be hope for all — but only if we work with, and not against, each other."

In the months that followed, Khatami and Chandra studied the records together, learning the timing and the mechanism of the next planetary cleansing. They learned how to alter the programming and thereby prevent their own annihilation. The purge was scheduled for the very day they planned to depart this world for their return trip to Earth.

Khatami, Niles, Devlin, and Chandra became nearly inseparable friends during that time, spending the greater part of their off duty hours together. Inevitably the discussions centered around what they called the Cathdenian Dilemma. Khatami and Chandra had told all to Niles and Devlin, but they felt it necessary to keep the fate of the Cathdenians a secret from the others lest problems arise from the realization that the proverbial Sword of Damocles hung in the sky over all their heads.

Recalling his Hindi upbringing, Chandra compared the Cathdenian satellite to Vishnu, one of the triad of divinities comprising the ancient trimurti: Brahma the creator, Vishnu the preserver, and Shiva the destroyer. Given to symbolism, he pointed out that the dancing Shiva bore an extra pair of arms, which he compared to the Cathdenian physiology with its six adroit members. A Cathdenian could easily have imagined his own body set in the traditional pose of Shiva dancing within a ring of perpetual flame. Khatami had to admit that the image was reminiscent of the schematics which depicted the satellite in action, though he had difficulty envisioning its lasers as eternally purging flames. Chandra even equated the aftermath of the planetary cleansing to Brahma and Vishnu bestowing new life and protective vigilance, respectively. Khatami humored him for the most part, though Niles and Dr. Devlin actually enjoyed such flights of fancy. Niles teased the Hindu, pointing out that these gods were male but also had female aspects; Chandra agreed that the gods differed in their definitions of "normal," just as he and Khatami once had done.

The members of the small but intimate group debated nightly, considering the dilemma from every possible approach. Each took turns playing the

SELF-CORRECTING MECHANISM

Devil's advocate in these discussions, as they proposed various approaches to the philosophical problem. None of them would champion the Cathdenian's own solution but conversely, none felt they had the right to halt the periodic planetary "cleansings."

The day arrived when "Vishnu" altered its position in preparation for the next cleansing. The group had predicted the event, telling the others that the satellite was only performing periodic self maintenance and overhaul.

Khatami and Chandra made the subsequent trip to Vishnu in a gnat craft specially modified to carry passengers. The satellite dropped its impenetrable protective shield as they approached, and for three days the two humans endeavored to reprogram Vishnu's prime directives. Niles and Devlin greeted them upon their return, and over dinner the four of them toasted the success of the mission. They were scheduled to leave for Earth the following morning.

After a long series of pre-flight tests, the Perspective rose from Cathdeny's surface. A nearly audible sigh of relief resounded through the spacecraft as the passengers and crew congratulated each other at finally heading for home. The crew members on duty were so distracted that none of them noticed when Vishnu began transforming into Shiva. Nor did anyone notice that the Captain, the scientist, and their mates had not joined in the festivities; they were gathered in the captain's quarters. They had been faced with an awesome decision and were now praying they had made the right choice.

Silently, in the pitch black void of space, hundreds of nearly invisible hatches opened on the surface of the Cathdenian satellite; metalic rods tipped with mirrored discs extended from each hatch to form a shining ring around the newly enlivened craft. Six larger mechanical appendages burst forth, four rising like arms from an area near one end of the hull, while two other protracted like legs from the opposite end of the satellite. Moments later, the discs flared to life as if activated by some unseen hand, each simultaneously emitting fulgent beams of deadly heat that burned inside the tiny spacecraft as it attempted to escape the gravity of Cathdeny.

The Shiva satellite now prepared to continue its dance of cosmic purification on a distant world called Earth, a purification based on the new instructions implemented by an entity that referred to itself as Chandrakhatami. His cleansing flames would purge that world too, rendering it pure for subsequent renewal by Brahma and Vishnu, another dire error of Nature corrected.⬖

181

Famine Wood

After receiving several polite brushoffs and having a few doors slammed in their faces, two novice members of a religious group that recruited door-to-door were shocked to find themselves warmly welcomed by Abe Camden, an elderly gentleman who responded when they knocked upon the door of his somewhat isolated farmhouse. Not only did the man appear receptive to their pitch, he ushered them into the parlor, seated them both in an antique 'love seat' and invited them to present their well-rehearsed rhetoric. The farmer, thought the visitors, must be desperately lonely as everyone else they had approached had abruptly turned them away.

The pair bombarded Camden with religious information, then tried to draw him into a discussion of the finer points of their church's teachings. But to their surprise, the initially quiet and patient old gent suddenly seized the conversational reins. Before they realized what was happening, Camden had taken off at a verbal gallop that defied interruption.

"I've heard of Yahweh's Children before, but you are the first I've ever met," he began. "And I appreciate you young fellers coming all the way out to the middle of nowhere, especially considering Madland County's reputation. Sometimes I think the great state of Ohio would be very relieved if this here county just up and disappeared!

"Now don't let on like you don't know what I'm talking about, 'cos *everybody's* heard rumors about how, shall I say, peculiar, the folks of Madland are, and I admit there's a certain amount of truth to what they say!

"No sir, there ain't many willing to venture into these parts, particularly not to spout religion to the locals! You see, folks 'round here don't cotton much to what you'd call traditional religion. We've got a church here, but I suspect you'd take exception to the liberties Reverend Petersen takes with the Lord's word in his sermons.

"None of my family were churchgoers, so I've got to admit I never give much thought to religious matters. But after listening to you two, I'll allow there's a certain appeal in some of what you say. I'm particularly interested in the part o' your spiel where God forgives even the worst of sinners when He's asked to."

The wizened old character paused for a moment, seemingly lost in thought, then chimed in again loudly at the first indication that either of his guests was about to make comment. "You see," he continued, "something happened a number of years back that still weighs heavily on my mind. I just can't seem to shake the memory of it, though I was not much more than a foolish teenager at the time. I know I'd feel a whole lot better if I just put it all behind me, but to date I haven't been able to do that.

"If you boys wouldn't mind listening, this might be a good opportunity to get some of it off my chest. They say confession's good for the soul, and at my age a man's got to fess up to his shortcomings least they haunt him all the way to the grave ... and maybe even beyond."

The two youthful guests glanced at each other nervously. The worm had obviously turned in an unanticipated direction. They had been instructed to maintain total control of the situation while peddling their propaganda, but they had never actually gotten this far before and thus had no idea how they might regain the upper hand. All they could really do was sit quietly and listen, least the old man think them rude. If they passively listened and observed, maybe they could discern some means to deal with such dilemmas in the future.

When his visitors did not protest, Camden smiled. "No doubt you never heard of Famine Wood, but that's no surprise as folks don't like to talk about the skeletons in their closets, and the people around here are no exception. Well, I don't mind telling you about Famine Wood, but first I'm obliged to provide you with a bit of background.

"The first whites in the Ohio territory were nothing but trappers and fur traders, daring souls who risked their lives avoiding the various native tribes in hope of stockpiling enough cash to make good lives for themselves when they returned to more civilized parts back East. Still, there was one brave group of six families that lit out on the Ohio River to look for greener pastures. They made it all the way down here to the Mad River Valley before dropping stakes. Now this was right when the French and English were both finagling to claim Ohio for themselves. They were ruthless, turning the Indian tribes against each other 'til it turned into a full-scale war, the French and Indian War. The Shawnee, Miamis, Wyandots, Delawares, Mingos and others were already fighting each other tooth-and-nail, not realizing they were being used by the Europeans to bolster their own claims to the territory. So when the six families arrived, they were all on their own in the midst of a wilderness war zone.

"The Miami tribe let them settle here but only in a part of the forest they considered unnatural. The Miamis claimed their 'Master of Life' had warned them to avoid that particular patch of wood 'cos the spirit of the place was only half-formed and not willing to accept intruders. The Shawnee held the territory before the Miamis, and they too claimed their 'Great Spirit' had warned them away from the place for the very same reasons. So the Indians didn't mind white families as long as they restricted themselves to the wood they themselves considered off-limits. The settlers were neither French nor English, but the Indians figured the spirit would surely make short work of them. And, as it turned out, that proved to be the case."

Camden paused to settle in his seat, confident his listeners were becoming caught up in his tale. He continued, "Everything went pretty well for the new-comers 'til 1762, about a year before the end of the war. Crops failed through-out the entire Ohio Valley due to a terrible drought, and it wasn't long after that famine set in. To top it all off, both the Indians and the Europeans began to drop like flies from the smallpox. The Miamis turned to the English since they'd helped them send the French packing, but the Brits ignored them. The Miamis in turn didn't give a hoot when the settlers looked to them for aid. Before winter was over, every member of the six families had either starved to death or succumbed to the killing force of the cold.

"The British settlers that came along later found the wretched remains of the six families and buried their bodies right where they lay. They vamoosed out of there right after, claiming something about some of the bodies didn't look quite natural. Even later, when more whites moved into Valley, they heard enough spooky stories to stay clear of the Wood where the families were bur-ied. A cloud of superstition hung over the place. Some said the soil was tainted, having soaked up the excruciating hunger of those who starved to death, and that's how the place came to be called Famine Wood.

"It wasn't until more than a score of decades later, during the Civil War, that anyone actually entered Famine Wood again. Word got around that a rogue troop of Confederate soldiers had been spotted in the area, and they probably saw the Wood as a good place to hide out while they'd planned some mischief. They were seen marching into the Wood, but nary a one of them ever came out. It was like they just vanished into thin air!"

The speaker halted to clear his throat before plunging back into his narra-tive. "My buddies and I weren't old enough to have good sense, and we were curious about the yarns we'd heard concerning the Wood. We didn't believe in ghosts, so despite the warnings, we were stupid enough to decide we'd go out there and take a look around just for the heck of it.

"Me, Roscoe Masters and Tom Tucker had grown up together, so we were more like brothers than friends. Heck, it was Roscoe that first showed me a man's pecker was good for more than just draining his bladder! But it was

FAMINE WOOD

Tuck and me that ended up fooling around two, three times, 'til I got tired of such shenanigans. Tuck didn't want to give it up, but, well, I got this sudden interest in girls. Roscoe swore Tuck never got over me and, mind you, though I wouldn't have hurt the lad for worlds, I just considered it puppy love. Well, no doubt you know how it is with us fellers at that age!"

Noting the scandalized expressions on the faces of those he addressed, he further remarked, "Then again, judging from the set of your mugs, maybe you don't know. Don't know at all!" The old man laughed uproariously.

While Jim struggled to regain composure that he might offer some intelligent response, Mike maintained his dumbstruck silence. Jim finally tendered awkwardly, "Ah, so you, ah, committed the sin of homosexuality and that's what's been haunting you all these years?"

Camden hooted, "Hell, no! There ain't no sin in chums getting intimate! Tuck and I shared everything; I mean *everything*, and I don't regret it for an instant. The bond we forged was a rare and precious one that neither one of us ever regretted!" Agitated now, he closed his eyes and shook his head. "I guess I shouldn't of brought it up," he harrumphed, "I just felt it necessary to emphasize the fact that Tuck and me were as close as two folks could be."

Seeing the way the two inched away from each other in the love seat, the frowning Camden continued his narration. "Anyways, Roscoe picked me and Tuck up at my folks' place around noon that day, and we took a round-about dirt road to the Wood so none would suspect we were going there. Not that anybody would have tried to stop us if they'd seen us; they'd have just figured we were out of our minds and left it at that.

"Roscoe parked the truck 'neath a nest of trees right up next to the seven-foot storm fence that closes 'round the eight or nine acres of Famine Wood. Just who put that consarned fence there is anybody's guess; it's been there since long before anyone can recall different. All around the Wood is open pasture, so we guessed the fence was meant to keep livestock from straying into the Wood. But we were soon to learn the hard way that there was a damn sight more to it than that!"

The speaker lowered his voice and paused to observe his guests momentarily. As expected, both remained silent, obviously intrigued by the unraveling tale.

"That darn fence was a bitch to get over. Storm fences are made of real fine metal mesh that's meant to catch debris so as to clog up when there's a flood; that way it acts like a damn to keep back the water. It's pretty flimsy, though, and wobbles like crazy when a body tries to climb over it. The outside was clean but for rust, as you'd expect, but the inside was bound tight with vines and brambles enough to hide pretty near every inch of the actual fence. Seemed like more was trying to get out than trying to get into the place.

"Once inside, everything changed. The Wood's a shadowy, sinister kind of place where nature's turned all dark and brooding. Put me in the mind of some kind of ancient, evil womb.

"Right off we saw the trees were bigger than any we'd ever seen, and a dang sight older too. The bases of some of those giants were as big around as houses and the trunks were twisted and deformed something awful. For sure none had suffered the hand of man since the time of those doomed first settlers. The boughs of those trees met way up above, locking together like spooky fingers serving to blot out as much sunlight as possible. What feeble light managed to filter through lent a nasty, kind of jaundiced glow to that awful place. The air was stagnant, still and muggy, making every move a sweating effort. We got the feeling right off that the place was watching us, ready to pounce at the first opportunity. I admit I had to fight to keep from turning tail and heading for the openness still visible on the other side of the fence.

"Aside from the buzzing of insects, it was unnaturally quiet in there too, like a graveyard at night. Not a single bird sang in the whole place, and we never saw any kind of animal either, which was awful strange. There should have been squirrels, rabbits and chipmunks everywhere in a wood as wild as that, but we didn't see hide nor hair of a single creature the whole time we were there, not even a 'coon nor a 'possum. We couldn't help but feel we were trespassing where we ought not to be, but we still kept going.

"Darn near every inch of the boggy ground was covered with a layer of dead, rotting leaves to a depth of better than a foot in most places, and more leaves were constantly raining down from above, like sallow snowflakes gliding silently through the air. There wasn't much in the way of grass or weeds able to penetrate the leaf blanket, though fungus, moss and toadstools grew all over everything else. And since it was warmer inside the Wood than outside, there were bugs everywhere, flies and gnats. Even the mosquitoes were bold enough to be out and biting in the daylight. What with the yellow light, mugginess and eerie quiet, there was a hatefulness about the place that didn't sit well with us at all.

"But we'd come to explore, and, sure enough, it wasn't long before we came across the remnants of some of those first settlers' cabins. Not that there was much left after all that time but a couple boulder chimneys and piles of decaying logs. One site had three walls still standing, and with a bit of kicking around, Tuck exposed a section of crude flagstone flooring that remained intact. The highest of the walls only came to about shoulder level and, of course, nothing was left of the roof.

"Roscoe struck out on his own, but it wasn't long before Tuck and I heard him let out a yelp. We went running to see what the problem was, only to find him stuck half in the ground, nearly up to his waist, screaming and cursing like all get out.

"Seems those that buried the dead settlers just sort of packaged them up in cheap pine boxes and plugged them in the ground right where they fell, and none were buried too deeply. Roscoe had stepped on one of the makeshift coffins and his foot went right through the rotten wood. His leg was cut up but he'd only started screaming when he tore the lid off the box as he tried to pull free. When his weight was applied to the old bones inside, the top half of the skeleton rose up as if to grab him, the round yellow skull lolling to and fro on the tip of the spine. The sight of the damned thing scared Roscoe nearly half to death, it did! It took some finagling, but we eventually pried him loose, calmed him down and stopped the bleeding. It was obvious to Tuck and me that the main bone in the lower half of Roscoe's leg was badly broken, so we couldn't expect him to walk.

"Well, the two of us heaved and hauled him over to that three-sided cabin I mentioned, but he griped so much about the pain and how the hardness of the stone floor made it worse that we finally lugged him outside the shelter and propped him up against the trunk of an ancient oak. We used a bottle of cheap gin that Tuck always toted around with him to disinfect the wound, but neither of us knew how to set the bone.

"Tuck had the best sense of direction in the bunch, so he lit out for the truck, thinking he'd drive on in and pick us up rather than the two of us carrying Roscoe. If he couldn't find a hole in the fence, he'd find a means to lay it down somewhere and just drive the truck right over it. All Roscoe and I had to do was stay put.

"I parked my butt on the dead log near Roscoe, thinking I'd make a comfy spot for myself by stripping the bark off the trunk. But when I pulled off a hunk, I saw there was a whole slew of bugs lurking beneath, frenzy-feasting on the wood. More ants, grubs, beetles, and mites scrambled off that log than you could shake a stick at; the mass of them had chewed and riddled the wood so much it reminded me more of pulp mush than the remains of a tree. It was enough to make a body's skin crawl, so I chose to plop down a few feet away, on the hard flagstone of the old cabin."

The man lowered and shook his aged head as he emitted exasperated sounds. "Shouldn't a taken him long to get back, but it was over an hour before I heard Tuck shuffling through the leaves.

"I started to ask why he hadn't brought the truck, but the puzzled look on his face silenced me. He grumbled about how walking straight in any direction should bring a body to the fence sooner or later, but it didn't in the Wood. No matter which direction he went, he ended up confused and all turned around until he finally ended up right back here where he'd started. He said he'd felt light-headed and dizzy, but he was still sure he'd been going straight in one direction. I recall him saying it was almost as if the space within the fence was distorted in a way meant to keep anyone from leaving once they were inside, like it was some kind of trap.

"Sounded like nonsense to me, but the sun was going down, leaving us no choice other than to drop stakes for the night right there. We assured Roscoe we'd get him to a doctor first thing in the morning, but he'd gone all quiet, like he was in shock. Tuck and I built a decent fire, then doled out the sorry sandwiches and snacks we'd brought before settling in for the night. Tuck and I decided we'd rather sleep on the cabin floor than stretch out on the open ground, regardless of the hardness of the stone. We'd given up trying to move Roscoe inside with us by then, but we figured he'd be okay since he was only a few feet away from where we settled.

"Judging from the glimpse of moonlight I caught through the thickness of the branches above our heads, I'd guess it was about midnight when something woke me up. The highest limbs of the trees surrounding us commenced to creaking and crackling something awful. But there wasn't a hint of a breeze, which meant wind wasn't the cause. Still, the ruckus continued incessantly for what seemed like at least an hour. All that rustling and moaning in the branches was awful queer, even to a country feller like me; I'd never heard such carrying on before. Tuck sat bolt upright and took notice after a bit, but neither one of us dared speak a word. After a while, I got the feeling the trees were sharing secrets among themselves, things we humans could never understand."

The man fidgeted in his chair, a gesture that added odd emphasis to his words. His audience remained silent, anxious to hear what happened next.

"After a bit," Camden mumbled, "Roscoe started groaning in his sleep, almost like he was reacting to the clamor in the trees above. He talked a bit, but I couldn't make out much. I'm pretty sure he cried either "Get out" or "Get away" a couple times, and Tuck whispered that it sounded to him like Roscoe was gibbering something about getting out before it was too late. I'm not ashamed to admit we were both so spooked by all this that all we could do was scoot closer together and try to stop shivering.

"Then it all stopped at once. The sound of the trees and Roscoe's moans cut off at exactly the same instant. If that wasn't eerie enough, all the chirping,

buzzing and croaking of the night halted right then as well. It was as if every ounce of life had suddenly dissipated from the world around us. I could hear only Tuck's rapid breathing over the pounding of my racing heart. The two of us lay there, clutching at each other like terrified kids. I guess we nodded off after a while, but we sure didn't sleep soundly.

"Come dawn, I was still nodding when Tuck let out a yell to end all yells. Seems he woke up before me and decided to check on Roscoe's leg before disturbing me. By the time I rushed to his side, he was swatting like the devil at a cloud of big fat blowflies that rose up from Roscoe's leg in a black swarm. They were all over Tuck, buzzing around his head like hundreds of angry bees. We'd cut Roscoe's jeans the night before, slitting the leg from the bottom to just above the knee, so when Tuck'd flipped the loose flap of pant leg aside to check on the wound, the flies that were feeding on the wound came at him. By the time I got to him, I'm not sure whether he was screaming more because of the flies or because of what they'd left behind."

The elderly gent looked much older as he swallowed hard and continued. "You'll recall me telling you earlier about what lay beneath the of bark when I stripped it off the oak tree. Well, once the flies disbursed, I could see that Roscoe's leg looked pretty much the gawdawful same; the flesh had turned all soft, yellow and putty-like, and every inch was crawling with maggots, ants and grubs gobbling up the pus that was leaking from the wound. They'd drilled a honeycomb of tunnels into the skin and the muscles so's it looked more like Swiss cheese than a man's leg. I tried to brush some of the bugs off, but I stopped when a chunk of Roscoe's calf muscle tore right off in my hand like meat falling off the bone of a well-done roast."

Camden's eyes closed as he spoke and his body convulsed as the painful memory sent a shiver the length of his body.

The two representatives of religion experienced a wave of nausea as they pictured the scene in their minds. The rather large lunch they had eaten earlier suddenly did not sit so well in their stomachs.

"Roscoe'd been lying on his side. I guess I must have been whimpering like a baby when I rolled him over and called to him by name. I thought at first he might be in a coma, but one glimpse at that blank, bluish face told me he was a goner. He wasn't breathing, his tongue lolled out one side of his mouth all gray and black, and when I lifted an eyelid, the pupil had rolled back in his head. It was a shock more horrible than I can describe.

"You can't imagine how Tuck and I felt," the farmer exerted, "Roscoe, our best friend, gets his leg all messed up, yes, but not bad enough to kill him, and certainly not to change him into a corpse that looked for all the world like it had been laying there dead for days! None of it made sense to us, no sense at all! Tuck, well, he got sick as a dog, but I just stood still for a while, not really feeling anything but numb. When I finally snapped out of it, I tried to make sense of what was going on as we couldn't just stay there like that; we had to get the hell out of there as fast as possible."

He sighed heavily. "I finally was able to speak, though for the life of me I can't recall what it was that came out of my mouth. Next thing I knew, Tuck was pulling at me and screaming that we had to escape that accursed place before we ended up like Roscoe. He rambled through a plan he'd been mulling over, a way we might be able to reach the fence. He'd once read something about space being curved or something like that, and that's what he thought was going on around us in some distorted way. That's why, he said, he'd ended up back in the same place when he walked in a straight line earlier. If we walked toward the rising sun, he said, and used it as a guide, we should be able to stay on course and make it to the fence. I didn't know anything about curved space, so I didn't understand what he was talking about, but as I had no better idea, I went along his idea.

"We didn't waste any time covering Roscoe's body with a coat before high-tailing it out of there. The body reeked of compost and there wasn't no point in trying to take him with us. We daren't run, since the leaf-covered ground was damp and mushy soft in places. We were scared we might trip or fall and end up not being able to walk, so we took it slow and easy."

"You must have been frightened out of your wits!" cried the sympathetic Mike, noting how very frail their host suddenly appeared.

In confirmation, Camden yelped, "More than words can relate! And if it wasn't bad enough already, Tuck accidentally kicked up the remains of one of them fool Johnny Rebs who'd hid in the Wood during the Civil War, the bones still wrapped in a tattered uniform. We feared we were going to end up the same way."

Sighing, Camden rested further back in his seat.

"Tuck must of been right about the curve thing 'cos before long we spotted the fence. We couldn't help but start grinning, whooping and hugging like idiots, we were so relieved."

His voice dropped to a hush as he confessed, "It was then I knew Roscoe'd been right about the feelings Tuck and I shared for each other." Shaking his head sadly, he added, "It's a crying shame how folks tend to refuse to admit their true feelings for one another until it's too late." He shot a challenging glance at his audience. "There ain't no finer bond than what we had, and it didn't make a lick of difference that we both were fellers. You youngings'll be damn lucky if you ever have a relationship that even approaches what Tuck and I had, regardless of whether it's with a woman or another feller."

Mike detected tears glittering at the corners of the old man's eyes. He turned to his frowning companion and was relieved to see he wasn't going to comment.

"Please, go on, sir," Mike urged, "we're listening."

The wary speaker nodded, acknowledging his gratitude.

In calmer tones, Camden complied with the request. "We lit out for the fence at top speed, but when we were less than three or four yards of reaching it, the ground beneath our feet began to heave and drop down and away. It sucked at our feet like quicksand, trying to drag us down into the rotten leaves and soil. We could barely pull our shoes free long enough to keep moving. Before long, we were sinking all the way to our knees in the muck.

"I heard once it's best to stretch out flat over quicksand, so I called out to Tuck as I sprawled out onto the surface as best I could, telling him he should do the same. He was too panicked to pay attention to what I was saying though, and before long he'd sunk darn near up to his waist."

Camden's listeners trembled with anticipation.

"I sprawled out over the soft dirt in an attempt to reach a gnarled-up tree root jutting out of the ground. I managed to anchor myself by holding on to it. I don't know how I managed it, but I slowly pulled myself across the muck, crawling up the root to the trunk of the tree. Once there, it took every bit of strength I had, but I climbed up to the first big limb. Then I shimmied out as close to the tip as I could so's my weight would bend it down toward Tuck. I threw my weight into the branch to make it bob up and down, all the while calling out for Tuck to catch hold of the end of it. If he could get a tight grip on the tip, all I'd have to do would be back up and let the branch pull him up out of the spongy ground. Once we were both on the limb, we could shimmy up a bit higher to a branch that stretched clean over the fence. We could scramble to safety without having to set foot on the tainted earth again."

As he struggled to continue, the older man's voice betrayed an even greater solemnity. "Tuck'd been swallowed up beyond his waist, nearly to his armpits, but he still managed to get a grip on the nodding limb. I held my breath and commenced to retreat back toward the trunk."

The old man suddenly stopped, as if he were incapable of going on with the story. To the relief of his listeners, however, he continued after a moment. "He started rising up, just like I'd hoped, but he didn't respond when I called out to encourage him to hang on. Something about his silence gave me the willies and I feared he was about to lose hold. I thought about inching out to catch his hand, but every time I moved forward at all, Tuck's weight drew the branch back down toward the muck.

I couldn't see much in the dim light and the damn foliage kept slapping me in the face, but his body started to twirl around in a circle at one point. He managed to get his belt off using one hand and whipped it around the branch, securing his wrists so he could slide a little at a time without fear of losing his grip. That belt was probably the only thing that kept him from tumbling back into the grasping earth below. He slid a couple times, but I could see he was gradually rising up and pulling free, which gave me cause to take heart. I'll never forget the terrified, pleading look on his face when the shadows parted just long enough for me to make out his features. I called out softly, encouraging him by telling him he was doing fine and we'd soon both be safely out of that hellhole."

Camden suddenly choked with passion to the extent that he was forced to stop until he could regain his composure.

Finding himself confronted by a much older stranger completely overcome with emotion, Mike leaned forward compassionately to whisper, "It's okay, sir. Take a deep breath and then just take your time; there's no need to rush. It must be very painful for you to relive such a horrendous experience." He then glanced at his companion, noting the irritated impatience apparent not only in his cross-armed position but in his expression as well.

Camden again nodded to silently acknowledge his gratitude for Mike's sympathetic words. After a weighty silence, he managed to resume his narrative in agonized tones, "Tuck's head popped through the greenery so I could finally see his face clearly; I almost didn't recognize him. He began crawling toward me, but then he turned to peer behind momentarily before crying out as if in agony.

"When he looked back at me, his face was even more contorted, like he was in unspeakable pain. He uttered something I couldn't make out. I asked if there was something more I could do to help him as I reached out with one hand, ready to grab him at the first opportunity. All he did was groan and scream at me to leave him behind and not look back."

Wiping the tears from his eyes as inconspicuously as possible, Camden sat upright in his chair, declaring loudly, "To this day I can't recall exactly what happened next. All I know is that I must have scrambled up to the higher limb and run like a jackrabbit. Hank Danner stumbled across me toward sundown on his way home from hunting pheasant. He said I was sitting on the ground crying and jabbering like an idiot just a few yards from the fence. When he tried to get me to my feet, I started screaming and shrieking like a madman to the point he finally had to knock me out. Right before he'd spotted me, he'd passed Roscoe's truck, which was parked right where we'd left it. He dragged me to it, tossed me in the back and drove straight to the Sheriff's office. When I came to, the doc gave me a shot to calm me down enough to allow me to describe what had happened as best I could, but there wasn't anything they could do until the next day since nobody's fool enough to set foot in Famine Wood after dark.

"The following afternoon, the Sheriff and a couple others came back with Roscoe's and Tuck's bodies. I was kept locked up for nearly a year after, but not for any crime; the Sheriff declared that, after what they'd found in the Wood, there was no way I could be held accountable for either death. Still, they kept me under wraps until they felt confident I wasn't going to do myself any harm.

"I've never been able to remember what possessed me to turn tail and abandon poor Tuck there to die, though I've tried 'til it hurts. No matter what the Sheriff says, 'til I actually can recall what happened, I can't forgive myself. I can't believe I'm such a coward that I could just up and leave my best friend to die," he choked, "but maybe I am."

Contrary to everything the church taught about how to present himself as a missionary, Jim could contain himself no longer. He jumped up abruptly and shouted, "Mike, we're leaving, right now! I don't believe a word of the swill this old bastard's been spitting out." Turning to address Camden, he yelled, "You're mad as a hatter, you know! You'd have to be crazy to believe the story you just told, and the worst part is, I think you actually do believe it's true! But it's not, it's garbage, all of it. There's no such thing as a man-eating wood, and if you're convinced what you're saying is true, then you know what that makes you, don't you? Not just a coward but a murderer as well. I don't care either way, I just know I'm getting out of here right now. Come on, Mike, let's go."

Mike made a feeble attempt to calm his friend, despite the reeling confusion Camden's confession had set off in his own brain, but Jim was determined.

Camden simply sat and stared at his accuser, unable and/or unwilling to even try and defend himself.

Jim pulled Mike to his feet and all but dragged him to the door. He turned as they exited to shout one further remark. "If there's even a shred of truth to that black fantasy of yours, Camden, then you better hope God can find it in his heart to forgive you because I sure as hell couldn't."

Pulling his friend roughly along, Jim marched to the car. He jumped inside, slammed the door and started the engine immediately. Fearing he'd be left behind, Mike hopped into the passenger seat.

Jim prattled on incessantly about how Camden had suckered them into wasting an entire afternoon listening to a load of absolute drivel. The old codger, he declared again and again, was obviously insane and probably should be put away.

Mike, on the other hand, felt troubled and downtrodden over the entire experience. He was certain they had abandoned an extremely lonely man in desperate need of counseling and comfort of some kind. What was the purpose of their missionary work if it not to help troubled people like Camden find some sort of inner peace. Mike found his companion's attitude contemptible, and he was ashamed that he had allowed Jim to rail so caustically at a man unable to defend himself. The disillusionment he felt toward his partner had reached its zenith by the time they reached town.

Immediately after Jim dropped him off, Mike phoned Reverend Pauly, explaining the events of the afternoon and Jim's tantrum-like reaction. When the Reverend sided with Jim, Mike immediately proffered his resignation, not only from the missionary work but from membership in the church as well, explaining that he now realized his personal goals radically conflicted with those of Yahweh's Children.

Three days passed before Mike found an opportunity to return to Madland County. The pain he had seen in Camden's face haunted him continuously during those days, and he was determined to apologize and do whatever he could to undo at least some of the damage he and Jim had inflicted upon the old man. Mike had taken a few psychology classes in college and was convinced Camden was an extremely disturbed man, despite the fact that Mike could not bring himself to accept Camden's tale of horror at face value. Obviously something dramatic had happened to the man that had left him grievously traumatized and in dire need of help. Mike hoped that, given further opportunity to speak with Camden, he might be able to discover the underlying cause of the man's guilt and, with any luck, help him find a way to deal with it. It is impossible to predict how any particular person will react in an emergency, and surely the authorities would have pressed charges had they deemed Camden guilty of any wrongdoing.

It was only when he pulled up to Camden's farmhouse that Mike's determination began to fail him. The front door and windows had been boarded-over and the walkway leading to the front porch was cordoned off with yellow police tape. After staring dumbly for a few moments, Mike spun the car around in the dirt driveway and returned to the main road. Unable to just let the matter drop, he headed directly for the small police station he recalled having passed a mile or so down the road. He prayed he and Jim were not responsible any sort of tragedy.

* * *

Mike parked in front of the small, rundown building labeled Madland County Sheriff's Office, got out of the car and nervously approached the door. His knock elicited an immediate response from somewhere inside as a voice called out, "It's open!" He entered, suddenly unsure of what he would say to the capable-looking officer seated behind a cluttered desk.

Without looking up, the officer asked, "What can I do for you?"

Mike's hesitation caused the man to glance at his visitor. A look of moderate surprise crossed his face when he did not recognize the face of the young fellow standing before him. "You lost or having car trouble, son?" he queried.

"No, sir," Mike mumbled, noting the officer's uniform identified him as the County Sheriff, "nothing like that." He paused momentarily before blurting out, "I've just come from Abe Camden's place and, seeing the house closed up and cordoned off, I just thought I should check to make sure Mr. Camden is, well, all right."

"I can't say I've seen you around here before. Mind if I ask who you are and why you're so interested in Abe Camden?" inquired the Sheriff.

Camden had obviously been right about outsiders not being overly welcome in Madland County. It occurred to Mike that maybe it might have been a mistake to come back after all, but now it was too late to turn back.

In gentler tones, the Sheriff advised, "Take it easy, son. I'm only asking because Abe's been holed up in that house all alone for so long that I'm surprised to learn he had a friend."

The sincerity apparent in the man's voice had the desired effect; Mike identified himself and explained how he had come to know Camden. He explained that he had come back to check on the old man, to make sure he was okay. His friend, Jim, Mike further related, had reacted poorly to an unbelievable tale Camden had told them, and Mike confessed he felt bad about the way Jim had treated him.

When the Sheriff asked if Camden had told them about his experience in Famine Wood, Mike nodded enthusiastically. He started to repeat what Camden had told them of his experience in Famine Wood, omitting only the part about his abnormally close relationship with Tuck, but he did not get far before the Sheriff waved for him to stop.

"I know the rest, son. I know it only too well. Before I say any more, I think I should straighten you out on one important point. You referred to Abe as an old man, and that's quite understandable in light of the way he aged prematurely, almost overnight, after the incident he described to you. Truth is, I'm thirty-two and Abe was five years my junior. You seem to have the impression that Abe and his friends went to Famine Wood twenty or thirty years ago when, in fact, it was only seven years ago. I was one of the two deputies who accompanied Sheriff McKinny out to the Wood the morning after Hank found Abe and brought him back here."

Shocked, Mike whispered, "The man we spoke to is only twenty-seven years old? My God, I'd have guessed he was closer to sixty."

"Nope," replied the Sheriff as he swiveled his chair around to access the file cabinet immediately behind him. He thumbed through a mass of folders before pulling one file from the drawer. Placing it on the desk before him, he opened it and handed the top page to Mike. It was the notice of report of investigation, including basic information on those involved. The dates and overall information confirmed what the Sheriff had just told him.

Indicating a wooden chair in the corner, the Sheriff said, "You'd better sit down, son. You're looking a mite pale." Mike took his advice, pulling the chair nearer the desk before seating himself. The Sheriff immediately continued.

"I wish I could account for it, but as you must realize by now, Madland County isn't quite like other places and neither are most of the folks who live here. There's something strange about this place, maybe something in the air, the water, the soil or, well, possibly in them all. Things happen here that happen nowhere else, and most of the time those things are bad, sometimes really bad."

"Sheriff, it sounds as if you are about to tell me the story Camden told Jim and I was true, that the soil of this county eats the residents," Mike challenged.

The Sheriff leaned forward intently. "You can hear what I have to say about what we found that day in the Wood or you can read the official report. It's up to you, my friend."

"Okay," Mike shrugged, "I'm sorry. I'd rather hear it from you, sir."

Relaxing in his seat, the Sheriff smiled encouragingly before continuing.

"Like I said, it was the next morning before we took a ride out to the Wood. Sheriff McKinny and Hank led the way with Tom Riley and me following in a second car. Once Hank showed us where he'd found Roscoe's truck, it wasn't difficult to locate the spot where Abe and the others had climbed the fence. We followed suit, although Hank insisted on remaining outside. It was like a jungle in there, so overgrown that neither fresh air nor much light penetrated the heavy foliage, but we soon found the boys had left a clear trail through the mud and leaves. To make a long story short, it wasn't long before we stumbled upon the skeleton of a man lying on the ground, propped up against a tree.

"Yeah," he added, noting Mike's apparent bewilderment, "just a skeleton. Every bit of flesh, organs, and what have you had been stripped from the bones. Nothing was holding them together but a green-gray fungus that had grown over nearly half of the body. Tom and I put the remains in a body bag we'd brought along, though it wasn't exactly the most pleasant in the world. Lucky for us, we'd brought gloves along, because the skeleton fell to pieces as soon as it was touched and that fungus wasn't something either one of us wanted to contact directly."

Mike interjected to ask, "Were the remains of an old cabin nearby, maybe three partial walls with a stone floor inside?"

Without pause the Sheriff confirmed that they had encountered an old ruin just a few feet from the corpse.

"Sorry to break in," Mike apologized, "I just remembered Mr. Camden said they'd left Roscoe's body fairly close to a ruined cabin, a leftover from the earliest settlement in the area."

The Sheriff smiled indulgently. "As I recall, we'd pretty much confirmed everything he'd told us before we left, actually more than we would have liked.

"Later, after we got back to town, the doc did an autopsy of sorts on the bones. He claimed he'd never seen anything like it. There were no teeth marks, so no animals had been gnawing on the body, and the only way thing he knew of that could clean a set of bones that quickly would be a strong corrosive, like acid or quicklime, the latter taking days. Either way, nothing would be able to grow on the bones for weeks or months after due to the chemical residue, so he was also at a loss to explain how a fungus could cover so much of the corpse in just a few hours. Sure as hell there wasn't anything natural about it, so we couldn't blame Abe. Hell, the only way we could even be sure it was Roscoe's body was by the gold tooth in the front lower jaw."

"But what about Tuck?" Mike demanded. "If what Camden told us is true, he panicked and left Tuck to die. He claimed he couldn't remember why he'd lost his nerve when he was within inches of rescuing Tuck. That was what really haunted him."

His head lowered, the Sheriff sighed deeply. When he looked up, his entire face seemed to have changed due to his own recollection of that aspect of the story.

"I know. I was coming to that. Poor Abe never stopped torturing himself over Tuck's death despite our desperate attempts to explain what we'd found. Nothing we said or did consoled him. He had to remember that moment for himself, which he never did.

"We found Tuck's body, just as he described it, tied to a tree limb with his own belt. It was dangling from that limb just a few yards from the fence."

He fell silent for a moment, then he raised the file from his desk and handed it to Mike.

"We took photos of both bodies before removing them. The photos are there, so you can see for yourself what we found."

When Mike made no move to open the file, the other man felt obliged to describe what he wished he could forget.

"As we saw it, when Tuck ordered Abe to leave and save himself, Tuck already knew he was a dead man. It wasn't until the boughs parted that Abe saw enough to understand, and what he saw was enough to drive any man mad.

"As the photos show, only half of Tuck came up out of the swampy soil. I can't explain how he held on long enough to warn Abe, but he did. But whatever he'd sunk into had already gotten to him. There was nothing left of his body from just the rib cage down; the entire lower half of his body had been eaten away, bone and all.

"That's what Abe saw and that's what caused him to run away. I don't know if he let on about how he and Tuck felt about each other, but everyone knew they loved each other; that's not something we frown upon around here. So keep in mind when you consider what that moment must have been like for Abe, to see Tuck half gone and ordering him to go. If you can look at it that way, then I think you can understand why he couldn't live with that memory. He did his best by blotting it from his conscious mind, but deep down it was still there."

An ominous silence followed until Mike finally whispered, "He's dead, isn't he? Mr. Camden, I mean."

The Sheriff lowered his head as he nodded in confirmation. "Yeah, he's dead. He put the business end of a shotgun in his mouth three days ago and pulled the trigger. I guess he just couldn't take it anymore."

"And our visit was the last straw. He begged us for help, yet Jim all but spit in his face. I'm no better, though, because I just sat there and let him do it."

At that point, the Sheriff reached across the desk to Mike, placing his hands on top of Mike's.

"When you first told me about your visit and how your buddy went off on Abe, I confess I thought the same thing, son, but now that I've relived the whole thing in my mind, I recall something Abe said to me. We'd already shown him the photos, hoping to convince him he was not responsible for Tuck's death, but he remained inconsolable."

"What did he say?" Mike asked reluctantly.

"He said he could see how the three of us could go into the Wood to fetch the bodies and get out without being affected since it was daytime and we were only there for a short time. What he didn't understand was how he, unlike Roscoe and Tuck, had escaped the Wood's unquenchable hunger. He couldn't understand why it hadn't overtaken him as well."

Mike stared solemnly at the officer, unsure of his point.

"Don't you see? He didn't escape the Wood's ravenous hunger any more than the others did. It ate Roscoe and Tuck right then and there, but it got inside Abe somehow without his knowing it, and it remained there, slowly eating away at his mind during all the years that followed. I'd like to think he finally realized that in the end, so it wasn't himself he killed, it was the ravenous, cancerous hunger that fed on his brain day and night that he was determined to kill when he pulled that trigger. It was the only way for him to free himself and finally find some real peace." ✦